SISTER

SWITCH

SISTER SWITCH

BETH GARROD

SIMON & SCHUSTER

First published in Great Britain in 2021 by Simon & Schuster UK Ltd

1 3 5 7 9 10 8 6 4 2

Simon & Schuster UK Ltd
1st Floor, 222 Gray's Inn Road
London WC1X 8HB

www.simonandschuster.co.uk
www.simonandschuster.com.au
www.simonandschuster.co.in

Simon & Schuster Australia, Sydney
Simon & Schuster India, New Delhi

A CIP catalogue record for this book
is available from the British Library.

PB ISBN 978-1-3985-0024-2
eBook ISBN 978-1-3985-0025-9
eAudio ISBN 978-1-3985-0067-9

Printed and bound by CPI Group (UK) Ltd, Croydon, CR0 4YY

To Rose – the most magical person I know.

CHAPTER ONE

If I'd ever wondered what could be worse than being laughed at by my sister in front of my life-icon and her terrifying sibling, now I knew. Being laughed at while wearing a beard.

As Erin cackled, Frankie pretended to take a selfie (but was a hundred per cent filming me) and Nic looked like she might be mid-swallow of a wasp. I tried to focus on the most important thing.

Breathing could wait.

Getting my sister back was *everything*.

Five hours earlier

'So you're sure *sure* I have to do this?' I asked, even though we'd already been driving for ten minutes.

Mum adjusted the rear-view mirror. We both knew she was just making sure I could see her giving me *that* look.

'Sisters together. It'll be fun!'

Erin and I together? That hadn't been fun since I was eight and Erin was nine – and ever since I'd started senior school with her, it had upgraded to a full-on nightmare. But when Mum made her mind up there was no changing it.

'Fun as in . . .' I got distracted by the weirdness of seeing my reflection in the car window – a semi-bald wig covered where my ponytail usually was . . . 'worst day of my life?'

I was *meant* to be spending the day prom shopping with Micha and doing the Saturday usual: eating chips, hanging out at the skatepark and writing something for my blog, while my best mate laughed at videos of people falling over. But oh no.

Here I was on the way to a Shakespeare convention looking like my sister's sweaty sidekick.

A *Shakespeare convention.*

On a *Saturday.*

Full body shudder. And the worst thing about it was that after twelve years and fifty-one weeks I was no longer surprised. My family had given up trying to be normal a looooong time ago.

I brushed my fingers through a dangly bit of hair below the wig. It felt like carpet. Was this my real follicles matted together or the fake stuff? Either way, the wig glue was itching and made me reek of marker pens. At least I'd convinced Erin

I didn't need the beard. It was lying abandoned on the seat next to me like a deflated gerbil. I stroked it. *Sozzee, beardio.*

Mum cleared her throat. Uh-oh. This was never good.

'Worst day of your life, Lily? Good to see you're not being dramatic.' I huffed silently. 'And perhaps you could stop that huffing too . . .' *How can Mum's ears detect even the* thought *of a huff?!* 'Maybe you could be a little more mature considering what you put your sister through.'

How many times?! I *genuinely* thought I was doing a good thing showing Erin how to create a treadmill on the kitchen floor using washing-up liquid and some water. How was I to know her boyfriend, Ben, was about to walk, with surprising speed, into the room?

Yes, we could *all agree* it was bad news he'd broken his wrist. But I did *keep* reminding everyone of the better news. It was 'probably going to heal *even after* being fractured in five places'.

'It was an accident,' I muttered for the billionth time. I should get it printed on a T-shirt.

I swear Erin whispered, 'Just like you.'

I kneed the back of her seat as hard as I could while pretending to stretch. I gripped my skull. As in the one in my hand. It was a prop Erin had handcrafted. Ben was meant to have helped but my sister said his one-usable-hand technique was 'compromising its anatomical accuracy'. He was supposed to be here today but was having his hospital check-up. Lucky him.

I slumped back and tried not to get my foot tangled in the blue skirt spilling out from Erin's seat. A massive poofy dress with a fitted bodice thing wasn't exactly my sister's style. But with her permanently perfect bob, freshly done cropped nails and simple chain necklace, she made the whole thing somehow look the height of fashion. Not that she cared. Erin never cared what anyone thought. Unless it was a teacher wondering whether her A was an 'outstanding' one or a 'mind-blowing' one. I only really got As when teachers wrote 'A disappointing effort'.

Which sucked, because I *totally* cared what people thought. And right now I was wearing the Elizabethan man costume Erin had bought for Ben – an eye-melting combo of pantaloons and velvet jacket (both four sizes too big), with long white socks and pointy shoes as long as Toblerones. Complete with actual ruff. A *ruff*?! I didn't even know what one was until Erin was clipping it round my neck, an evil glint in her eye. Sorry, ye olde people, but why was wearing a massive folded party plate round your neck ever a good idea?

When I'd seen the outfit laid out on my bed I'd gone mute for two hours. Dad had said the experience could 'make a cracking feature for my blog'. Dad was wrong.

When my voice came out of hiding, I'd immediately called my angel-human best friend, Micha, to ask if she could speak to her lawyer mum about whether divorcing a whole family was a thing. Sadly she said it wasn't, and then asked

4

why there was a paper plate around my neck. Although she calmed me down a bit by pointing out that at least being at a random exhibition centre out of town meant no normal people would be there to witness how I looked. Like the perfect person Micha is, she even offered to come with me, but there was no way I would put her through this. Mich was most precious and needed to be protected at all costs. So we'd agreed to meet at hers after.

My phone buzzed. Probably another motivational penguin GIF from Micha – they had been really helping.

But it wasn't from her.

> Erin: Cheer up. You might even enjoy it

I started to reply, peering over my ruff, making sure Mum didn't spot I was on my phone. She hated when Erin and I messaged each other around her. She said it 'makes her feel we're saying things she wouldn't approve of'. She was absolutely right.

> Me: Enjoy it?! A neck satellite dish just tried to suffocate me
>
> Erin: #prayforLily
>
> Me: #prayforanewsister. This is going to be a weirdofest
>
> Erin: Weirdos like you 😜

Even though we were only born thirteen months apart, we couldn't be more different. Erin was fourteen going on forty and breezed through life. Even when she was doing something completely cringe (hello, today!), she managed to carry if off in an annoyingly cool way because she was so confident. She was a hundred per cent our parents' favourite child. They said they didn't have one, but they also said that about our grandparents and then called Grandma 'Grandmoan' when they thought we couldn't hear. Plus teachers *loved* Erin. Last term they invited her to join them for lunch as they wanted her tips on 'effective classroom control'. But me? Most teachers only knew me as Erin's little sister (normally accompanied by a slightly sad look in their eyes). Or the girl who once ran in late to assembly wearing slippers.

'I'll pick you up at five, by that drop-off point?' Mum pulled the car up. I felt instantly sick. We were here. The hordes of people wearing hats with feathers and clutching oversized quills should have been a sign. And the man in pantaloons holding a MUCH ADO ABOUT SOMETHING placard was most *definitely* a sign.

But what was that?! I grabbed the door handle to steady myself as I dealt with what I'd just spotted.

Next to the pantalooned man was a super-smiley woman in a red crop top and matching pleated skirt, waving pom-poms and cheering, 'I'm loud! I'm proud! I can cheer the crowd! CheerCon is thissa way!'

CheerCon?! Was in the next hall?! In the same building?! This was a disaster. *The biggest.*

Micha had been wrong.

People *were* going to be here. And not just any people. One particular people. Person.

Cheerleading superstar and all-round terrifying human. Frankie.

Aka Frankie-who'd-had-it-in-for-me-all-term-especially-after-I-accidentally-wore-her-PE-kit-and-she-got-forced-to-wear-something-soggy-from-lost-property.

She'd made sure the whole school knew that the new cheer team she was captain of were the CheerCon guests of honour. Frankie could *not* see me! She'd never let me forget it!

And noooooooo. I splodged my face on to the car window. Frankie would probably tell her big sister Nic.

Aka Nic-who-was-so-legendary-she-didn't-even-need-to-write-a-surname-on-her-schoolwork-and-was-my-actual-life-icon-who-I'd-been-trying-to-impress-for-years.

WHY, CRUEL WORLD? WHYYYYY?

Pom-pom lady beamed a massive smile at me even though my face was now sliding down the glass, making a small squeak. I ducked down and tried to urgently get a grip.

Give me a C. Give me an A. Give me . . . Oh forget it. Just give me a massive CATASTROPHE.

If Frankie saw me here, in this outfit, my life would be over.

'Just to double-check,' I said, grabbing Erin's headrest.

C'mon, sister. Hear my desperation! Take pity! 'You *definitely* still want to go?'

Erin turned and glared at me. 'It's not a case of *want*, Lil. What I *want* is to get the part of Titania in the school play. What I *need* is to impress Mrs Saddler.'

Mrs Saddler was our terrifying English teacher and deputy head.

'And she is going to know you did this ... *how*?'

'Because she's doing a panel here and we're going to be front row. That's how.'

Forget Shakespeare's tragedies. My life was the ultimate one.

'And I *definitely* can't get changed?' I looked at my stuff next to me, ready for Micha's later. Normal human clothes, how I longed for thee.

'Come on, Lily.' Mum turned off the engine. 'It's time to stop moaning and get out of the car. Just think of poor Ben.'

I hadn't stopped thinking about Ben! Safe, warm, in shoes not the length of a large salmon, enjoying having his bones reset. I'd done him a favour getting him out of this! His wrist would (should) recover. My dignity was going to be damaged for *life*.

I had to make sure I wasn't spotted.

Which meant I had no choice. I was going to have to go full disguise.

I grabbed the beard, peeled the sticky backing off and pushed the hairy monstrosity on to my face.

It felt ... surprisingly cosy – like a tiny chin scarf.

'And to confirm,' I hissed at the back of Erin's head, 'after this, I'm free from all guilt trips?'

But she just replied with, 'Maybe.' I really should have negotiated this first.

Peeping up from the bottom of the window, I scanned for any sign of Frankie. Nothing. It was now or never. Keeping my head low, I opened the car door and, with as much speed as I could muster, sprang out of the car and stumble-sprinted towards the entrance, hunched over like a famous medieval squirrel hiding from a whatever-it-is-that-eats-squirrels.

'Way to go, old man!' The cheerleader waved her pompoms at me. 'You've got this!'

She couldn't have been more wrong.

The only thing I had was intense fear of running into Frankie.

Deep regret I hadn't brought deodorant.

And absolutely no idea how bad things were about to get.

CHAPTER TWO

Macbeth burgers? Tick. A *Romeo-and-Juliet*-balcony-themed photo booth. Yup, although I was staying *well* away. I couldn't have ANY photo evidence of today leaking out into the real world. We even sat through a two-hour panel on words Shakespeare had invented. (Which included swagger and bedroom and eyeball. *What on earth did they call eyeballs before him?!*)

Despite being the absolute worst event I could imagine – and I'd once gone with Dad to his work exhibition on 'The Joys of Concrete Through the Ages' – the massive hall was packed. We had to push through crowds to get anywhere, there were cheers every time an event was announced, and if I heard 'there's no way you can be Bard here!' one more time, I might weep. At least my beard could act as a face sponge.

It was torture. Torture in a ruff. My wig had fully tangled into my hair, I'd developed a sweaty beard rash and the safety pins in my pantaloons had pinged off so material was now flapping round my legs like calf sails.

Erin, though, was having the time of her life. But finally, after what felt like three-and-a-half weeks, it was time to leave. I *had* to be back in our parents' good books after this! Especially because at the end of Mrs Saddler's panel I'd waved super hard, skull aloft, so Erin had been picked to ask her question. When she heard it, Mrs Saddler did one of those deep, dramatic, satisfied-English-teacher inhales then gave an answer that felt as long as a play. But she did end with something cryptic about finding the perfect Titania. Which was the part Erin wanted! *Result.*

Out of all the things my sister was amazing at, she loved acting the most. She was incredible at it. In the last school play, even with her small part, she'd blown me away. Not that I'd tell her that. And now Erin was in Year Ten she could try out for Chinyere Okafor's Drama Academy that ran after school. Competition was fierce, but it was the thing Erin wanted more than anything in the world, and she was doing whatever it took to get a place. Starting with trying to get her first major role in the school play to film for her audition.

'Don't suppose I can talk you into an extra hour?' Erin leant beside me, prodding at some fake ivy on the fake pillar we were leaning on. 'There's a comedy-improv set happening – kind of rapping with classic lines from plays.' She nudged me. 'I'm *sure* your internet friends would love to read about it.'

Here it came ... the wink.

Erin had never even bothered reading my blog, GettingLilyWithIt, but she still found it a source of constant entertainment. I didn't have the energy for yet another argument about it, so ignored her.

'Is that a yes then?' Erin never had a problem asking for what she wanted – or getting it. But oh no, sisterio, not this time.

'It's a no, because ...' *Being here was a crime against weekends?* 'In seven minutes Mum is picking us up, and Micha is waiting. So we'd better head.'

I tried to look as disappointed as someone who was a hundred per cent the opposite of disappointed could do.

'Oh, okay.' She shrugged. 'Wouldn't want to hold up your big night of doing bad, bad dance challenges with Micha.'

Erin always took the mick out of my stuff, but today she'd been extra annoying, probably because we both knew if we argued then all the good I'd done by coming would be cancelled out. But a deal was a deal. She left me with most of the bags, and the skull she'd got signed by everyone we'd met, and popped for a last-minute loo break.

I edged forward so I could see the road outside. Freeeeeedddooooommm.

Although freedom meant one last hurdle. Making it out of here undetected by Frankie.

I was secretly hoping there had been an incident with some overly flammable pom-poms and CheerCon had been

12

evacuated, but, oh no, I couldn't be that lucky. There were *hundreds* of perfectly dressed, gorgeous cheer crews milling outside. I wasn't following Frankie, but knew what her handle was, and checked it for the hundredth time today.

There she was. Having the time of her life, her massive group of friends all in matching, custom-made, bright blue crop tops. How was it possible to have hair *that* perfect when she'd been out all day?! Mine didn't even look that good by the time I made it downstairs in the morning!

They were in the queue for a signing of someone who seemed to be able to touch their head with their foot.

Although ...

If Frankie was in a queue, it meant she wasn't outside. About to see me!

Now was my time to run!

My heart started to race. I looked round for Erin. No sign.

Hurry up, sister! But a minute later, she still hadn't emerged.

I shuffled nearer to the exit trying not to trip over my stupid pointy shoes, which I couldn't see over my beard and ruff. Erin's bags weighed a ton – all packed with books. How she had so many I had no idea – it wasn't like Shakespeare had written any new ones for four hundred years.

But as I peered round a giant cardboard Shakespearean head, I spotted something beautiful.

Heaven had arrived, in the shape of a K-reg blue car.

Mum's Volkswagen. Aka my chariot to freedom.

By my calculation it was about thirty metres away.

If I scurried I could be inside it within twenty-eight seconds.

Should I stay and wait for Erin?

Or make a mad dash while the coast was clear?

It was a no-brainer.

I gripped on to the bag handles and pelted as fast as I could out of the door.

I felt the wind in my fake hair.

I felt the refreshing breeze of freedom in my beard.

I felt the thrill of the finish line as I grabbed the car door handle.

I'd done it!

'Muuuuum!' I didn't mean to wail with happiness as I flung the car door open, but that was what a day being held hostage with people who laughed at Erin's jokes had done. But I'd made it!

I threw my stuff down and clambered in. I couldn't spot my clothes so was going to have to get Erin to dig them out of the boot for me. But who cared?

I was freeeeeee!

I clipped on my seat belt as all the energy today had sapped out came back in one big burst.

'Pheweeeeee, what a day!' But where to start? I *could* tell Mum the truth. How I'd had to recite some of Dad's positive mantras to stop myself climbing out of the toilet window. But no. I'd survived today! Anything was possible! It was time to show Mum I wasn't her walking disaster daughter. I could be just as good as Erin.

'I honestly had *such* a great time, Mother dearest!' I sounded so enthusiastic! Maybe the acting workshops Erin had forced me to go to earlier had worked? 'Who knew Willy Shakey could be *so* good?' I was panting, which was slightly worrying as I'd only run for twenty-eight seconds. 'Erin was right, you know . . .' Time to lay it on extra thick. I shook the headrest of her driver's seat. 'You really can't *get bard* when there's so much Shakespeare to have fun with!' Nailed it! And for the first time I laughed at that joke.

But Mum didn't.

In fact, she didn't do anything at all.

Because . . .

Oh no. No. Nooo. NO!

I actually froze.

In the front seat wasn't Mum. Or Dad. Or *anyone* I'd seen before.

And now, come to think of it, didn't we have grey seats? Not black ones.

My blood turned to slush.

What.

Had.

I.

Done?!

'I'm sorry.' A confused-looking man turned round in the driver's seat. That I was still clutching. 'Do I know you?'

He had shoulder-length blond hair in an old-school Harry Styles-esque way. I must *not* tell him I thought he was my mum.

'I thought you were my mum.' Right. Well done, me. 'Not because of the hair. Although it does look a bit like Mum's.' I gulped. 'In a good way.'

I didn't know who was more shocked, him ... or me. I guessed it wasn't every day a sweaty stranger in half a beard and a droopy ruff thought they were your offspring.

'So I *don't* know you?' The look on his face suggested I hadn't really cleared things up. Shakespeare would probably have described him as 'most alarm-ed'.

Should I leave? Or was that even ruder?

'I ... er ... don't think so, no.'

I peeled my fingers off the headrest as he slowly turned to the passenger seat. The whole time he kept me in his sights, as if I might be about to attack. 'And she's not one of your friends?'

Oh holy pantaloons, he was talking to someone else?! There was another person witnessing this?! How had I not spotted them?! I blamed the ruff.

The person in the passenger seat shifted into the middle. As they swivelled round my stomach flipped. And then went off for a cry.

I knew *exactly* who they were.

And I also knew I'd just made the biggest mistake of my life.

CHAPTER THREE

I'd launched myself into a car with Nic. Amazing Nic. Coolest person I knew, writer of my favourite blog in the universe and all-round iconic human.

I'd been trying to impress her ever since I started senior school.

And I'd just called her dad 'Mum'.

I'D CALLED NIC'S DAD MUM.

'Nicole?' Her dad sounded calm yet confused. 'What's the deal please?' They were both staring at me – the hairy, historical mutant sitting uninvited on their back seat. All these years I'd wanted Nic to notice me, but I had *not* meant like this. 'Do you guys know each other?'

I said a definite, 'Yes,' as Nic said an even more definite, 'Absolutely not.'

Positive: she didn't recognize me.

Way less than positive: I needed a genius idea as to why I said she would. Despite me visiting Nic's website every day and giving Micha almost hourly updates on what she was up to, our only contact to date *had* been me once offering her the last pasty in the canteen – and her saying thanks but she was vegan.

'I offered you a pasty.' No flicker of recognition. 'On October fourteenth.' It was Micha's birthday, which is why I remembered. Blank faces all round. Where was my sister when I needed her?

I had to get out of here as quickly as my salmon-feet would allow.

'I'm sorry. I er ... thought this was my mum's car.' I fumbled around for the bag handles, but the ruff made it hard to see anything. 'So I'm just going to get my ruff – sorry, stuff – and say sorry again, and er ...' I tried to think of anything Shakespeare. 'Bid you adieu.'

I clambered out of the car so fast I lost my balance and splatted on to the pavement. I felt like a lamb I'd seen in a video of a sheep giving birth, limbs flopping everywhere as it plopped to the floor. I lay on the ground, in the middle of everyone walking past, and tried to use whatever sisterly connection I had to summon my sister.

ERIN! HELP NEEDED! HEAR MY SILENT CRIES!

But there was no sign of her, so I scrambled up, waved apologetically at Nic and backed away. My shoes were making me jerk-bow with every step, which didn't help me look any more normal.

Why had I said October fourteenth?!

I tried to breathe.

Why was I still waving?!

Still there was *one* good thing. At least Frankie hadn't put in an appearance. And maybe, just maybe, if I didn't mention pasties or mums ever again, Nic might never figure out who I really was.

I really should stop waving at her.

Should I crawl into this large bin? It couldn't get any worse.

'Lily?'

Or not.

'LILY MAVERS?! Is that youuuu?!'

I didn't need to look to know *exactly* who it was. I would recognize that voice, that laugh, *anywhere*.

I was in *serious* trouble. I put on the best game face I could and turned to face her. It was time to be the most confident, calm and composed I'd *ever* been.

But my fake beard didn't get the memo and some of its fluff did a samba up my nose, making me sneeze six times (a personal record, but this was no time to celebrate).

'Oh ACHOO, hello ACHOO, Frankie.' Oh no. It wasn't just Frankie. She had her whole cheer team in formation behind her.

Of *course* this was the moment she'd arrive.

She looked me up and down with the *exact* same expression my sister uses when she watches documentaries about undiscovered sea creatures.

'Can I ask why you're dressed like that?' Frankie's cheer

team were looking at me as if I was a mouldy sock they'd discovered in their kit bag.

Say something funny, Lily. Nic's window was open and she could still hear every word.

'Can I ask you the same?' I laughed.

Frankie and her friends didn't. In fact, the one at the front hissed, 'Because it's our award-winning cheer costume?' which suggested she hadn't grasped the concept of a joke.

'So *this* is how you spend your Saturdays?' Frankie sniggered as she looked round at the MUCH ADO ABOUT SOMETHING signs behind me. '*Interesting.* I didn't even think you were any good at English?'

Just what I didn't want Nic to hear. My one dream was to be considered for the writing team for her online magazine, TheNicReport.

'No, I am. English. Good at.' Er, thanks, words, really backing me up there. 'My sister made me come. After an incident. A washing-up liquid incident.'

Frankie wound her long ponytail round her hand as she looked at the space either side of me.

'Your sister . . . *right.*' I agree – the evidence wasn't exactly compelling. Where was Erin?! 'What even *are* you?' Frankie looked back at the car behind her. 'Nic, any ideas?' I didn't like how firmly Nic shook her head. 'Like, is that even a jacket?'

'It's a doublet,' I replied, a little too quickly. 'And pantaloons.'

Frankie wrinkled her nose as if she'd smelt something bad. She probably had – my general waft of wig glue. 'What it is, *Lily*, is a fashion disaster.' And without warning she stepped beside me, putting an arm under my ruff and round my shoulders. Frankie looked at her friends as she held out her phone, 'Can someone pleeeeease get a picture of me with it?!'

Was I the 'it' or did she mean the doublet? It was hard to tell when she was laughing so hard.

'Er, I'm not sure . . .'

I tried to wriggle free, but Frankie's back-flipping arms were pure muscle that had clamped me to her.

The photo was happening whether I liked it or not. What if she showed someone back at school?!

But one of her friends was already zooming in the shot.

I had milliseconds before my semi-bald, fully bearded, pantalooned self was immortalized. Right next to the perfection that was Frankie.

I had to do *something*. So with all the speed I had, I pulled at my wig to whip it off.

Yank.

But the wig didn't shift.

The glue had welded it to my scalp.

And all I did was yank my head sideways so hard I gave myself whiplash.

At the exact moment the photo was taken.

Y-owwwwch.

I rubbed at my scalp, as Frankie and her friends gathered

round to look at the photo. And maybe it was okay, because they were smiling ... But as the smiles turned into tears of laughter, I wasn't exactly reassured.

'Lils ...' Erin's voice cut through the hysterics. Finally! At least now everyone would see her costume and have proof I'd been dragged here by my sister and I was actually a very nice, and normal, human being. 'You all right there?'

No ... *She hadn't?!*

That was why she'd disappeared for ages! Erin was in jeans looking like a totally regular person coming to collect me from my solo day of fancy dress fun.

'ERIN!' I shouted so hard a chunk of beard flopped off.

She shrugged as if I was being dramatic. 'You didn't say you were meeting friends?'

Before I could reply, Frankie spluttered, 'Friends?! Let me stop you right there.'

I knew we *weren't* but ... ouch.

Erin didn't miss a beat. 'Well, why are you taking photos with my sister then?'

Oof. Just like that Frankie stopped laughing – and suddenly I was glad Erin was here. My sister unleashed her signature move – a withering eyebrow raise – and Frankie stepped back. Never had I seen a cheerleader look less cheerful.

'You coming then, Lils?' Erin looked towards the bus stop in the distance as a car beeped. Mum's car. My actual mum's car. *Why two minutes late, Mother? Whhhhhy? You're never late, so why today?!* You might have thought there was no harm doing a quick tidy of bits of paper by the phone, but alas, those two minutes had changed the course of my life!

I scurried towards the car as fast as I could, feeling Frankie's glare follow me like a laser beam.

I just had to hope she had an ounce of humanity and kept that photo to herself. It was bad enough her cheer friends witnessing the whole thing, but if she shared it, come Monday my dream of surviving school would be over.

I sighed so hard my ruff rippled. *Why had I agreed to come?* Nic was never going to talk to me now, let alone want me for her website team.

'Did you have a nice day, girls?' Mum wound down her window. Despite everything I still needed to put on a smile and carry on the plan to get in her good books.

'Great day.' Erin beat me to it. 'Although, Lils –' she leant on the car roof – 'I thought you said Frankie was a nightmare? She seemed nice enough to me?'

Eurgh! Why was Erin always like this?! So smug and so perfect with her easy-peasy life?! I glared at her. She winked right back. Would trying to strangle her with my beard count as 'mature enough' behaviour for Mum?

'And not to change the subject, but have you seen my skull anywhere?'

And that was when I realized I'd left her prop in Frankie's car.

And that was when Erin said innocently that I'd have to hurry or I might lose her precious signed artwork.

So instead of putting this whole thing behind me, I had to chase-limp after Frankie's car, my costume billowing around me, then hammer on their back windscreen and wait as Nic wound down her window. I think she was expecting me to say sorry, not, 'P-please can I have my, er . . . skull back?'

As Nic passed it to me, Frankie waved from the back seat, her phone up. Great, more photos.

'See you Monday, Lils.' Frankie sounded like butter wouldn't melt in her mouth. But as I gulped, she looked me right in the eye and grinned. 'Smile for the video!' And blew me a kiss. 'XOXO.'

RIP life as I knew it.

CHAPTER FOUR

'We can fix this.' My best friend could *always* be relied on to be positive. Micha and I had ditched our usual lunch spot to sit on the wall round the back of the main building. Some people would call it hiding; I thought of it as visually obscuring. I'd skated so fast into school to try to avoid any sighting of Frankie that my skateboard had felt like a hoverboard.

'How?' I'd gone through everything I could possibly think of. Including googling head transplants and how far off we were from time travel (although the fact no one seemed to know made me think the answer was 'for ever'). 'You saw the look Frankie gave me in assembly.'

'The big smile as soon as she saw you?' Micha nodded solemnly. 'Worrying. Very worrying.'

'The *most* worrying.' I tried not to think about the footage Frankie had of me. Or that she had about one zillion followers online. Or that for some reason this whole term she'd full-on hated me.

'Although –' I looked around to check we were still alone – 'if, y'know, she *did* show anyone the video –' *full body shudder* – 'it wouldn't be *that* big a deal . . . would it?' My voice was so bad at lying it went all squeaky.

'Of course not,' Micha said with her big, reassuring smile, even though we both knew the real answer was: 'The deal would be so big it would change life as I knew it.'

'And we've always got these.' Mich held out some cling-film-wrapped Cadbury Fingers. 'Frankie might take away our freedom, but she can never take away our snacks.'

'St-unning.' I popped one in my mouth and instantly felt a tiny bit better. 'And by tonight this –' I wobbled my head, making the oversized knot-bun on top of it bounce from side to side – 'will have been chopped out of existence as well.' The fluff monstrosity on my head was a mix of my real hair and fake hair all glued together. Never again would I trust Erin when she said best-before dates were 'just guides'. Over the weekend the wig glue had evolved into cement. Mum and Dad hadn't exactly been sympathetic – they'd mainly shared pictures against my will on the extended family WhatsApp group, and overused the crying laughing emoji. There was a glimmer that Dad *had* been concerned, but it turned out he was just investigating the hairy knot for ideas to share with his colleagues on their 'Concrete Chat' forum. Sometimes I felt the only one who truly cared about me in this family was Barry the Hamster. And he died four weeks ago.

I would never forgive Erin for this. If her boyfriend hadn't broken his wrist on my experiment, and she hadn't forced me to wear that stupid outfit then had an overly long wee, this would never have happened.

We hadn't spoken since Saturday, despite Mum and Dad hurling comments at me including, 'Is it mature to ignore your sister?' and, 'How do you dissolve industrial glue?'. Erin and I were both going to the hairdresser's tonight after school. I didn't want to hang out with my sister but I did want to get a brush through my hair again. It had been two days.

'Exactly.' Micha put another Cadbury Finger in my mouth. 'Hair today, gone tomorrow. And you always said you wanted Nic to know you existed.'

Ever since we'd started senior school, Micha had been helping in my attempts to get Nic to notice me. Nic had a whole committee of students who worked on TheNicReport – all totally different, and all totally brilliant. Nic set the agenda and together they made the site a mash-up of writing, filmed stuff, animation, photos – whatever Nic thought people should know about. Actual Billie Eilish had once commented with 'mind blown' and last year Nic blocked Lewis Capaldi for being 'too chatty in the comments'. There was nothing I wanted more than to write for TheNicReport. But if Nic figured out I was the Lily Mavers who clambered into her car, there was no way she'd talk to me again, let alone think I could one day be part of her team.

As much as I wanted to cry, change my name, change schools, maybe even countries, instead I bit into another

Cadbury Finger and told Micha that maybe she was right. The last thing I wanted was to let Erin ruin my life *and* Micha's lunch hour. Yes, my best mate was always positive on the outside, but behind her big smiles I knew she was really stressed. She'd been falling behind in chemistry and this morning Mr Sharma had said that if she didn't get her grades up he was putting her down a set. And if Micha dropped down we both knew what her parents would do – stop her playing football. They'd done the exact same with her older sister and her filmmaking. It wasn't that her parents weren't supportive of what their children did. It was just that they had one condition. Good grades came first. And football was the thing Micha loved most. Her dream was to play for the Aston Villa youth team – and go on to be selected for the England squad (I was the only person outside her family who knew Mich slept in an England shirt with 'Ndiaye' on the back to try to manifest it all happening). And she was *so* close to getting there. This Sunday she was playing in the Inter County Cup – a huge tournament that the Aston Villa scouts would be at. My shambles of a life could wait.

I put my arm round her.

'You're right. And when it all goes to plan and I dazzle Nic and she asks me to guest-edit her site, my first feature will be "Why Micha Is So Awesome" told through the medium of Chase Cheney GIFs.' He was an American pop star who we were both ob-sessed with.

Mich smiled, happy she'd cheered me up.

'Would definitely read.' She waited a moment. 'So in the meantime, what are we going to do about your sister? And y'know.' She lowered her voice. 'Frankie ...'

We both made the same tongue-out 'erghk' noise.

'Erin? I'm not sure ... *yet*.' She'd spent the car journey home telling me to chill out, and to write up what happened into a 'life fail' piece for my blog. *Thanks for nothing, sister.* 'And Frankie? Well ...' I took a deep breath and did the impression of her that always made Micha laugh. *'Well, she is like the meanest person I know, so I'm going to have to avoid her at all costs or –'* I flipped my head just like Frankie always did – *'my life won't be worth living, XOXO.'* I even did the X O finger movements.

But Micha didn't laugh. She just kicked me hard in the shin. And considering she was top goalscorer in our school, that was quite hard.

'What?' I asked, confused. But Micha kicked me even harder. With a growing sense of dread, I turned round.

Uh. Oh.

'Cute,' Frankie smirked. She flipped her hair so hard she whipped her best friend PJ in the eye. He didn't even say ow.

Please don't let Frankie have heard every word?!

'Think I do it better though.' She held her fingers up. 'X and indeed O.'

She'd heard *every* word.

I actually whimpered. But Micha smiled as if I hadn't put my foot so far in my mouth I looked like the lady at

CheerCon. 'You guys want anything?' She jumped down from the wall and grabbed her football boots. 'Cos we were about to head off.' She sounded impressively breezy.

I silently slid off the wall. Could I absorb into the brickwork?

'No biggie.' Frankie smiled the hugest, fakest smile. 'I was just trying to decide something and thought maybe you two could help?' She paused. 'Nice hairstyle btw, Lil. Very ... *experimental.*'

I gulped so hard I choked on a bit of rogue biscuit.

'So whaddya think ... ?' Frankie held out her phone. Whatever was on it switched off Micha's permanent smile.

Years of experience of Erin's tricks meant I knew *exactly* what this was. A trap. We needed to find an escape. But all I could spot was one open window above us.

'To post or not to post – that is the question?' Frankie laughed, triggering her mates to do the same. 'It's *Shakespeare*, Lily. But you'd know that.'

She turned the screen to face me. A video was playing. Of me grabbing Erin's skull through their car window, my face scrunched like a historical gremlin, my beard flapping in the wind. For added effect Frankie had even made my eyes red. And it was playing on loop, the UPLOAD button flashing away below it.

My blood ran cold.

The world could *not* witness this.

'Obviously it's really funny –' *lie, lie, lie* – 'but I don't think anyone else needs to see it.' I didn't want to beg, that would only make Frankie more likely to do it.

'Agreed,' Micha backed me straight up.

Frankie wrinkled her perfect eyebrows, in fake deep thought.

'Weird, huh ... cos I thought the *exact* opposite.' Her finger hovered over UPLOAD as my stupid face lurched back and forth on the screen.

'It's gold, Franks.' PJ leant over. 'I mean, no offence, Lily, but what were you thinking?' Offence taken. 'You *gotta* share it.'

Frankie nodded solemnly. 'It *would be* rude not to, *wouldn't it?*' She moved her finger closer to the screen. 'Give the people what they want and all that.'

'Er ...' I couldn't just stand back and watch my life get ruined! Could they be reasoned with? 'Do you really have to ... ?'

Frankie cut me off. 'Well, I wasn't *going* to ... I *thought* we could just have a chat. That's why I came looking for you.' I didn't believe a word. 'But then I heard you call me the – what was it ... ?' She tapped her lip. 'Oh yeah, "meanest person you know", and well, I wouldn't want to let you down now, would I? And I'm sure my 37,453 followers –' she refreshed the screen – 'oh no, 37,454, will love it.'

As PJ led their friends in a chant of, 'Do it, do it, do it!' any hope I had crumbled like the emergency Cadbury Finger I'd just panic eaten.

31

'This is ridiculous, you know.' Micha's brown eyes narrowed. I'd never seen her look so furious.

Frankie shrugged. 'Is it? Or is it really, really funny?' She raised an eyebrow. 'I mean, fair's fair after that little impression of me.'

'But you'd already made the GIF. Posting it was your plan all along!' Mich made an excellent point. 'C'mon, Lil, let's go.'

Mich's hand was out but walking away meant giving up on any chance of stopping Frankie. If she posted it, I'd never live it down.

'DO IT, DO IT, DO IT!'

The chanting was now a shout with an added slow clap. Okay. Time to beg.

'Please, Frankie? You *know* I'm sorry about what happened in PE. I've said it a million times!'

'*As if* this is about PE . . .' She scoffed. *What did that mean?!* But her finger was almost touching UPLOAD. She was doing it as slowly as she could, loving every second.

I could hear my own heartbeat, it was thumping so hard. Micha was still beckoning for me to leave.

'DO IT, DO IT, DO IT!'

Argh! I couldn't think straight over the noise!

Which was why, before I could stop myself . . . I reached and grabbed Frankie's phone.

Well, that was what I *meant* to do.

Turns out I didn't grab the phone. My fingers were so

32

shaky and sweaty they slipped right off it – and all I did was knock Frankie's arm. *Hard*.

Her phone went flying.

Was it just me or did the whole world pause as it sailed through the air?

The chanting *definitely* stopped.

Please let it land on something soft!

Frankie's friends' hands had all paused mid-clap.

I swear even birds stopped flapping about.

The handset somersaulted through the air, looking like Tom Daley at the Olympics. But a phone.

Should I throw myself on the paving stones as a human sacrifice for it to land on?

But instead of landing gracefully in water to ten out of ten scores, it landed face down on the paving stone with a massive crack.

Silence.

Followed by a long, loooooong shriek from Frankie.

The phone was as smashed as my chances of making things better with her.

Actual chaos broke out. Her friends all started screaming at me as Frankie waved her shattered phone in my face.

'I CAN'T BELIEVE YOU'D DO THIS!'

She had a point. Nor could I. It really had been an accident.

Frankie looked as if she might cry. Well, that made two of us, not that anyone was listening to my apologies.

But something else shut everyone up. A massive squeak.

Our heads all snapped up. The window above us had swung wide up and open, and out of it dangled a very red Mrs Saddler.

The one teacher everyone went silent for.

'WHAT ... IS ...' She was so twisted she was struggling to yell. 'ALL ... THIS ... SHOUTING?' Quite a weird question to ask at that volume.

None of us said anything.

'And *who* has a phone out in lunchbreak?' She glared at Frankie, who was holding hers up to my face. 'Frances?'

PJ stepped forward. 'It's mine, Mrs Saddler. Sorry. It won't happen again.'

But PJ should have known that sucking up bounced straight off our deputy. 'You're right it won't. Patrick, it's noble of you trying to save your friend, but next time make sure you're not holding your phone at the same time.' PJ mumbled something and shoved his phone in his pocket. 'Now ...' Mrs Saddler left a dramatic pause. 'Will *someone* tell me what's going on?'

There was silence. No one wanted to be the first one to speak, and if I opened my mouth I'd probably only make things even worse.

Mrs Saddler sighed. 'Fine. We'll do it the hard way. Frances, why is your phone broken?'

'Lily threw it on the floor,' Frankie answered immediately. Thanks for that.

'It was an accident,' I said, getting a sense of déjà vu.

Mrs Saddler leant further out. 'And why did this *accident* happen . . . ? Anyone?'

What could I do? Explain that Frankie had been about to post a video of me when I'd begged her not to? But if I did that, Frankie would never forgive me.

But Micha spoke up.

'Frankie was threatening to post something about Lily. And then the phone just sort of . . . fell. Well, flew, really.'

Wow – my best friend really was the best for a reason. Telling the truth meant she had now joined me as Frankie's joint-least favourite person. I pressed my foot on to hers, my way of saying a secret thanks. She wiggled her toes back.

Mrs Saddler rolled her eyes. 'Lucky me. Another exciting day in the dramas of Year Eight.' She sighed. 'I'll make this quick. Frances, L . . . aura?'

Frankie shouted, 'Lily.' Yup, my own teacher didn't even remember my name despite hearing it ten seconds ago.

'Yes, you two. You know the rules. No phones, no fighting, no –' she poked her arm out to wave her hand dramatically – 'any of *this*. You need to sort out whatever it is you've got going on.' Frankie coughed indignantly as if Mrs Saddler had just suggested the impossible. The first step would be me getting Frankie's phone repaired. The parentals were going to kill me and I could already see Erin's face. She was going to *love* this. I'd have to do *so* many chores to earn the money back. RIP fun, it was nice knowing you. 'Now, I can't make you be friends, but what I *can* do is make you find a

35

way to work together.' She paused. 'So my office, eight thirty tomorrow, and I'll let you know what I have planned.'

Extra school time?! With Frankie?! In the morning?! Horrific! With a capital H. Still at least a teacher being there meant Frankie couldn't actually murder me.

I rubbed my face as Frankie hissed, 'This is all your fault,' at me. But when I looked back up Mrs Saddler was squinting – right at me. 'You. Laura. You're Erin's sister, aren't you?'

Uh-oh. That question was never good. I nodded and Mrs Saddler's face brightened right up. 'Excellent! That's given me the perfect idea!' Perfect? Or perfectly terrible? 'No need to come to my office tomorrow. From this moment on, you two can consider yourselves to be . . .' She drummed her fingers on the window. 'Backstage crew for the play!'

My mouth fell open.

Giving up all my spare time? To work on my sister's play? With Frankie?

There was *no* way.

And by the look on Frankie's face, she felt exactly the same way.

But Mrs Saddler just smiled. 'Excellent. I'll take that as a yes. You can be the first two.' She lowered her voice. 'Maybe only two . . .' She coughed and remembered we could hear, 'And, Laura, we just announced that your sister got the role of Titania.' Of *course* Erin had got the part. We were like a see-saw – the more she excelled, the more I flat-out failed.

'The most pivotal role of the play. I'm sure you're going to love supporting her.'

She clearly knew nothing about me and Erin.

'Can we do detention instead?' I shouted up. Weirdest plea ever. 'Please?!'

Frankie and I sitting in silence, trying to ignore each other's existence felt dreamy in comparison.

'No, you cannot.' Mrs Saddler looked at me as if I was a piece of hardened food on one of her textbooks. 'First full rehearsal is tomorrow. Main hall, quarter to four. And if you're going to do this kind of thing again, can I at least advise you to have the common sense not to do it under the staffroom window?'

CHAPTER FIVE

Today had gone from bad to worst to worsterer. Still, at least I was on the verge of getting one thing fixed – my hair. My head tuft was so knotted it had separated into two furry pom-poms. Even Micha, the kindest person in the world, had said the look was 'brave'.

Once school had finished, Dad drove Erin and me to town. We were in no doubt of the plan. We weren't just going to leave the hairdresser's with a new cut – we had to have seriously made things up. Did Mum and Dad understand a haircut didn't mean a total change in personality? But Dad was seriously cross – not just pretend cross to please Mum. When I'd told him about having to get Frankie's phone fixed, he'd gone silent and nose-breathed for a full minute. He was so furious he didn't even register Erin chuckling away.

I was *so* over my sister. Especially as she'd followed my confession by declaring she'd snagged the 'most wanted' part in A *Midsummer Night's Dream*. They'd been rehearsing the play for weeks, swapping everyone in and out of roles, and even though she was one of the youngest in the cast Mrs Saddler had apparently said Erin was 'the stand-out choice for Titania'. I'd never seen my sister so smug. It was enough to tear my hair out – except I physically couldn't as it was glued to my head.

But when we got to Anita Haircut the whole place was shut up. The only sign of Anita, who we'd been going to for ever, was a note stuck to the door.

Had to shut early. Sorry!
To my lovely customers, I'll be open as normal
tomorrow (if we get out of A&E in time)
Anita xx
PS If you see the pictures on the
internet, remember, things always
look worse out of context!
PPS If you're the person coming to try
to get the blood out of the carpet,
then text me for the key. And
if you find a small bit of

(her handwriting went very small)

ear

(it went back to normal size again)

then give me a ring!

'So . . . guess we're not having our hair cut then.' Erin looked delighted that my hair misery might continue after all.

A vein had popped out on Dad's head, which meant he was trying hard to hold in a swear.

'I think it means –' the vein pulsated – 'we come back tomorrow.'

I clutched my skateboard tight. This could *not* be happening. I'd rather have half an ear than ever-growing cooker knobs sticking out of my head.

'But, Dad.' I lowered my head so he could get a good look at them. 'These *cannot* live to see another day. They're hair-endous.'

Normally I'd be happy to dodge an evening activity with my sister, but facing Mrs Saddler and Frankie tomorrow was bad enough without these monstrosities getting even worse. Dad scanned up and down the high street, as if he might spot a big sign telling him what to do.

'C'mon.' I needed to get him moving before Erin talked him into going home. 'There must be *somewhere* else we can go, even at –' I looked at my phone – 'five p.m. on a Monday.'

The signs weren't looking good, but then again neither was I. Determined to fix this, I marched off, leaving Erin and Dad no choice but to follow. But after trying the only three places still open, all we got was helpful advice to, 'Not leave it so late next time' and, 'Have you thought about a hat?'

'Well, we tried.' Dad had walked us back to the car park. 'Your mother is not going to be impressed but maybe Erin can help you do something with –' he peered at my head – '*them* tonight.'

But Erin was squinting up at the huge railway bridge that stretched above us. 'One sec ...' She sped off around the corner, before jogging back looking pleased with herself. 'Panic may be off. There's one there ...' She pointed to one of the arches where little businesses had started to pop up. Wow, she was actually being helpful for once. I hurried over – there was a cool coffee place, a dog-yoga place called Feeling Ruff and ... yes! A hairdresser: The Hairy Godmother.

Sure, as we walked nearer it looked more and more weird, and less and less as if there was a single customer in there, but still ... It was time to say goodbye to my head-hogs!

'I hope their speciality is mullet,' Erin whispered. Had she really only suggested it as she thought they might make me look even worse?

'You're in this with me,' I hissed as Dad pushed the door open.

TINKLE DING!

The high-pitched chime sounded like a pretend wand I had when I was little.

41

Where was anyone? Was it even open?

'Er . . . hello?' Dad called out, his words echoing round the exposed brickwork and empty chairs.

The coolest woman I'd ever seen not-on-the-internet materialized.

'Welcome.' She stuck her hand out for Dad to shake. The three of us looked round – where had she come from?! 'I'm Agatha.'

Agatha had a shaved head, stripy top, black dungarees and trainers that looked as if they'd had a lifetime of all the best festivals. Agatha was amazing. Like on-a-level-with-Nic amazing. Even Erin lost a bit of her cool at this goddess appearing out of what felt like thin air.

It must have been her desk. Yes. Agatha must have been behind it while we were looking at the framed pictures on the wall. Inspirational quotes and pictures of her clients, smiling as if they'd had the greatest hour of their life in her chair. Maybe, just maybe, Erin's sabotage plan had backfired.

'So what can I do for you?' Agatha smiled gently.

'My sister needs something doing with this.' Erin pointed at my head.

'And *my sister* can let me speak for myself.' I smiled back, although I realized Erin had basically summed it up. 'But, er, yes. I do need something doing with this.'

Dad rolled his eyes, embarrassed a stranger was witnessing what he saw all the time at home. It wasn't my fault my older sister was a maniac.

Agatha nodded slowly. 'Okay.' She prodded one of my head pom-poms. 'So are you looking for a big change?'

I shrugged. 'Just something normal would be good. This was . . .' How to explain? 'Just an accident really.'

'Another one.' Erin smiled sweetly.

'You can talk! It's all your fault?!' Gah! Erin wound me up so much!

'Girls, PLEASE,' Dad boomed. 'Enough!' He did one of his in-for-four out-for-four breaths and composed himself. 'Sorry about that, Agatha. It's lovely to meet you. I wanted to see if you had time to fit them both in? That is if you even want to after that little display. I'm not sure –' he looked around the empty salon – 'if you or your team have space?'

He was giving her a get-out – I crossed my fingers we hadn't put her off.

But Agatha smiled, another very calm smile. 'Don't worry, I can squeeze them in now. If you come back in ninety minutes, we should be done.'

'Perfect. Much appreciated.' Dad put a hand on my shoulder, and one on Erin's. 'And, you two, remember, when I pick you up, no more . . . *this*. Okay?'

By 'this' he meant drama.

'Sure thing, Dad.' I gave him a firm nod. With my birthday, and prom, looming, I urgently needed to get back in the parentals' good books – or at least out of the terrible ones.

No sooner had he walked out of the door than I was in Agatha's chair. I couldn't remember swapping my school jumper for the wrap-around gown, but it looked cool. All moons and stars.

Agatha put down a hot drink in front of me, then one by the sofa Erin was sitting on. It smelt of liquorice and chocolate and marshmallow. Yum. I took a sip as Agatha undid my head tufts. How was she running her hands through my hair when I'd broken a brush just trying?! She made eye contact in the mirror.

'So then, Lily.' Wow, I didn't even remember Dad telling her my name. 'What are you after?'

I always found this bit embarrassing. What I *wanted* was to walk out looking the coolest I ever had done – but I wasn't sure how much making my hair strands slightly different lengths could do that.

'Er, just something good. Something y'know ... That's ... I dunno.' *A style to stop Frankie in her tracks?* 'Less terrible than this.'

'Gonna be hard,' Erin muttered under her breath.

Agatha turned to look at her, but didn't say anything before slowly swivelling back to me.

'You're sisters, correct?' Agatha asked as she washed my hair. We'd moved to the sink.

Her head massage felt so good all I could reply with was, 'Mmmhhrgghhha.' Which was an error – I'd given Erin an opportunity to answer for me.

'More's the pity,' Erin said as she flicked a page in a magazine.

'She's always like this,' I said quietly enough for just Agatha to hear – but she didn't react, clearly not wanting to get caught up in it. And soon I was back in the chair, a damp towel round my shoulders, with Agatha snipping into my wet hair. I'd never seen this place before and I wanted to know more about The Hairy Godmother. Agatha didn't say much, but did explain that she'd just opened the salon, as she normally visited homes or did backstage at events. I fired loads of questions at her, especially ones about the celebs she'd worked with as I *swore* she'd let the name 'Chase' slip. But Agatha was more interested in my life, and soon I'd told her all about Micha, and her football tournament, and GettingLilyWithIt, and what had happened on Saturday, and how I'd accidentally made Frankie even madder at me. In what felt like minutes, not only had I told her my whole life story but my hair was cut, dried and looked the best it ever had.

'Wow,' I whistled as Agatha held the mirror up behind me. 'You're some kind of scissor wizard!'

My brown hair was trimmed to past-shoulder length, the tufts totally gone. It was so shiny it was almost reflective.

'My pleasure.' She grinned. 'A new haircut can make you feel like a new woman, right?' I nodded – it sure could. I already felt a bit less worried about tomorrow. But my time was up – Agatha was gesturing for me to swap with Erin. I picked up my mug so as not to leave the cold drink in front of them, but it was still piping hot.

Weird.

I flopped down in the swivel chair next to them, keen to chat more to Agatha. Maybe I could come back and do a blog post about her? But Erin was taking out her super-neat French plaits and moaning that her long bob looked a bit flat (even though her red hair never looked anything other than perfect). Now she'd seen what Agatha had done to mine, she was clearly looking for some of the same magic. But as Agatha started pasting on some purple goo, Erin and I glanced at each other. Dad was going to be here in forty-five minutes – did we have time for this?

But soon Erin had the most amazing deep-red lowlights and there was still . . . half an hour left. Phew. I must have got the time wrong. As Agatha blow-dried Erin's hair I studied the most amazing tattoo on the side of her arm. Sort of like a flower, but with symbols in it.

'What's that?' I asked, hoping I wasn't intruding.

Agatha lifted up her arm. 'This?' She held it up to the mirror. 'What do you think?'

'Is it a puzzle?' It was my only guess.

'Kind of.' Her eyes sparkled.

Erin squinted. 'It's letters, right?'

'Kind of.' Agatha laughed.

But then I saw it in the reflection – and it made sense. It was a picture of a mirror made up of the letters of Hairy Godmother. 'Oh I seeeeee. It's the right way round in the reflection!' *See, Erin, you're not always the smartest one.*

46

Agatha chuckled. '*Exactly*. Sometimes it's easier to understand things when you look at them a new way.'

I had no idea what she meant, but in my opinion anything she said was gold, so I nodded hard in agreement.

And by the time Agatha had finished perfecting Erin's extra bouncy bob, my sister was fangirling as hard as me. Sorry, Anita, but you and your ear-chopping days were behind us.

'Thank you. Seriously . . .' Erin flicked the ends of her hair. 'I didn't know it could even look like this!'

'Well, *I* always knew, Erin.' A weird thing for Agatha to say considering we'd only met an hour and a half ago. 'But now you see it you can believe too. Anyway . . .' She walked over to the desk, Erin and I suddenly beside her in our jackets even though I didn't remember standing up. 'Your father will be here soon – so are you going to do what he asked?' Agatha typed something into the bookings screen. 'I don't want him cross at me too!'

'Oh deffo.' Agatha had cheered me up so much, I'd almost forgotten I was mad at my sister. 'Honestly, you've saved the day. Completely.' I checked myself out again in the big wall mirror. 'No more looking like a total weirdo for me!'

Erin laughed. 'Well, no more than normal anyway.'

And just like that, the zen of Agatha poofed into thin air and normal Erin-rage resumed.

'All right, *sister*. Let's not forget you're the one who dragged me out in that stupid wig in the first place.'

Erin folded her arms. 'It was *funny*. Not like you breaking my boyfriend's wrist.'

'That was an *accident*!'

'Hello, catchphrase.' Erin's eyebrows wrinkled. 'Wonder if Frankie would say that about her phone?'

I *knew* she'd loved hearing about that. But there was one thing Erin didn't know.

'I'll ask her tomorrow. The two of us are doing all the backstage stuff now.' I paused to let it sink in. 'Mrs Saddler asked for me by name.' True on a technicality (even if she did think it was Laura).

Erin looked horrified. *Good.* Although within a millisecond she'd composed herself. 'Fingers crossed there'll be no disaster with the special effects this year.'

She had a point. Working backstage wasn't just time-consuming, it was dangerous. Last year a flame-throwing prop had charred both of Singed Simon's eyebrows (I was pretty sure his real name was Pete but no one could rhyme anything eyebrow-related with that). Singed Simone wasn't a look I could ever live down.

'Girls.' Agatha stepped between us. Cringe. '*Please.* Your dad will be here any second. You should be supporting each other.'

But maybe Agatha, who hadn't taken sides this whole evening, was the person to finally make my sister realize how she acted towards me. 'Well, I would, but Erin never takes a moment off from reminding me, reminding *everyone*, how much better she is than me.' I sighed. 'It's as if she doesn't realize how much harder life is when you're not the over-achieving big sister.'

Erin spluttered. 'Harder? I just *try* more. If you stepped it up a bit, maybe you'd find all your accidents magically stopped happening?'

But Agatha didn't say anything. Instead she lifted up two handheld mirrors.

'Look.' She had one in each hand. 'Both of you. Take a moment to look in the mirror – at each other.' And we did. Something about Agatha made you want to do whatever she said. 'Do you see each other differently when do you it this way?' Erin and I scowled at each other. 'Because you cannot see unless you *try* to look.' Agatha paused. 'I know what having a sister is like. But no more arguments. Not like this. Let that be your promise to me.'

Erin and I both nodded.

Maybe we were as tired as each other of all the bickering?

Agatha looked pleased. 'Good. Trust me, if you try to understand each other more, I promise understanding will flow back.'

I had no idea what she was on about but it sounded good.

But the second she looked away and Erin shot me her smug little smile, I had a suspicion that not even Agatha could stop our feuding.

TINKLE DING!

Dad pushed open the door and almost tripped over his

own feet with the shock of me and Erin standing calmly together, my tufts a thing of the past.

'Wow.' He looked super pleased. 'Agatha, you've really worked your magic here!'

'It's what The Hairy Godmother does.' Agatha smiled gently. But as we thanked her again, and went to follow Dad out of the door, she blocked our way.

'Erin. Lily. I'm glad to see you leave happier than you came. As I said, a new haircut can make you feel like a new person.' I did like Agatha, but she couldn't half say some odd things. Anita normally just told us to come back in twelve weeks and not to worry if our hair didn't look quite symmetrical for at least three washes. 'But . . .' Agatha lowered her voice so Dad couldn't hear. 'Remember your promise. I would not want you to realize the hard way that what you look like on the outside is only half the story. Understanding comes from really seeing – not just looking at a reflection. Good luck.'

Yup, she was bonkers. But I loved her.

And as Erin and I jumped in the car (her shotgunning the front seat, of course) things did feel a little less tense between us. Dad seemed positively victorious. As I stared out of the window, Erin chatting away about playing Titania and getting full marks in her geography test, I couldn't help but wonder.

Maybe this was a turning point for me and Erin, just like Dad and Mum and even Agatha wanted?

CHAPTER SIX

My alarm went off early. Too early. And three hit-snoozes later I was still mad at it. But I needed to drag myself out of bed. Today *had* to go well.

After the news about Frankie's phone, last night's dinner had been a mix of frosty silence mixed with Mum and Dad listing chores I could do to earn back the money. So with Mrs Saddler holding me hostage at school with play rehearsals, if I wanted to get *any* spare time back to have a life, I needed to make them all less cross at me. Starting with getting up early to fit in making myself look presentable, mentally preparing to see Frankie and making it on time for school for once. Mum and Dad had begrudgingly agreed I could swap my normal last place in the shower queue for first to help me out.

Half asleep, I grabbed my towel, tightened my wonky ponytail and fumbled my way into the hall. But there was something at the end of it by the towel cupboard.

My sister.

'I'm first, remember?' I croaked, sounding like a swamp thing.

'But I've got my first read-through as Titania,' Erin said, taking a step forward and holding out her perfectly folded towel as if it were evidence she deserved my place.

Sorry, but how did that beat my Frankie issue?

'No, Erin. Not today. We agreed, remember?'

'Did we?' She knew full well we had. Just because no one was around to hear her, she thought she could get her own way like normal.

But nearly thirteen years of dealing with her meant I knew what this was. A distraction technique.

And as she scoped out the bathroom door I knew *exactly* what she was planning.

A sprint to the bathroom.

No way. I was not having it. We'd all agreed!

If she was going to play dirty, so was I.

I ran. Fast.

But so did my sister. And instead of being first to hit the shower, the only thing I hit was her head. With mine.

BANG.

Ow.

Owwwwwwwwwww.

Did I pass out?

I couldn't be sure, but when I stood up I felt weird. The world had gone blurry.

Dizzy, I staggered into the bathroom, feeling Erin do the same next to me.

'You . . . okay?' I clutched my head. My hair was messy and loose – my ponytail must have fallen out.

'Errrrrr,' is all I heard my sister say.

Well, not strictly true – she then flicked the light on and screamed. Incredibly loudly.

What was up? I leant against the sink, looked up and blinked hard. There we were, in the mirror. No blood. We both looked fine.

But my head did hurt. A lot.

As I heard the shuffle of Mum and Dad getting up, I kicked the bathroom door closed. I didn't want to have to explain yet another argument to them.

So why was Erin still screaming?

I rubbed my head again, willing it to stop throbbing.

Weird. My hand in the mirror wasn't moving.

But . . .

No.

NOOOO!

In the mirror, Erin's hand was.

And now Erin was saying, 'Erin?! What is happening?!'

Which were the exact words I thought were coming out of *my* mouth.

I did the only thing I could do.

Scream.

CHAPTER SEVEN

'Unless John Legend himself has decided to have a singalong in our bathroom at 6.53 a.m., I'm expecting a *very* good reason for all this racket.'

Dad had stormed into the bathroom in his Yoda dressing gown, green hood and ears pulled up. But this was not the most traumatic sight here by a loooong way.

Because I WAS STARING AT THE MIRROR AND MY SISTER'S FACE WAS STARING BACK AT ME.

This could *not* be possible.

I prodded my face. Erin's reflection did the same.

What was going on?!

I looked at the person standing next to me. It should be my sister – neat red bob, slightly smug face. But no. It was brown-haired, shocked-looking and most utterly and definitely . . . *me*. Its face looked as freaked out as I was feeling.

Had the mirror got confused?!

Was that a thing?

I raised a hand. And dropped it when I saw Erin's reflection do the same.

'Erin?' Dad asked, alarmed.

Was ... I ... In ... Erin's ... Body?!

This couldn't be right.

'Lily?' Dad followed up.

I opened my mouth. Then shut it. Then made a noise that sounded like a balloon deflating.

I had *no* idea what was going on. And *no* idea how big my nostrils got when I looked shocked. No wonder Erin used to call me Lilydactyl.

Breathe, Lily. Don't panic. Not yet.

I must be hallucinating.

I mean, I had eaten a lot of broccoli last night. Was a side effect accidentally swapping souls with your sibling?! I didn't see anything on the label, but who knows!

Or were my eyes playing up from lack of sleep?

Mum appeared behind Dad, rubbing her eyes. 'Erin. C'mon, we agreed Lily could go first.'

I *knew* it! I smiled, happy that even in the middle of this disaster, I was right. But Mum was giving me evils.

'C'mon then ...' she snapped, pushing the door open. 'It's not like you to be okay with running late for school.'

What? It was my *dream* to run late for school! Run so late that I ran right past it and straight to dinner time.

Dad tapped his watch, 'Come *on*, Erin.'

55

Oh, riiiiight! They thought I was Erin! They were seeing this weirdness too!

So even though I was the one in the right for a change, I was *still* the one in trouble.

Oh, how stupendously brilliawful.

I looked at my sister – who worryingly still looked very much like me. A very alarmed me.

C'mon, Lily . . . think.

There *had* to be an explanation.

Am I just dreaming? I pinched myself hard. Ouch. So it wasn't that. Next option . . .

'Quick question.' Argh?! I even sounded like Erin. 'Family quiz . . . is eating too much broccoli . . .' There was no other way of saying it. 'Dangerous?'

From the looks on Mum and Dad's faces, the answer was 'No'. And also 'Please never ask us something that weird before seven a.m. again'.

Okay. Maybe we just bumped our heads too hard? Making this all a freaky concussion dream, just like when Dad stood up into a shelf and spent ten minutes having an in-depth conversation with a cushion.

Yes. That must be it. So this was fine. Allll fine. And even better, I could prove it. I just needed to hit my head again and everything would snap back to normal.

I smiled calmly at my family and pulled my shoulders back.

'Sister. Parents. Prepare for things to get normal.'

I took a deep breath and ... ran. Full-on pelted as fast as I could. Right into the door frame.

I felt majestic!

Right until I bounced straight off it and back on to the floor.

Ow. Ow. Oooooow.

I opened my eyes, excited to see the world back to normal.

But the person staring down at me was ... me.

NO, EYES, THIS IS NOT OKAY!!

I snapped them shut. They didn't deserve to be open if they weren't going to show me better things.

'Are you all right?' Mum sounded seriously worried. I prized one eye back open – she was crouched over me, Yoda next to her (but I thought/hoped that was just because Dad's hood had fallen too far forward). 'I'm starting to really worry, Erin ...' Mum rubbed at the bump on my head – if she was worried about that, imagine if I told her my entire soul and being had somehow swapped into the body of my sister.

'I'm fine ...' I started to say. Nope, hearing Erin's voice was still too weird. 'Sorry.' I stopped again. 'This is too *major* weirdio.'

My sister glared at me, but it was too late. Our parents had already twigged that Erin had never said 'major weirdio' in her life. 'To, y'know –' I tried to laugh, which was hard when you were lying down, and your head felt as if it'd been bashed into a door frame, because it had – 'quote Lily.'

'Darling.' Dad crouched down. 'Is everything ... okay?'

'If everything was okay, would she have run into a door?' my sister said, which in fairness was a pretty accurate assessment.

'Is my voice *really* that high?' I sat up, only to get an extra clear view of Erin shaking her (my) head in despair.

Dad clutched Mum's arm. 'The doctor doesn't take appointments for an hour!'

'She's fine,' Erin said sternly. 'Aren't you, Lil . . . er . . . Erin?'

I got what she was trying to do – get our parents out of the way so we could figure this out. And for once, I agreed with her. I wasn't sure she needed to add the kick to my bum though. Mumbling something vague about being too focused on today's rehearsal, I clambered up and staggered to my room.

Phew.

It was such a relief to open my door and finally be out of sight so I could properly think.

'Erin, why are you going into Lily's room?' Mum called down the landing.

Oops.

I turned round. Quick, brain. What would Erin definitely not have in her room, but would a hundred per cent be in mine? 'Just wanted to borrow an unwashed sock,' I said with the most reassuring smile I could manage. 'For an art project.'

And feeling Mum's eyes boring into my back, Erin's back, *somebody's* back, I escaped into Erin's room.

I fell back against the door, and looked down at the body below me.

What *was* going on?!

And how could Erin and I fix it the second she was out of the shower?

I flumped on to my sister's bed, but it was already made way too neatly, and smelt weirdly clean, so I sat on the floor in front of the mirror instead.

How was my sister looking back at me?

I didn't like this. Not. One. Bit.

I patted my hands over the body I was in, prodding my face and pulling at Erin's fringe. It all felt so wrong.

By the time Erin got out of the shower, I knew *exactly* how I handled a crisis. By lying starfished on the floor repeating, 'This cannot be happening,' and stress-eating Hula Hoops I'd sneaked and got from my school bag.

Erin darted in, quickly closing the door.

'So ... *this* –' She pointed up and down her body – 'is weird, right. *Hella* weird.' She looked down at my starfish formation. 'And *please* tell me you haven't dropped crisps on my rug.'

I had, but I'd do as she'd asked and not tell her.

'It's *more* than weird, Erin.' I sat up. 'Weird is like when Dad tried growing a ponytail. Or your creepy rock collection. This ... ?' It was hard to describe what it was, when it made no sense at all. 'This is a *disaster*. Have you got *any* idea what's going on?'

Everyone knew my sister was the clever one – surely she had *something*?

But all she did was shake her/my head.

'Nope. I mean, I know you're always getting yourself into weird situations, but this one seems way off, even for you.'

Wait. Was she blaming me?

'Erin. You know this isn't my fault, right?'

'I've heard that before.' Wow, she couldn't drop it even for one second. She breezed on. 'At first I wondered if my brain was playing up, but I got Ben to message me some quiz questions and I got them all right.' She sighed. 'So that's that theory out.'

Great. In moments of crisis I lie on carpets. My sister? She does quizzes for fun. How did we have the same parents?

'And just to check –' I lowered my voice right down – 'to make sure I'm thinking what you're thinking –' in fact, maybe I should just mouth the rest – 'you and me ... well our bodies have ... s ...' But my mouth wouldn't go there. Admitting it made it even freakier.

'Yup.' Erin nodded firmly. 'Despite it defying *all* laws of life and science, we've somehow switched bodies.' She shook her head. 'And yes, I'm aware how ridiculous that sounds. Which is we can't tell *anyone* until we figure out how to switch back.'

'Agreed. And that needs to be *as soon as possible!*' I was grasping on to my latest theory that a good sleep would put everything right. So maybe we just had to try to keep calm until then. Although did that mean spending a night in Erin's room? I looked round at the trophies and certificates (trying to avoid the creepy rocks), and picked up the photo

60

by her bed – Mum and Dad smiling with their arms round her just after she came off stage last year. And a thought hit me: if it was just for *one day*, it could be fun getting a glimpse of life as the favourite child. 'And who knows, maybe it'll be interesting to see how much easier life is when everyone thinks I'm perfect Erin.'

Erin raised her (my) eyebrows. 'Be my guest ... how does Year Ten chemistry sound?' Awful. 'And Les Quizerables practice this lunchtime?' Like torture? Hanging with Erin's school quiz team should be an illegal way to spend lunch. Still, at least it couldn't get any worse. 'And of course after school it's the first play read-through ...' Okay, that was worse. 'Uh-huh.' Erin nodded, watching the realization hit me. 'Then Ben and I were going to hang out for an evening of Castles! Chaos! Cows!'

GAH! An evening playing a strategy board game that was something to do with building castles and breeding wooden sheep while pretending to enjoy Ben's company?! I could never!

AND WHAT IF HE TRIES TO KISS ME?!

That was it. I needed to get back in my body *now*.

I collapsed on Erin's bed in horror. My first kiss was *not* going to be with my sister's boyfriend. That was even more wrong than the montage of 'Fun geography facts!' pinned by her headboard.

Erin smiled sweetly.

'Soooo, if you get through that little lot I'll try and get to grips with . . .' She pretended to think. 'Your mediocre grades and zero responsibility. Going to be really tough. Oh.' She flicked my foot. 'And don't mess up my bed per-lease.'

But I couldn't react. A horrifying thought had hit me (would the horrifying thoughts just stop for a minute?).

And it was the most awful one yet.

Never mind me having to hang out with Ben. Every second I spent being Erin, meant she was on the loose in *my* life. And I was meant to be seeing Micha tonight! Surely it was my duty to protect my best friend from my sister's rock-based chat? Was I going to have to bail on her for the first time ever?!

Any positive thoughts I'd had about this experience withered to a speck of dust. A really small piece of dust. That had been cut in half.

I grabbed Erin's/my arm.

'ERIN, WHAT ARE WE GOING TO DOOOOO?'

'Well, thanks to you, we can tick running into solid objects off the list. Any other ideas?'

I shrugged. 'YouTube tutorials on how to switch bodies with your sister?' Desperate times.

'Even with private browsing, I'm not typing that one in. Anything else?' If Erin was asking me for advice, we really were in trouble. Big trouble.

I slid off the bed and stood in front of her mirror.

'It makes no sense.' I pushed at the nose on my face. It squished differently to mine. 'As *if* I can be you? You watch *Mastermind* . . . for fun. And you don't believe in the concept of slippers.' I stuffed another BBQ Beef Hula Hoop in my mouth – which made me remember she was veggie. 'I can't even have a bacon sandwich to cheer myself up!' I was almost wailing. 'I don't even know how to do your hair.' I tugged the bits hanging in front of my face. 'I'm a ponytail or nothing kind of person.'

But Erin was giving me a funny look.

'You *might* have just given me an idea . . .' She flicked the ends of my hair. 'The Hairy Godmother!' *Agatha?* What did she have to do with this? 'Go with me here, Lil . . . No idea's a bad idea, remember?'

'That's what Dad always says, but he once had the idea of microwaving his socks to dry them.'

'Okay not *all* ideas. But looking back, didn't Agatha say some . . . *weird* stuff?'

I scrunched my face.

'Hmmmmm. Not really. Only something about –' I thought back – 'great haircuts making us feel like new women.' Was there anything else? 'And something about us not arguing . . . or was that about mirrors?' Maybe there was a lot to choose from after all. 'And there was that thing about seeing each other in a new way . . .'

Erin was nodding as if she'd found out they'd invented a new letter just so she could get better than an A* on a test.

Oh, hang on . . .

Was she saying Agatha had made this happen? On purpose?!

'Could *this* –' Erin pointed at our reflections – 'be us

getting to know what it's *really* like to be each other? To be in each other's shoes? Well ...' She looked down. 'In each other's everything.'

Everything? *Ewww.* I had *not* thought about spending the day in Erin's pants. And now I had, I knew it wasn't an option.

'I don't care if they don't fit, Erin, I'm wearing my own pants.'

'And to be clear.' My sister sat down in her desk chair and spun round. '*That's* your biggest worry right now?'

'Well, no ... Obviously the biggest one is that we potentially had our hair cut by a person who has channelled some sort of dark magic into us and altered the course of our lives for ever.' I folded my arms. 'But also pants, yes.'

'GIRLS? Fifteen minutes till we're out the door,' Mum yelled up the stairs.

Erin and I chorused, 'Coming.' We never normally walked to school together, but today every second together counted.

Because by the time we got there we needed to have agreed on something for the first time in for ever.

A plan.

CHAPTER EIGHT

'Well, that went well,' Erin said, slamming my skateboard into my chest as we cleared the view of our house. We were walking the long way through our estate, to avoid running into anyone and giving us maximum time to plot getting to The Hairy Godmother salon as soon as school finished.

'You think?' I tried to wedge my skateboard under the straps on Erin's school bag, but it was bulging with books and was already five times as heavy as mine.

'No, you napkin.' Erin turned into the footpath. 'Mum and Dad were one broccoli question away from ringing 999. And that was before the whole skateboard thing.' She might have had a point there. Out of habit I'd grabbed it, but then I'd had to immediately pass it to Erin who had wobbled her way straight over Barry's grave and into a hedge. 'We're going to have to be more careful around them.'

She was right. Mum had almost tripped backwards over a cheese plant when she'd seen me come downstairs. Even though I'd tried my hardest to be neat like Erin, apparently my sister had never looked 'so dishevelled'. Mum then *did* trip backwards on the cheese plant when her youngest daughter appeared asking for the iron. Erin and I had grabbed toast and ran rather than stay and deal with her confusion.

I couldn't blame Mum. Despite Erin promising me she'd dress relaxed (her actual words had been 'a mess'), never had my shirt been so tucked in or my hair so well plaited (and my chin so free of accidental toothpaste splashes). Micha wasn't going to recognize me.

'If you want us to be careful, I suggest not thinking *that –*' I prodded her in the arm – 'is an acceptable way to look when I have ... or you have' (it was all so confusing) 'got to spend the day dealing with Frankie.'

Erin laughed through her nose. 'I really don't think Frankie is going to be bothered about your jumper, Lil.' How little she knew. Frankie once dumped a boy because he squirted ketchup weirdly.

'In that case, don't mind if I make this a little bit better.' I reached to untuck her jumper. We'd made a pact that if we had to endure today as each other, we'd both try to get through it without doing any long-term damage to each other's lives.

'All right!' Erin rolled her eyes. 'A deal's a deal. But can we leave the Lily-izing till we're almost there?'

'You mean de-nerd-ifying?'

She gave me a withering look. Fine with me. Withering I

could take. Frankie making my life more of a misery I couldn't. As we walked in silence, I fired off a message to Micha.

> Me: Sorry for not meeting. Parentals made me walk in with Erin
>
> Me: And if I'm at all odd today, I didn't get any sleep. Tomorrow will be better. PROMISE. 😴

She messaged straight back.

> Micha: u okay hun?

I replied with a GIF of a confused waking-up dog. It seemed easier than saying, 'No, the entire universe has gone wrong and I fear I've been magically enchanted by a very cool yet all-powerful hairdresser.' It wasn't even eight a.m. but not being able to hang out with Mich, or tell her what was going on, was already torture. I had to make sure Erin knew how much she couldn't mess anything up with my best friend.

'Look, Erin. We both hate this as much as each other. So I'm serious about our deal. I'll be as *Erin* as I can in your lessons.' I had no idea how, but it was definitely going to involve pretending I found very boring things interesting. 'As long as you call off the date with Ben.' *Full body shudder.* 'And be nice to Micha, avoid Frankie and just be ... normal, okay?'

'Sure.' Erin nodded. 'Or as you would say, *dealio*. And

when we get to Agatha, I'll do the talking. You've already got us into enough of a mess.'

I stopped. 'You *really* think this is my fault?'

Erin nodded as if it was a stupid question. 'Of course. You're a walking disaster – even Agatha could see that. So until she fixes us, can you try not to mess up my life like you do your own?' I was so annoyed I grabbed a postbox for emotional support. 'Starting with the play. It's a big deal to me and I can't have you doing anything to jeopardize it.'

I didn't know which bit to argue with first.

'Well, you need to try as well. Because my life is also *full* of very important things.' It would have been useful if any came to mind. 'GettingLilyWithIt to name one.' I tried not to notice Erin's eye-roll. I worked really hard on my blog even if she didn't take it seriously. My sister had her acting, but for me being a writer was the thing I wanted most, especially after my 'Top Fifteen Dog Walkers Who Look Like Their Pets' piece had gone viral at the start of term. It was pictures I'd taken on the walk to school of dogs and their lookalike owners. Apparently the woman I put in the number one spot still got called Cockapoo Karen. A true compliment . . . I thought. Apparently she was less pleased. Thousands of people had read it – but my sister wasn't one of them. She'd never read anything I'd written. 'So the last thing I need is you making things even harder with Frankie. Or –' even more dreadful – 'Nic. So just stay away from them, okay?'

But my timing couldn't have been worse.

Because as we turned the corner, there, standing right outside the newsagent's, bag of Haribo in hand, was Frankie. For someone so scary she made excellent breakfast choices.

She saw us and smiled.

'Well, look who it is. Phone Smasher and her superstar sister.' She scanned Erin up and down. 'Nice style today, Lil. Shame I didn't get the memo mega-nerd was back in fashion.'

I sped up. The quicker we walked by, the less my life would get ruined further.

But Erin stopped.

Why had she stopped?! And why was she smiling at Frankie?! Had she forgotten our deal already?! Rule number three – avoid conversation with Frankie *at all costs*.

'Dress smart, *think* smart.' Oh no, Erin was talking. 'That's what our dad always says.'

What about rule four. *Be normal?!*

I kicked Erin in the shin. This was *not* what I meant by not making things worse. But it was too late – Frankie's mouth had already dropped so far open it had revealed a semi-chewed cola bottle.

'She's joking.' I smiled at Frankie, which felt all kinds of ick, but had to be done for the greater good of keeping the peace and stopping more footage of me dressed as Shakespeare appearing on the internet. 'She's just in a bad mood after I dared her to dress like me for a day.' I laughed. Too hard. No one else did. *Quick, move the conversation on.* 'Aaaanyway, I heard about backstage – I'm sure you two will be great. Really great.' I eyeballed my sister. 'In a kind and respectful way –' I was speaking slowly, trying to spell it out – 'that will definitely not involve any drama from either of you.'

Judging by the glare I was getting from Frankie . . . chances were slim.

'Okaaaay, weird sisters.' Frankie got back to chewing. 'Guess being strange is genetic.'

It was odd – I minded being called strange a lot less when I was Erin. Still, I wanted to get out of this situation before any more damage was done.

'So this has been lovely.' I grabbed my sister's arm. 'But we'll be off.' Erin stumbled slightly as I tugged on her elbow. Finally there was an advantage to my body being the weakling one. But I was too late.

'Oh, hey.' Nic walked out of the shop and right into our conversation, as if this was not the exact opposite of okay! She peered at me. 'You're in my science group, right?'

'Nooo—' I started to say, but felt a nudge in my arm. This whole being Erin thing was way too hard. '—oooyes.'

'She means she is.' My heart rate tripled in speed. Having Erin talk to Nic was about as relaxing as when Dad says, 'Isn't it time you let your ol' dad join in with one of these dancing videos.' 'Top set for everything,' my sister said happily. As if those words would ever come out of my mouth!

I had to stop this conversation. And fast. We had to get out of here before Nic recognized my body from Saturday.

'I see . . .' Nic gave us both a funny look, but lingered

on my sister. Uh-oh. 'And no way … Aren't you that girl who …'

Could I jump in?

Has that really successful blog.

You should get to write for TheNicReport?

Or at least … *You've never seen before in your life?!*

C'mon, Erin. I willed her to pick one, any one!

'Climbed in your car and called your dad Mum?' Erin actually bowed as she said it! 'The very same.'

What was that stabbing feeling? Oh yes, another Shakespearean knife in my back.

'Which Lily is very sorry about.' I yanked my sister's bag so hard it fell off her shoulder. 'It was totally out of character as she is actually a very competent yet also funny young woman.'

This would have been more convincing if Frankie wasn't now snorting with laughter.

Nic just hmmed. 'To be fair, you do look a lot better without the wig.'

'Thanks.' Erin said it as if it was a compliment. If I glared at her any harder, one of my eyes might plop out. 'Y'know, you missed *quite* an event. The freestyle sonnet slam was *mmm!*' She did an actual chef's kiss.

Did she *really* think this was making things better?!

'What my sister means is …' I pressed so hard on her foot, I heard a small crunch. 'It was obviously awful, but she liked that it inspired another brilliant post for GettingLilyWithIt.' Erin

71

raised her (my) left eyebrow. I didn't even think that eyebrow would raise! How was she better at being me than me?! 'That's her blog, and it got loads of hits, so all worth it really.'

Frankie looked like I was talking in Latin. But Nic ... well, Nic had tilted her head and was staring at my sister.

'So GettingLilyWithIt is you?'

This time I grabbed a bollard for emotional support, except it turned out to be an annoyed Great Dane. But who cared? Nic had heard of my blog! I didn't think she knew me or my blog existed!

'Uh-huh.' Erin nodded.

'Someone sent me the link to that pets thing.' Ahhh, so Nic had seen the pets who looked like their owners post. 'It's decent.' Decent? NIC THOUGHT IT WAS DECENT?! This was peak epic st-unning-ness!

Full body swoon!

But Frankie had curled her lip, unimpressed.

'It's the worst thing on the internet,' she spat. 'And you know it, Nic.' But Nic didn't react – and I was too busy dealing with my ego fanning itself (and the Great Dane now sniffing my trouser pockets) to be bothered about what Frankie thought for once.

In this disaster of a day, *finally* something great had happened.

'Nah, Franks. It's funny stuff.'

What came after a full body swoon? Full body meltdown? Whatever it was, I was on the verge.

'TheNicReport is genuinely the best *ever!*' I blurted before I could stop myself. My voice was super squeaky – Erin's body clearly had no experience of handling genuine excitement. 'That post about Chase Cheney was *epic!*' My sister coughed. Oh yes, real Erin wouldn't recognize Chase Cheney if he jumped in front of her wearing an 'I'm Chase Cheney' T-shirt, let alone write an eight-thousand-word post on the way he blinked (I'd got 134 comments on it). I cleared my throat and tried to think of something boring and Erin-appropriate instead. '*I mean,* I've never read it. Obviously. Too busy working on my rock collection. I was just quoting my sister.'

Erin slapped a smile on. Here it came – her acting. 'Lol. OMG. TSF.' I knew from her face she'd made that last one up to annoy me. 'Too right. Squeal. Chase is *maje dreamio.* Still not over not having a ticket.'

Chase Cheney was playing the Artemis and Athena Arena this Saturday, the day after my birthday. It was the biggest concert we'd *ever* had around here. Micha and I had tried *everything* to get tickets but they'd sold out in milliseconds. Not exactly helped by Erin kicking me off the family computer so she could do her homework. Her priorities sucked. The rumour going round was that Chase had got in touch with Nic to ask for a video feature on TheNicReport, but she'd said she was busy and could only do a phone call. Mich and I, along with the whole school, had been trying to find out if it was true for *weeks.*

'Chase is actually a good guy.' Nic said it as if she was

talking about her dentist, not the world's biggest pop star. 'Not my music at *all* but still . . . and my sister was more than happy to take those backstage passes off my hands.'

OMG, so it *was* true! Chase and Nic did know each other! What could I say to that other than ohmerrgeeedwhat?

'C'mon, Nic.' Frankie sounded annoyed. 'I'm not exactly a *Cheneyator*.' That was what his fans were called. Frankie said it as if it was tragic, knowing full well I was a proud member. 'But backstage should be jokes.' Frankie pouted at my sister. '*Such* a shame you couldn't get tickets, Lil. Guess there are perks to having a geekazoid sister after all.'

How she could say that about Nic – literally the coolest person in school?

The only perk I got from being Erin's sister was . . . Nope. I had nothing.

'Well, have a great time,' Erin said, completely unbothered. 'I'm busy anyway. I've got some rocks I ordered arriving.' Who bought rocks? They were literally free from all gardens and paths! 'I can't wait to start getting them identified.' She cracked her knuckles. 'Hours of fun.'

Right, that was it. Our deal for me to suck up to Mrs Saddler later was *off*.

Nic was *never* going to speak to me again.

'Ooookay, so this conversation is not getting any less weird.' Frankie hoisted her bag on to her shoulder and looked at Nic. 'Shall we head?'

But Nic didn't move.

'One sec.' She held up hand. 'Lily, not sure it's your scene, but if you're up for it we're trying out some new writers for TheNicReport. I'm always looking for fresh perspectives and you've clearly got a *unique* take. Fancy sending me some stuff to take a look at?'

Sorry, had my ears heard that right?

Had Nic really just asked me to try out for her site?! In a way it was lucky it wasn't up to me to answer. I was speechless. I turned to my sister – surely for once, she'd know exactly what to say. Yes. A massive, big YES!

This was *everything* I'd dreamed of!

I held my breath.

But ... Erin looked puzzled. What was there to think about?

Nic picked up her bag. 'I need to warn you. It's a lot of work. And a big commitment. So if you're not up for it, that's fine.'

I couldn't be more up for it if I'd tried. So why hadn't my sister said yes yet?! Didn't she realize that TheNicReport team only took on new people once a year?!

We all looked at my sister, waiting for her answer. Finally Erin noticed my manic blinking and nodded as if she'd got my sister-signal of what to do. Phew.

'Thanks for the offer, Nic, but my sister and I have a deal.' She smiled at me. 'So I think I'm going to have say ... no.'

No?! NOOOOO!

With a wave and a, 'Fine,' Nic and Frankie walked off.

Along with everything I'd ever wanted.

CHAPTER NINE

How bad could pretending to be my sister pretending to be Titania be?

Answer: so excruciating I got stress hiccups.

I'd wanted to bail, especially after what Erin had said to Nic, but it turned out my sister had honestly thought she was doing the right thing. She'd thought my blinks and weird staring were reminding her about our deal. Where I'd asked her to stay away from Nic.

For someone so clever, she could be entirely un-clever. I was fuming, but when I'd told her my dream was to write for TheNicReport she seemed genuinely sorry. So in a bid to stop anything getting even worse, we agreed to stay out of each other's business entirely for the rest of the day, including all talking to Micha and Ben. Not that I had time to talk to anyone because between lessons teachers kept trying to chat to me – for fun! I'd planned to spend lunchtime secret-spying on Micha to check she was okay, but Mr Sharma grabbed me for a Les Quizerables 'cool crib session'. After over thirty minutes of sitting with Erin's teammates, clicking through a never-ending 'quiz' ('quiz' is definitely just a way of making 'test' sound more appealing), all I'd learnt was that *hippopotomonstrosesquippedaliophobia* was the fear of long words and that being in the computer room at lunchtime with a teacher yelling, 'Go, Quizheads!' was not my idea of fun.

Yet somehow this rehearsal was even worse. I thought we'd all just be saying hi, or doing warm-ups pretending to be trees or something normal like that, but oh no. Now the parts had been officially decided, Mrs Saddler had two weeks of intense rehearsing planned out. All starting now.

'So let's hear that scene again. And remember ...' Mrs Saddler paused with a dramatic raise of her hand. Everything she did was dramatic. She probably made tea by throwing the bag in from another room. 'This needs to have the audience on the Edge. Of. Their. Seats.'

If I had to go through with this play, the only way the audience would be on the edge of their seats was if they were about to run for the door.

Come on, Lily. Only a few more hours to survive and this will be over. Just focus on the book in your hand, not the person millimetres behind it. Harley. Harley Grayson. Not only the best-looking boy in our school but also funny, smart and had a dog called Kettle that looked like a burrito.

And right now Harley was smiling. Right. At. Me.

The only time he'd even looked at me before was when

I'd picked up a wireless earbud I'd thought he'd accidentally dropped in the bin and asked, 'Is this yours?'

He'd replied, 'What, that used chewing gum?'

And I'd panicked and said, 'Just wanted to check you didn't still want it.'

How had Erin failed to mention Harley was in this play with her, let alone playing her husband?! Thank goodness I could deal with this situation in private.

Oh no, that's right – Harley and I were in the middle of the stage, a spotlight shining right on us, the rest of the cast and crew standing around us in a circle. Staring. It wasn't exactly not off-putting to be being watched by myself either. I would love to say my sister was using my body to give me supportive looks, but from the way she mouthed, 'Don't mess this up,' 'threatening' was more accurate. At least Frankie was distracted by her phone.

'Relax,' Harley whispered, making sure Mrs Saddler couldn't see. 'You've got this.'

Nope, Harley. You couldn't be more wrong. The only thing I *had* was an inability to speak, the wrong body and a chronic case of stress hiccups. I looked up into his green eyes. Micha would not *believe* I'd been this close to him. Or that I'd had my entire body swapped with my sister. But the Harley thing was a close second.

No, Lily! Stop thinking about Harley and start reading these stupid lines in a suitably dramatic way. If I got Erin kicked off the play she'd never forgive me.

With a deep breath I went for it.

'Would imitate, and sail up on the land to fetch me ... trifles?' Who knew Shakespeare liked sponge fingers?!

'Erin, it's not a question,' Mrs Saddler snapped. '*Why* would you say it like that? It's *obviously* a declaration of friendship.'

'I see.' I didn't. Mrs Saddler pushed her glasses further up her nose (dramatically) and stared at me as if I must now deliver such gold it would gloss over the shaky start.

I started to read again. The words made zero sense. Should I look annoyed? Or happy? I went 'cross with a touch of disappointment while smelling some toast burning' and hoped for the best. I stuttered my way through as Harley delivered everything word perfectly.

Thank goodness we were finding Agatha and swapping back this evening. I could *never* do this again. I'd had a taste of life as Erin – and it was worse than celery.

At least when we finally got to the end everyone clapped – slowly, like a tap dripping, but still. I'd kept my promise to Erin. I looked over at her to get her reaction but ... she'd gone. Where was she? *Uh-oh.* At the side of the hall. Talking to Frankie. And ... laughing?!

My brain tried to compute what it was seeing. *Me and Frankie hanging out?!*

What on earth could the two of them be talking about?! They had nothing in common!

I didn't take my eyes off them for the rest of the rehearsal. Even when I sneezed. It was a painful sixty minutes, but at least

I'd officially survived the worst after-school activity of my life (which included when Micha and I cleaned out lost property and discovered a cheese and ham sandwich from 2012).

Mrs Saddler summoned us together.

'Same time on Thursday.' She pointed round the room with the pen she kept behind her ear. 'We've got less than two weeks till we're doing this for real, so total commitment please. Backstage crew, we'll be going through prop design, and, principle cast, I'll expect you to be able to run today's scenes without scripts. Okay?'

A boy called Mark punched the air and said, 'Let's do this.'

Enthusiastic Mark was on Erin's Les Quizerables team. Clearly he'd never been asked the question, 'How many punches of glee should be allowed in response to a teacher comment?' (Answer: zero.) The girl next to him rolled her eyes – then grinned when she realized I'd noticed. I think she was called Lou. I smiled right back, even though that was exactly what Erin *wouldn't* do. She'd probably loudly ask why no one had already learnt all the words.

'So, Erin.' Uh-oh. Mrs Saddler had followed me over to the side of the hall where I was packing Erin's bag in double time to flee. 'How are you finding Titania's *motivations*?' *Motivations*?! I stared at her in horror. Before today I'd only experienced a teacher voluntarily coming over to talk to me once – to ask if I knew I had a pair of pants bunched in the bottom of my tights. 'Now you've got the part, do you feel as if you're starting to get under her skin?'

Ermmmmm. Erin would say something impressive, but all I had in my head was, 'How could someone not notice they had a pair of pants in their tights?'

I attempted a smile. 'Well, I er ... definitely feel as if I know what it's like to be in someone else's body ...'

Mrs Saddler closed her eyes and exhaled, a smile on her face. Although the exhale went on so long I started to worry she was deflating. '*Delighted* to hear it. I *knew* you would. To be honest, I *was* worried about today's performance. Not at all your usual standard. By a long way. But if it's all part of your "creative process", I can't wait to see you unleash your full talents next rehearsal.'

I nodded, relieved that by tomorrow I'd be back safely in my own body.

'Don't worry. I'll be a new person by then,' I said with a genuine smile. But I wasn't free just yet – I had to wait for Erin to clear the hall. So I headed outside and stood by the bins where no one would see me.

What a day. Definitely my second worst school day ever (the day I'd accidentally thrown a javelin into our sports teacher's thigh was still clinging on to first place). Being Erin was *exhausting.* I'd had questions fired at me all day and in maths I'd had to pretend I'd got sudden cramps when I'd got asked what was the value of 'x'. It didn't help that I'd had to sit front row for every lesson as they were the only seats left for me, so I hadn't even been able to have any secret sleeps with my eyes open. Finding Agatha couldn't come quick enough. So when I eventually heard Erin's footsteps, I jumped right out.

Into the person who was speed-walking while typing into their phone.

Who wasn't Erin.

She actually screamed.

'I'm *so* sorry, Nic. I didn't mean to scare you.'

'Really?' Nic looked genuinely shocked. 'Hiding round corners and jumping out on people tends to do the trick.'

But she was grinning. Phew. Maybe it was now or never to try the idea I'd had to undo the damage from earlier?

'Weird coincidence though. I'd been looking for you . . .' Here went nothing. 'After we left you this morning Lily told me she'd made a big mistake. A massive one. The most massive-est.' I was speaking so fast I sounded like someone had doubled my playback speed. 'She'd actually *love* to try out for TheNicReport . . .' Gulp. 'If the offer's still there?'

Nic's eyebrows raised.

'Are you sure? She didn't seem that keen. Normally people jump at the chance . . .'

I wanted to scream, 'TRUST ME, NORMAL ME OR NORMAL ANYONE WOULD!' but instead I nodded my head furiously.

'I dunno . . .'

I felt sick.

'Honestly, she really would love to do it . . .' I was

one sentence away from begging, but Nic's phone had started ringing.

'Tell you what.' Nic clearly had to go. 'Let Lily know I'll keep my eye on GettingLilyWithIt for the next few days. And, if I see anything I like, I might track her down. Maybe.'

Maybe?!

Maybe I'd take! *Maybe* was AMAZING!

Nic answered the call, and distractedly waved goodbye, which was lucky as it meant she didn't see me grinning from ear to ear.

Maybe everything wasn't lost after all!

Maybe after finding Agatha and ending this nightmare, I really could get my life back on track.

CHAPTER TEN

If we wanted to get to The Hairy Godmother before it shut we needed to leave *now*. But I was missing one crucial thing.

My sister.

Where was she?!

I looked back towards the big school fire doors, the evening sun bouncing off them, but there was no sign of her. *Eurgh.*

To calm myself down I messaged Micha. I'd never gone this long without talking to her (which included the time she flew to Australia, as she left me voice notes to pick up every hour).

> Me: For no reason at all just wanted to say
> PORCUPINE WIFE 4 LYF 🦔

A hedgehog emoji was the nearest we could get to a porcupine, which we'd called each other ever since Micha once asked me what they sounded like, but our smart speaker thought she was asking it and had played a porcupine squeak at full volume to my whole house. It sounded like Barry the Hamster (RIP) crossed with Dad when he once inhaled helium. She replied straight back.

> Micha: I missed you on the walk back. Can't
> believe you've got to de-fluff your dad's
> socks tonight!!

Mich knew I had punishment chores to do, but washing dishes and doing the bins couldn't take *all* night, and this was the only other thing that had sprung to mind when I was messaging her earlier.

> Me: ikr. Unbelievable.
> Me: How was chemistry???

Yikes. *Error!* I regretted it immediately. Could I un-send?! I should know about chemistry as I was *technically* in that lesson this afternoon. But it was too late. Micha had already read it. I had no option but to dig even deeper.

> Me: as in, did Mr S say anything else to you?!

The next few chemistry lessons were crucial for Micha if she wanted to stay in top set – and keep playing football.

> Micha: One sec ... Abdou is trying to put Dave in
> the toaster

Abdou was her four-year-old brother and Dave was their gerbil, so I thought it best she went.

> Me: 🧎☠️🔥⊝

Micha's timing was perfect as Erin finally appeared. After taking a moment to deal with the weirdness of watching myself leave school, I ran over.

'What took you so long?' Despite practically shouting, my sister didn't even flinch. 'We've only got fifteen minutes to get to Agatha!'

'Hello to you too, sister.' Why did she look so calm? It was frightening. 'And stop freaking out. Google Maps says it'll take eleven minutes walking my pace. If you'd wanted me out quicker, you could have helped me stack the chairs.'

And spend time with her and Frankie? No way. I grabbed Erin's arm. 'Walk quicker. And tell me what happened!'

It was the first chance we'd had to catch up in private.

'With what?'

I didn't like it when Erin was like this. Which was all the time.

'With EVERYTHING! Micha? Frankie? Lessons? Did anyone speak to you at the lockers? I need *everything*.' I took a dramatic deep breath. 'Every. Single. Word.'

But Erin just shrugged. 'Nothing to report. Although I heard you got almost twenty questions right for Les Quizerables?'

'Uh-huh.' I nodded, proud of myself.

'Out of two hundred.' Ah. No *wonder* it felt never-ending. 'Lils – they were multiple choice, even a monkey could have got fifty.'

'Yes, but I bet that monkey wouldn't also be texting its best friend explaining why they couldn't meet for lunch.'

'Ah.' Erin's face fell. 'Look, I didn't *technically* meet Micha, okay.' *What? This wasn't our deal!* 'But I wasn't to know she'd come and sit by me in the canteen.'

My mouth fell open. Did my sister *really* not know how best friends worked?!

'Please tell me you didn't do anything weird ... well, weirder than normal.'

'Calm down, Lil. For your info, I can report that neither Chase Cheney's blinking, Micha's new football trick nor how "weirdly into rocks" your big sister is was *that* interesting.' Er, *oops*. I'd been so busy worrying about Erin being weird to Micha I hadn't thought of all the secrets that might come spilling out back in her direction. 'And no, I will not dump Ben for Harley.' Wow, Micha really had covered some areas. 'And for the record, yes, of course my bananaphobia is real. Why would I lie?' Erin shuddered. My sister really did have no weaknesses except a weird, crippling fear of bananas. We weren't allowed them in the house and she avoided them in the supermarket too. So typical – even her one phobia was unique and sort of impressive. 'I made my excuses so I could go and do something fun instead.'

'So you abandoned my best friend mid-lunch?' What would Mich be thinking?! 'That is not okay, Erin.'

'But you told me to not speak to her?'

Arghh! She was so infuriating. 'Yes, but once you started, stopping was probably worse. And anyway, hanging out with my best friend is miles more fun than spending lunch finding out what *hippo . . . monster –*' I realized I hadn't even learnt that fact – '*squidophobia,*' I ended with a confident flourish, 'means.' I held out her school bag. 'Can we swap? This weighs a tonne.'

Erin sighed. 'Probably because it doesn't just have one mouldy apple, a packet of flattened Hula Hoops and *zero* books in it.'

We swapped bags just as the boys' football team walked by. I swear one of them shouted, 'Shouldn't you be reading classic texts?' *Weird.* Erin stopped to glare at them. But there was no time for dirty looks. Every second counted. Grabbing her arm, and pulling her after me, we turned on to the main road into town. I'd started to feel really nervous so to calm myself down, I opened my Hula Hoops and pressed my finger into the dust. Erin could take away my existence, my privacy, and cause dark magical forces to awaken, but she couldn't take away my crisps. 'So what were you and Frankie chatting about? When I left it looked like you were having a deep and meaningful.'

'Nah.' Erin had to shout over the noise of the cars. 'We

were just working through plans. I've drawn up a rota for prop production, set design and rehearsals and wanted to walk her through it.'

I couldn't help but groan. I bet Frankie *loved* that.

Erin rolled her eyes. Well, *mine*, which made it even ruder.

'Lil, please. Frankie's not a big deal.' No, she was the *biggest*. 'You just have to stand up to her, be her equal, that's all.'

'That's your opinion.' Today might have gone okay for Erin, but if she understood how much of a misery Frankie had made my life this term, she wouldn't be saying that. 'So did Frankie like the plan?' I had a feeling I knew what the answer would be.

'I think so.' Erin smiled. 'She kept calling me mini Mrs Saddler which was cool.' I sighed. If Erin was so clever, why couldn't she see this was just giving Frankie even more ammunition? Tomorrow morning when I was back in the right body, I was going to have to tell Frankie it was all a big joke. 'Oh.' We stopped to wait to cross over the roundabout. 'I also suggested Mrs Saddler schedule some lunchtime sessions to give the backstage crew a refresher on safety practices.' Wow, my sister had found a lunchtime activity worse than Les Quizerables? My last shred of hope that I could repair things with Frankie wilted and died.

But my phone buzzed.

Micha: Back.

Phew. Mich always cheered life up.

> Micha: You know that time you asked Mr Sharma
> why you could catch a cold but not a hot?

I did.

> Micha: To confirm, what you said in English
> genuinely outdid it. 😅 😵

It did?! Was I meant to have a clue what she meant?

> Me: Hahahha yes 😜
> Me: Also what exactly are you talking about?
> Mich: 😶

I waited.

> Micha: Asking Mrs S to stop playing the Romeo
> and Juliet film so we could study the 'classic
> text' instead.

I DID WHAT?! My frustration with my sister finally bubbled over. Well, more exploded like Mentos in Coke.

'Erin, could you not have tried a bit harder?!' I wasn't shouting. But I wasn't not-shouting either. 'To not ruin everything?' Or at least not undo all the hard work I'd done

over the years of trying to pretend I was normal. '*Classic text,*
Erin?? *CLASSIC TEXT???*'

She looked at me innocently.

'You're making a big deal out of nothing.'

'No, you're making a small deal out of everything!'

Neither of us spoke the rest of the way. When we got to
the railway arches, I sprinted past the coffee shop, straight
towards The Hairy Godmother. I'd never been happier to see
a hairdresser's in my life.

I honestly couldn't take another second of being my sister.
Of her being me. Of all of it.

And – relief! – it was open!

I pushed the door open and ran in.

'AGATHAAAA!' My voice echoed round the empty
room. Good. She didn't have a client which meant she
could help. 'HAAAIRRRY GODMOOOTHHHERRRRR?
We need your help. It's time to –' I dropped my voice a
little – 'swapusback!'

I said it quickly in case anyone else could hear.

'One second!' she called back.

Phew x infinity.

I instantly felt a weight lift. This nightmare was almost
over. An old woman shuffled out of the back room where
we'd had our hair washed.

'Hello, missy. Did you say it's Agatha you're after?'

'Yeah,' I panted. 'And it's kind of urgent.' I heard Erin
come in the door. Better late than never. But she marched

straight over to me and grabbed my arm. Couldn't she see I was busy with the nice old lady?

'Well, that might be tricky.' The lady smiled. 'This shop's been empty for years.'

'No . . .' I started to say but faded out as I looked around. What?

The.

Hairy heck?!

Then I realized why Erin's fingers were so tight around my arm. My blood – well Erin's blood – ran cold.

It had all gone.

Every trace of The Hairy Godmother.

The chairs. The mirrors. The desk. *Everything*. And in their places were old packing boxes, covered in thick dust.

The only things still here from last night were the frames on the wall, although the pictures in them now looked faded and old.

The lady's kind face wrinkled with worry. 'I'm afraid I don't know any Agathas. None at all. So I hope you didn't need her for anything too important?'

Oh no, nothing important.

Only the small matter of getting my body back . . . and evicting Erin out of mine before she ruined everything.

CHAPTER ELEVEN

My first thought when I opened my eyes:

Thank goodness for breakfast, or there would be no reason to ever leave bed.

The second:

Why is my room freakishly tidy and why is my alarm going off at 6.15 a.m.?

Ugh. The reality hit me like a netball in the face.

This wasn't my room.

And I was waking up early to memorize the lines Erin needed to learn. Because I needed to be word perfect by the second play rehearsal this evening. Because I was still stuck being her.

It had been a day and a half since we'd tried and failed to find Agatha, and with Erin busy doing my punishment chores (which, tbh, was the only thing I could really enjoy about this whole thing, especially as in a beautiful twist of fate she had actually ended up de-fluffing Dad's socks), and me busy trying to learn her lines *and* write new blog posts to impress Nic, we'd both been out of ideas and out of leads. Agatha's disappearance had made Erin think that the answer wasn't about finding her, while I was convinced the Hairy Godmother was the only person who could fix this.

I rubbed my eyes, trying to wake up. I *had* to get up. It wasn't just Erin's lines that depended on it. I needed to use the school computer room before registration to look for clues to help track down the Hairy Godmother. Erin said I was wasting my time, as apparently she'd 'already looked at over eighty per cent of the internet and found nothing', but I *had* to do something.

> Micha: Sersly Lils. Should I ask my mum if this is
> legal? There MUST be a limit to how much chore-
> age is allowed in a day!?!! 🦷 💩 🦨

Ding ding ding. My guilt-o-meter maxed out. I closed my phone, without replying. My reply rate to Micha was normally around 1.5 seconds, but these last couple of days it had been around the five-minute mark.

I'd asked Erin to avoid Micha where possible, which sucked, but I figured the damage of what Erin might say was worse than a temporary disappearance. So not only had I been exaggerating my chores to Mich, I'd laid it on even thicker, saying that, along with my backstage duties, Mrs Saddler had asked the teachers to report back about my behaviour in lessons. Which meant no chatting, no notes and definitely no plaiting my hair together with Micha's and seeing if we could get away with it.

Micha and I were always honest with each other, which is probably why she didn't question my terrible excuses. But it only made me feel even worse. Being with Micha was like eating toast. There was just no point in a day without it. Especially when she was having a rubbish time. Erin had told me Micha hadn't got good marks in the chemistry homework yesterday, so she was probably fretting more than ever about being put down a set, especially with the football tournament looming this Sunday. I'd promised I'd be there to cheer her on, help show the scouts she already had fans, so I *had* to be back in my right body by then.

I was desperate to hang out with Micha like normal. All my thoughts that I could share with her and no one else were building up and in serious danger of popping out in front of anyone.

- Is cereal soup?
- Did the bruise on my leg from running into the door look a bit like Chase Cheney's gran?
- Who invented garden gnomes?

My phone buzzed across my pillow, snapping me out of gnome thoughts.

Micha: oh and your new post? BEST YET.

She'd sent a screengrab: 'Ten Ways Having a Sister Makes You Want to Lick Biscuits Just so She Can't Eat Them'. I'd spent all night putting the finishing touches to it. I just hoped it made Nic laugh too.

Micha: MY BEST FRIED IS A GEEEEENIUS. Nic
will ♥ it!!!

I hoped she meant 'friend'.

Me: has anyone ever told you YOU'RE THE BEST?

I meant it. I'd only posted it seven minutes ago, but Micha had alerts set up. I just wished there was a way I could properly talk to her ... Although ... A most cunning plan came to me! I got my phone back out.

Me: I reckon I can sneak out for lunch. Want to
meet 1pm? In the usual?? Although be warned my
sister will be there 👽

I sent her a porcupine dancing GIF which summed up how I'd feel if I got to see her. Erin didn't need to know. We'd agreed to meet at lunch to debrief on any swapping-back progress, so as long as she stuck to our plan to meet at the same time and same place I'd just told Micha, life would be gooooood. Maybe Micha was right, maybe I was a genius! And I didn't stop genius-ing. Because I had another idea. Why learn the lines for tonight when I could scribble them in tiny writing on the inside of my wrists and get an extra hour's sleep instead?

Which turned out to be a lifesaver as when I woke back up and eventually went downstairs, I needed all the mental strength I could muster to deal with what greeted me in the kitchen.

Dad. Lunging. In Lycra.

And Mum totally ignoring the whole thing, eating some granola.

'Morning, Erin.' Mum squinted as if she were being asked to identify a rare six-legged hairy creature. And I was it. 'I really thought it was only your sister I needed to remind what a mirror was.' She had a point. After my extra-snooze I'd had to get ready super quickly, and all Erin's stuff was in weird places, like hung up in the wardrobe and folded in drawers. I tucked my shirt in to try and be more Erin. Out of everything, being around our parents was the hardest thing of this whole swap. I needed to switch Mum's focus to something else.

'Sorry, Mum, but how are you talking about what I look like when *that's* –' I nodded towards Dad – 'happening?'

Dad looked up at me from between his legs. 'Where your focus goes, Erin, your energy flows.' I couldn't help notice his socks were incredibly smooth. Good job, sister. 'It's my first Circus Skills class tonight.'

'I see.' I didn't. 'And what *exactly* does this mean?'

'It means –' Mum took a calm sip of her tea – 'your father is going to be spinning from the ceiling on ropes. And doing things with hula-hoops that I don't think a man who can't touch his toes should.'

Dad tutted as he tried to cross his legs over one another. 'Y'know, when you work in the fast-moving world of concrete it's not just your mind that needs to keep nimble.'

I thought concrete didn't move – wasn't that the point?

'Well –' Mum bent down and unhooked one of his feet that was already stuck – 'please keep all limbs functioning till tomorrow night. We're going bowling for Lily's birthday, remember?'

I *loved* birthdays. And Mum and Dad had made a special effort with this one after I'd missed out on Chase Cheney tickets.

'CANNOT WAIT!' I poured my cereal (or was it breakfast soup?!) into the bowl. 'I can't believe we got the UV lanes!' They were the Friday-night, once-a-month special. 'It's going to be st-unning!' Afterwards we were going to Slice, Ice, Baby! for unlimited pizza and ice cream. 'Dreeeeam city!' I was almost dribbling at the thought. 'That caramel sauceio better be ready for me!'

As the last of my Coco Pops hit the bowl, the 'plip' ringing round the silent room, I realized what I'd done.

Got so excited about my birthday, I'd forgotten I was in Erin's body.

Mum was staring at me, confused. Considering Dad was on the floor next to me trying to get a foot behind his head that must mean I really was being weird.

'But I thought you said you couldn't come because of a rehearsal?'

'I did ... yes.' Well, Erin did, but that was before the swap. And even though we should be back in the right bodies by this weekend, surely my sister wouldn't mind a backup plan so I didn't risk missing my own birthday? 'However, on reflection ... Lily is such a great sister. The best actually. So I will come after all. I'll just ask Mrs Saddler to be excused a bit early.'

Would Erin suggesting she leave something school-related early ring alarm bells? Mum had already asked if everything was okay last night when I'd switched off *University Challenge* to watch *World's Funniest Dogs* instead.

But luckily Mum smiled.

'Well, that will be lovely.' Wow, being my sister was really easy. Everyone was pleased with me all the time. 'I'm sure she'll say yes if you explain. Lily will be delighted.'

'About what?' My sister walked in, looking a total nerd-fest. I'd given up trying to make her look normal. When Micha had messaged saying she thought my new super-smart look was a 'brave act of sticking it to Frankie and her cool friends', I'd replied with a crying laughing face. Only the crying bit was true.

'Your birthday plans . . .' Dad answered from a position that looked like 'human pretzel'. Erin wrinkled her nose in confusion – before realizing they meant my birthday. Your sister's coming after all.'

'She is?' My sister shot me a major evil. 'But don't you want to be there for the ENTIRE rehearsal, Erin? Every last IMPORTANT second?'

I poured the oat milk on my cereal. 'Kind of you to care *so* much, but . . . no, I'd rather be there to bowl with you. Those UV lanes are hard to book.'

If Erin were a cartoon, smoke would be coming out of her nose.

Dad sat up. 'Well, I say –' he pulled an imaginary cord – 'ding-dong to full steam ahead on a family trip.' He scrambled to his feet. 'The Mavers engine is stoked – next stop Fun City. And . . .' He stopped to catch his breath. 'Erin, if you need a hand getting –' he winked entirely unsubtly – 'Lily's present, let's chat tonight.'

Of course! I'd be getting myself a present! Result! Erin's presents for me usually involved books – that she wanted to read. Or nice bath stuff – that she'd use up.

I gave Dad, then Erin, a massive smile. 'That would be *excellent*. Thanks, Dad. I thought after all the stress with Frankie, as well as all the really, really hard work Lily's been putting in to her brilliant blog, I'd go all out this year.' I pinched my sister's cheek. 'Expect something really special, sis.'

Like some new wheels for my skateboard. Ooooh, yeah. Or maybe some new nail varnish for prom? Or even just seeing how much pick 'n' mix twenty pounds could buy. Or crisps. A room full of BBQ beef crisps.

'Awesomeio,' Erin replied through gritted teeth. But what were savings if not to have your sister spend them on her own birthday present? 'And in return expect me to do *another* enthralling post about it.' She shrugged. 'Maybe even a celebratory dance video with Micha.' She waved her arms around as if that was as good as we got.

'That's the spirit, Lil!' Dad did a little shimmy. 'And if you want to sprinkle in some circus skills for your next video, I'm sure I can rustle something up.' He opened up Street View on his phone to show me the building where he was going. There were actual trapezes outside it. 'Doesn't it look great? I could be the new sensation!' Yes, Dad in Lycra hula-hooping on the internet might actually break it, but not in a good way. 'What d'ya say?'

The sheer horror on my sister's (well, my) face made Dad stop talking and slowly walk backwards out of the room. She then chewed her toast in a particularly annoyed way, as I dealt with a quick-fire interrogation from Mum about whether I'd filled in the forms to apply for Chinyere Okafor's Drama Academy programme and if I'd researched the scholarships. I said yes to everything, as I knew Erin would be on it. But all the talk about acting put me off my cereal (well, the second bowl anyway). The opening night of the play was a week on

Saturday, and it was being filmed for Erin's audition tape. We *had* to find Agatha. But Mum hadn't clocked that I'd sunk into a pit of despair and made us pose for a photo to show Grandma what a 'corner Lily had turned'. (I noticed Mum positioned us cleverly so Grandmoan couldn't see her eldest granddaughter had turned in the opposite direction.)

Once that was done Erin and I finally escaped off to school. My sister might have been even more rattled by the audition talk than me, as the whole walk she made me practise my lines. She said it was for 'constructive feedback' which really meant 'telling me I'm making a mess of them but in a way where I can't say anything and, worse, have to appear genuinely grateful'. But when I managed to reel them all off, Erin was impressed – as was I. I'd showered so quickly that ninety-nine per cent of my scribble had stayed on my wrist! Result! (For the play. Less good for my armpits.)

As soon as we got to school I headed straight to the computer room – and because I was in Erin's body not one person gave me a funny look for being such a keeno. I jumped on a computer but Google didn't have much in the way of 'how to swap bodies with my sister' and I'd already searched a thousand times for 'Agatha Hairy Godmother'. Still, I couldn't help but type it in again. Nothing. Although Dad had given me an idea – there was *one* thing I hadn't checked …

I went to Street View to see how Agatha's shop used

to look. Maybe I could get clues about when or why she'd popped up there? But in the image that came up neither The Hairy Godmother nor the dog yoga place had opened and the photo looked old ... four years old to be exact, as there was a poster outside the café advertising Chase Cheney's first album. I moved the camera round, but there was nothing out of the ordinary – just the exact same thing we saw on Tuesday evening: an empty, dusty shop, boxes scattered round the room. The old lady was right, it must have been abandoned for years. Which made *no* sense.

Although ... my heart jumped.

Was I seeing this right?

I leant forward and zoomed in on Agatha's shop. Hanging on the walls, just like on Tuesday, were the old pictures in frames. But in the middle of all the black frames was a gold one.

And in that frame was ...

I gulped so loudly the student teacher on duty shushed me.

It was the picture of me and Erin that Mum had taken! The photo from this morning!

Woooooah.

I rubbed my eyes and looked down at the keyboard in case I was having a hallucination. But when I looked back up, the picture was still there!

This wasn't just fishy, this was a whole ocean of marine life!

And it meant that whatever was going on, Agatha *did* want us to find her! That picture was a message to us!

'*Yessssss!*' I accidentally said out loud, causing the student teacher to do an extra-long shush.

But who cared! *I knew it!* Despite what Erin thought, I was right! The Hairy Godmother did want us to track her down.

And even better, I had a lead.

CHAPTER TWELVE

I couldn't *wait* to tell Erin the news, but decided to hold off till I could do it in person at lunch and fully enjoy her reaction to me being right.

It wasn't even nine a.m. and I was smashing today!

My heart raced.

Maybe this was the moment where everything started going right for me?

Maybe my latest post would do so well it really would impress Nic?

Maybe today really would be the day Erin and I swapped back!

Taking a deep breath, I refreshed my blog and scanned down.

OMG ... a hundred comments!!

Unreal!

Oh ... no. The counter actually said 000, but there was a bit of crisp on the screen at exactly the wrong place.

Guess you couldn't win them all. I'd just have to be content with today cementing me as a magical hairdresser detective. Triumphantly I headed to registration. Being first in the classroom almost felt weirder than seeing a photo of myself time-travel and appear on the internet in the past.

> Micha: Can't wait for tomorrow night!!!!! Bowling is
> right up my alley

Ha ha ha, I loved her.

> Micha: I'm going to request all the Chase
> tuuuuuunesss
> Me: Got to hope the speakers don't go
> on strike 🎳

'Hey, Erin.' Lou from the play sat next to me. She saw my *A Midsummer Night's Dream* book in my hand and smiled – she must have thought I was learning my lines, not hiding my phone. Erin and I had decided to sneak them into our lessons so I could message her whenever I felt a teacher was going to say 'Erin what's your take?'. In return I could remind my sister to stop answering every single question in mine.

Lou leant over her desk. 'Freaking out about this evening?'

I wrinkled my nose. 'I wouldn't say freaking out . . . but if I happened to fall into a manhole, I'd be very okay with that.'

She laughed. 'Same, but we'll get through it together.

Honestly, I'm only doing this after seeing you in *Sweeney Todd* last year. You were awesome.'

'Er, thanks.' My main memory of it was the small child sitting next to me breathing like Darth Vader. And that they'd said snacks were available in the interval, but then only had cheese.

'Yup, and that advice you gave me about "less expression sometimes being more" totally got me the part in this one. So . . .' Lou was almost blushing. 'I've been meaning to say a massive thanks.'

I couldn't help but smile, even though I wasn't sure real Erin would express such a level of emotion. 'No problem. Glad it helped—'

I broke off as something hit me on the arm. Someone's bag as they walked past to put an assignment on the front desk.

'Sorry . . .' they started to say, but as they did, we both did a double take. It was Nic. She stopped. 'Ohhh . . . Erin. I was hoping to see you.' She took off her jacket. 'Well, your sister actually.' Oh *riilllllly*. I crossed my fingers under the desk. 'I asked Frankie to keep an eye out for her but she said Lily hadn't been around much.' As if Frankie would do anything to help me out.

'Ah yes,' I tried to look as serious and believable as I could. 'I think Lily's just got some *very* important things on. That's Lily all over, you know. Always very busy with . . . er . . . very important things.' I shook my head and muttered, 'So impressive.' Lou was definitely giving me a strange look.

'Wow, that's cool of you to say. I figured you guys were like me and my sister.' Nic laughed. 'She can be an absolute nightmare.'

I tried to pretend this wasn't the most unsurprising thing I'd ever heard.

'No ... Who would have thought?' Answer: *me, me, me*. 'Anyway, is the Lily thing anything I can help with?'

'Maybe.' Nic shrugged. 'I've really been liking her posts this week –' *Whaaaat?!* – 'so was going to see if she would still be up for trying out for the TheNicReport.' Yes, she would! 'We're getting the three writers we like most to share ideas at the next editorial meeting.'

Thank goodness I was sitting down. I'd gone dizzy.

TheNicReport's editorial meetings were *legendary*. All Nic's team got together and went through pitches and their own ideas – and she wanted me to send some of mine in?! To maybe get a place on her team?!

Even Erin's abnormally large brain that I was brain-sitting couldn't cope with news this good!

I'd saved my chance with Nic! And Erin couldn't mess it up again, as I could send in my ideas from the safety of my laptop at home.

Woohoo!

Fingers clicked in front of my eyes, snapping me back to reality.

'Are you okay?' Lou looked concerned. 'It was like your screen had frozen. Although by screen I mean ... your face.'

The Nic news was so big it must have caused a temporary facial malfunction.

'Fine, thanks, Lou.' I tried to smile. See, the Mavers sisters could be normal! *Sometimes.* 'And, Nic, I think that's a great idea. Lil will definitely say yes. I'll pass it on immediately.' Nic smiled. She smiled! 'So if you see her you won't even need to mention it. Or even talk to her at all!'

But Nic had stopped listening, already opening up her phone calendar. 'Great. The meeting is the tenth.' Next Wednesday. Less than a week to come up with my best ever ideas. 'Can you ask your sister to confirm she's coming? She can DM me.' Nic picked up her bag. 'Oh, and tell her it's at mine.'

Wait.

WHAT?!

AT NIC'S?! So this wasn't happening via the medium of email?! I could *not* let my sister loose in the actual home of Frankie and Nic. School was bad enough! But their inner sanctum?! With their dad-mum who might recognize me?!

But . . . I also could not *not* let her go!

By the time I'd gathered myself to reply, Nic had gone. And Mrs Richardson had walked in. We all stood up.

'*Bonjour tout le monde! Asseyez-vous!*' I'd have had a much better idea what was she was saying if I studied French, not German. But seeing as everyone sat down, I did too, and tried to mouth along with whatever noises they were making.

As Mrs Richardson conjugated verbs as if it wasn't the

most boring thing imaginable (she even conjugated 'to be bored'), I tuned out and tried to work out what Agatha was trying to tell us. I needed the swap to happen tonight so I could enjoy my birthday tomorrow, watch Micha on Sunday, get to the editorial meeting next week, and return Erin to her beloved play.

'Erin.' Uh-oh. Mrs Richardson was staring at me as if she wanted a reply. Which was particularly difficult as I didn't know the question. Or speak the language. I mustered the only French I could remember.

'*Mais oui petit pois?*' A longshot answer considering it meant, 'But yes, peas?'

Mrs Richardson didn't react. Lou however hissed, 'She asked why are you being so quiet today.'

'But yes, peas?' *might* have been a slightly odd response, but for some reason it made Mrs Richardson want to converse even more, and she projected at least twenty seconds of pure sound at me. In desperation I dug out the last two French words I knew. '*Jambon-beurre ...*'

The room cracked up. Lou later told me she'd asked what career I wanted. Oh well, who didn't want to be a ham sandwich when they grew up?

Being Erin sucked, but the thought of seeing Micha at lunch kept me going. I practically ran to the meeting place and when I got there Micha was already waiting! Yes! Although where was my sister? She was never late and I couldn't *wait* to tell her my big discovery.

Micha gave me a big smiley wave. She always was much nicer to my sister than I was.

'Micha.' I pulled myself up on the wall next to her. 'I can't tell you how good it is to see you!'

Mich grinned. 'You too.' (Proof my best friend was an excellent exaggerator.) She opened her lunch bag up. Instinctively I popped open my lunchbox too. We always opened them at the same time, showed each other what we had and scored them out of ten.

'Obvs your jollof rice is a straight ten.' I was always so jealous when she brought in her leftovers. 'But my pasta salad is a solid seven, and the Penguin *and* Skips combo surely elevate it to a nine, right?'

Mich stared at me. I realized too late this was not normal behaviour for my sister.

'Er, yes. Nice choices, Erin,' Micha said politely. Ouch. I hadn't thought how hard not being my normal self around her would be. 'So er ... how are rehearsals going? Lily said it was really full on.' I'd been messaging Micha about it last night.

'Uhhmmmwwaffnne,' I said, strategically chewing to avoid putting my foot, or rather Erin's foot, in it further.

'Have your er ... *feet* got any better?' Ah yes. I'd forgotten I'd entertained myself by telling Micha my big sister was freaking out about discovering she had incredibly hairy toes. But surely in among all the disasters I was allowed to have some fun? What Erin didn't know could never hurt her.

'Why thank you, yes, I think I have them . . . well brushed.' But Erin's toes could wait. I wanted to make the most of my time with Micha. 'And what about you? What news?' I nudged Micha in the ribs as if that would somehow unlock the chat she'd normally have with me.

'Missing Lily.' Her words hit me like a punch. I missed her too. 'All the chores from your parents plus Mrs Saddler breathing down her neck have really wiped her out.' She sipped her Capri-Sun. 'Still, bowling tomorrow will be awesome. And then Saturday too.'

Saturday?! I stopped mid-chew. *How had I forgotten?!* The two of us were meant to be meeting after her football practice to spend the afternoon in town getting fifty-pence chips, picking up some new football socks for Micha's tournament on Sunday and shopping for a prom outfit. And then . . . oh no. My stomach flipped a full 360. We were meant to be having a birthday sleepover at Micha's too! We'd been planning it for *weeks*. But if we weren't back in the right bodies, there was no way my sister could spend the day, and night, with Micha. It would be a disaster! By Sunday Micha might have decided to trade me in for a new best friend!

How could I fix this?

'You know, not to be a Debbie Downer, or an Erin . . . er . . . Erin Erm-This-Isn't-Good-Newser but I'm –' I searched around for an excuse – 'er . . . not sure if there might be some extra rehearsals on Saturday.' I nodded seriously. 'A big one for backstage crew. That could go on into the evening.' I took a dramatic forkful of pasta, although a piece of cucumber undermined me by falling on to my knee. 'Maybe even ... the night? All night.'

But Micha didn't look fazed.

'Well, Lil can't be involved – she said just now she was really looking forward to it.' Did she?! Micha looked off into the distance, her voice dropping. 'Although ... when we were discussing prom, she *did* say going would mean missing the final of *Celebrity Mastermind*, which was ... *weird*.'

I was going to have to have *serious* words with my sister about what sentences should come out, and which shouldn't pass mouth security control. I knew she thought prom was lame, but couldn't she at least try? She could freak out our parents, make things even worse with Frankie, show off in front of the whole class, but whatever happened, she could *not* mess things up with Micha. Micha was as much a part of me as my thumb.

'To be honest, Mich –' I caught myself – 'a, between us, I think Lily is going through a weird patch. Y'know, with all the Frankie stuff and home things. So, er, stick with her.' Well, this was awkward. 'I know she thinks you're her, y'know ...' I hoped this wouldn't backfire. 'Porcupine wife for life ...' Nope, I instantly regretted it. 'Or something.'

I stuffed some more pasta into my mouth. Micha smiled ... but also looked as if she might be sitting on a drawing pin. My phone vibrated.

113

> Micha: Hurry up. NO offence but your sister is
> being weird

I pretended to be fascinated by a passing pigeon, and with my hand down by my side, out of Micha's view, I typed back with one thumb.

> Me: She's always weird. Just go with it. Sending
> you VIBESSSS 🐗

Although when I sneaked another look at my screen, my solo thumb work wasn't as good as I'd hoped. I'd actually sent:

> Me: She's always weird Josh GO WITHOUT.
> Sending you vibe sausage 🌭 🥴

I instantly regretted comparing Micha to my thumb. Micha would *never* do to this me. No wonder she was staring at her phone in confusion.

'Soooo ...' Time for a subject change. I could normally speak to Micha about anything, but now ninety-nine per cent of things were off limits. 'Did you see Lily's latest blog?'

Micha munched a large crisp and smiled (well, she actually jumped a bit at the extra loud crunch and then smiled). 'Straight ten out of ten. I wish she'd believe me when I tell her how good she is.'

The urge to hug her was so strong I had to sit on my hands.

'Totally agree. I know most people here talk about my grades, and my quiz team, and being put up a year, and my acting, but I truly think she's the talented sibling.'

My phone buzzed again.

Micha: you better be running

Urgent subject change needed. Again. But what? I wanted to know how things really were with Micha. If her chemistry grades had picked up, or if her parents had got a whiff she might be moved down a set. How she was feeling about the scouts on Sunday. About keeping her football dreams alive. But there was no way Erin should know any of that.

'So tomorrow then. How's your bowling? You know it's –' I cleared my throat – 'right up my alley.' Uh-oh, I was recycling jokes. I was becoming my dad. And way too Lily-like. Time to unleash an extra big dose of Erin. 'I've been working on my quads to get the right angle of projection. Should be a *thrilling* competition.'

'Yeah, should be good,' Micha started to say. But I cut her off.

With a scream.

An actual scream. Someone's arm was around me!

A boy someone!

A boy someone with a sling on his other arm!

I jumped off the wall and into the air.

'Excusssssse me?!' I shouted in the face of a very confused

person ... Also known as Erin's boyfriend of the last year, Ben.

What was he doing here?! My plan was to avoid him entirely until I was safely back in my own body!

'You okay, babe?' He was standing side on, legs slightly bent, non-broken arm out, as if I were a tiger that might bite his hand off. 'I mean, you do not seem okay.'

'Yes. Of course.' I threw my head back and tried to laugh but it came out like Siri saying, 'Ha ha ha.' 'Sorry ... b ...' Could I say 'babe'? 'Baaa ...' Could I? 'Baaaaa-sically –' No, I couldn't – 'I just wasn't expecting you. That's all.'

Ben scratched his head. 'But you said to meet here?'

'I *did?!*' I spluttered. 'Sorry, I mean ... I ... *did*. Yes.' How dare Erin invite Ben to our lunch? Me secretly inviting Micha was fine, but this was too far!

Ben went to reach his non-sling arm back round me.

'Hold up.' I jerked away, pulling myself back up on to the wall. 'Last night I did lots of rehearsing ... and I ... er ... think I might have bruised a ... er ... rib.' Ben's eyebrows shot up. I nodded seriously. 'I know, right – I think I might need to tone down my dramatic arm flings. Anyway, point is, best stay away.'

He stepped back. 'Sure.' The weirdest thing was Ben didn't even seem to think his girlfriend was being weird. 'Sorry I'm late by the way.' He ran his working hand through his jet black hair. 'Got held up. Found a killer article on Castles! Chaos! Cows! Did you know they were thinking about adding in mixed crop farming methods?' He shook his head in disbelief. 'Wiiiild.'

Wow, maybe Ben and my sister really were perfect together.

'Anywazzzz, Micha.' He shuffled towards me. I shuffled away to maintain a solid two-metre distance to be safe. 'Did I just hear you say bowling tomorrow?'

Micha nodded. 'Yup, Lily's birthday.'

Ben lifted his arm out of the sling and flexed his arm and fingers out. 'Awesome. Since she shattered my arm in three places I've been dying to see if it's back up to speed.'

'It was an accident.' I didn't care what body I was in, he needed to know. 'And also I'm not a hundred per cent sure bowling is still on.' There was no way Ben was inviting himself! He didn't even like me! He only tolerated me because I was his girlfriend's sister.

Micha looked confused. 'But you were just saying you'd been practising.'

C'mon, Mich – read my cryptic look! I'm actually Lily, and Ben coming bowling would mean spending my birthday being held hostage on a group date with my sister's boyfriend. But no, it seemed she just thought I had something in my eye.

'Bennnnn!' And *this* was the moment Erin chose to arrive. 'What a surprise seeing you here!' She grinned, not knowing I'd already rumbled her plan. It disappeared when she saw Micha. 'Oh, hi, Micha . . .' She lowered her voice and leant towards me. 'Guess great minds think alike.'

I turned my head so I could whisper back, 'Great minds

should be on time so they don't miss out on important news from the greatest of the two minds.'

Erin ignored me and said her hellos. It was a relief to see her doing just as badly at this whole body swap as me, because without thinking she went to hug Ben. He was so petrified he leapt backwards and stumbled into a bin. How refreshing if my sister was the one to break one of Ben's limbs for a change. Although ... Micha's already big brown eyes were even wider at the sight of her best friend trying to hug her sister's boyfriend. *Please* let that memory not be saved into a long-term brain folder.

'S-sorry, babe—' Erin stuttered, trying to gloss over it. 'Baa ... Babe-ybel is something that I would like for lunch. Is the thing I was saying.'

She actually winced. And as Micha and Ben stared and Erin rambled on about cheese I knew one thing for absolute certain.

Unless we found Agatha in the next twenty-four hours my birthday was going to be a disaster.

CHAPTER THIRTEEN

'I'm sorry, Mrs Saddler – it ... it's just a blip, I promise.' Standing in the middle of the stage there was nowhere to hide. *Why* did I write my lines on my wrist in biro, and not something that wouldn't smudge off during the day? In the whole first half I'd remembered about four words.

'Well, let's hope so.' Mrs Saddler's eye-roll was so big I wondered if eyeball dislocation was a thing. 'Recasting is always an option, let's not forget.' How could I? It kept me awake at night. 'You don't need me to remind you that your understudy Lou is exceptionally talented. And your sister could do with taking this more seriously as well ... wherever she might be.'

Where was Erin? She knew today was the big day to run through all the prop and scenery changes. 'Her detention isn't optional. I don't give out punishments for fun.' She literally did, and I could tell from Lou's hard stare at the floor she felt the same. 'So make sure she's clear about that or she could be looking at an even longer detention.'

Frankie popped her head out of the wings. 'Don't worry, Mrs S, I've got this. I know how important every second of rehearsal is, even if Lily *has* disappeared.' And the award for biggest suck-up goes to ... 'Look.' Frankie held up the schedule and detailed plan Erin had made for them. 'I even made this plan to make sure we have everything covered.'

I? It had all been my sister's work.

Mrs Saddler uncrossed her arms – her limbs were easily fooled.

'Well, that's great work, Frances. I'm *very* impressed with how you're applying yourself. I hope Lily will take a leaf out of your book.' *What?! To be a backstabbing-work-stealer?!* 'Although, please never call me Mrs S ever again. As in. EVER.'

As soon as I was allowed to leave the stage, I fled to the empty chair by Lou.

'Well, that was terrible.'

She nudged her knee into mine. 'We all have off days.'

That was one way of putting it. 'I just hope Mrs Saddler doesn't change her mind about me playing Titania before I get better.' Well, before Erin was back in the right body. She would never forgive me. Although, where was she? 'No offence or anything.' It wasn't Lou's fault she was my understudy.

'None taken. I want to keep playing Puck!' She gave me

a double knee nudge. 'But don't worry. You're the best actor in the whole school. Just remember what you said to me last term ... You can only eat an elephant bite by bite.'

It was one of Dad's phrases, although I never really understood what eating an elephant had to do with *anything*. And what would it taste like? Pork? Plus Erin was a vegetarian. You didn't get carrots the size of elephants. Not even large potatoes. Enthusiastic Mark slid his chair up to mine, making me snap out of my ginormous vegetable thoughts. He drummed his fingers on my script.

'Despite what everyone's saying, I thought you were okay up there.'

Right.

But I didn't have time to say 'thanks' or 'that's awful' or whatever the right response was, as Mrs Saddler was calling us all together.

'Today was ... Well ... I would say *a disaster*, but that conveys too much excitement. It's just over a week till opening night and there's *no* excuse for not knowing your lines.' Well, there was, and it was spelt 'b-i-r-o'. 'We only have six rehearsals left. Tomorrow night and every evening next week – then we're doing it for real at the Swan Theatre. So ...' She looked right at me. Like into my actual soul. 'I need to see *drastic* improvement. Understood?'

Was now the time to ask if I could duck out early tomorrow to go bowling? Almost definitely not, but I didn't have an option. To say Mrs Saddler was unimpressed would be an understatement. She actually pulled up a chair, sat down, closed her eyes and clenched her fist as she 'processed'. For over a minute.

I didn't know my lines but I did know two things:

1. I was pretty quickly ruining Erin's play and her chance of getting into Chinyere Okafor's Drama Academy.
2. The only way to fix it was to get back in my body.

As fast as I could I grabbed my bag and ran to find Erin. School was weird when it was empty, like when you see a teacher at the weekend in normal person clothes and it feels all wrong. I looked round all the ground-floor classrooms but there was no sign of life until . . . Ah! A light was on in the girls' toilets.

'Erin?' I pushed open the door. 'I mean, Lily?'

I had to hope no one heard that, as going into a room calling your own name was pretty strange even by my standards. But I'd found her. There my sister was, at the sinks.

'Found you!' I closed the door tight behind me. 'And don't think I don't know what you're up to.'

During Mrs Saddler's rant I'd figured it out.

'Which is?' Erin raised an eyebrow.

'Hiding out here to get me in even more trouble with Mrs Saddler.' Erin must have seen my terrible start to the rehearsal and decided to get her own back. 'I *know* that's the only reason anyone uses these bathrooms. To go undetected.'

'Or to wash out props ...' She held up what looked like a soggy mop. I *think* it was a wig. Well, either that or she'd resurrected Barry the Hamster (RIP) for a quick shampoo. 'So an apology might be in order?'

'An apology? Mrs Saddler is *fuming*. I swear she's about to extend your – well, my – detention.'

But Erin didn't look sorry – she looked ... confused.

'No way, Lil. You've got the wrong end of the stick.' She looked at me via the mirror. 'I went to rehearsal, but as soon as I got there Mrs Saddler asked me to go and wash these wigs out.' Erin smiled smugly. 'Apparently she wouldn't trust most people with them.'

And *that* was when I knew something was definitely up. That was *exactly* the kind of thing Mrs Saddler might say to Erin – but *never* to me. She'd tell me to keep a hundred metres away from anything that was vaguely dear to her.

'And who told you this?' I had a hunch.

'My backstage team.' My hunch became a stone-cold fact. She meant Frankie.

'Right after you gave Frankie the schedule?'

'Laminated schedule. Which FYI she loved.' Erin wrung some grey water out of the blonde hairy blob. 'And don't give me that look. I don't know what your problem is with her. She's actually really supportive if you get to know her.'

My sister could be really clueless considering she was so, er, clue-ful.

'Erin, you know Frankie wasn't telling you the truth, right?' I almost felt bad. 'Mrs Saddler wanted you at rehearsal. Not here.'

Erin shook her head. 'Honestly, Lil, no offence –' I braced to be offended – 'but I think I'd know if Frankie was taking me for a ride. You're just putting two and two together and getting five.'

I clenched my hands. Why could my sister never trust me?!

'Please just believe me on this. I *swear* Mrs Saddler is furious with you. Well, me. So instead of arguing about it, I'd reeeeally appreciate it if you could go and find her and try not to make my life any worse.' I flashed the nicest smile I could. 'Consider it an early birthday present?'

Erin sighed. 'Fiiiiine. I'll check in with her tomorrow.' She clearly didn't believe me at all. 'But in return you should give Frankie a chance.'

A chance?! A *chance*?! All term I'd given Frankie chances, and even once my lunch Twix, and she still hated me. Worst of all, I had no idea why. But Erin was having none of it. Fine, time to unleash the big one. My Hairy Godmother news.

But after my big reveal that I had single-handedly saved our chances of swapping back, all Erin did was frown and say 'We'll see.' *We'll see*?! Well, *yes, we will, Erin.*

And I had just the plan to prove it.

I grabbed some scissors from the first-aid box and held one of the wigs hostage until Erin sent a message I'd already composed to the Mavers Mayhem family group. For this to work, I needed Mum and Dad to think it came from Erin, not me.

> Erin: Rehearsal is running late. Is it okay if Lil and I
> walk back together?'

And bingo – because it came from my perfect big sis we got an immediate reply.

> Mum: 👍
> Mum: If the pharmacy's still open could you get
> some muscle rub? Your father is lying face down
> on the kitchen floor saying something about
> a hula hoop
> Erin: No probs.
> Mum: Thanks. I would send a photo, but probably
> best no one else witnesses this

We could see Dad typing.

> Dad: imok

Then a pause.

> Mum: TRANSLATION – he means 'I'm okay' but
> seems even his thumb is suffering

Lily: Ahhh Dad, don't worry. We can watch the
Christmas special of World's Funniest Dogs to
cheer you up

Lily: I could even de-fluff some more socks 😜

Erin's face scrunched as she read it. Blissful. If she could mess with my life and not believe me about Frankie, I could play with hers too.

'Dangerous game, little sister,' Erin said. 'If you're so certain about this clue leading us to Agatha, we could be back in the right bodies tonight.' She paused. 'And that sock fluff is no joke.'

But I'd give *anything* to get my life back, especially the day before my birthday, so even the threat of an evening with Dad's socks didn't put me off. In fact, I was in such a good mood about finding Agatha that I practically sprinted the whole way into town. My sister could hardly keep up, but it was a gorgeous hot summer's evening, and for the first time since the swap, I actually felt like something good was about to happen. By the time we turned into the railway arches, I was a fizz of nervous excitement.

I had no idea what we might find, but I knew that whatever it was, I wasn't leaving without being in the right body, or at least having a way of tracking Agatha down. And proving to my sister I could be right about something.

'So look, Erin.' I marched up to the door, excited to show her my big find. The door was locked, and there was no one

126

inside. Just the same old, dusty boxes we'd seen a few days ago. I got out my phone and opened up the photo Mum had taken this morning. 'This exact picture of us two is . . . right –' I pointed to the wall, to the frame I'd seen online earlier – 'there.'

But there was one problem.

The photo of us . . . wasn't there.

Erin leant forward, squinting. 'Should I be able to see it?'

This couldn't be happening!

I rubbed at the streaky window.

But no.

My one lead . . . had gone!

'Okay, I *promise* it was there!' I jabbed at the single gold frame in the middle of all the black ones as Erin made an unconvinced 'Hmmmmmmm'. '*Right there.* That gold one was the one that had our faces in . . . Look.' I opened the screenshot I'd taken of Street View this morning. Thank goodness I had evidence because as Erin looked down at it, then back at the wall, her face went from deeply suspicious to downright shocked.

Finally, she believed me.

I cupped my hands on the window trying to get a better view of whatever had replaced our picture in the gold frame. It looked like . . . a sculpture? 'Can you see what it is? Do you reckon it's another clue?'

Erin took a photo of it as her camera was better and shared it with me. 'I dunno.' She zoomed in. 'It looks like . . .'

The top halves of two stone women pressing their hands as if they were doing pat-a-cake?

'Statues?' She paused. 'Statues that look as if they're on top of something. A building maybe?'

Well, that narrowed it down to something that could be literally found *everywhere*. Agatha might as well have left us a picture of air. Or grass.

I sighed so hard the window steamed up. I'd been *convinced* that this discovery would lead us straight to the Hairy Godmother. That maybe once we got here, we'd turn round and she'd be behind us saying, 'Well done,' and, 'Here are your bodies back.'

'So after all this.' I let my forehead fall on to the glass. 'All we've narrowed it down to is . . . Agatha wants us to find some *statues*. Somewhere in . . . the *world*.' All my happiness at the thought of being back in my body for my birthday drained right out of me. In fact . . . was I going to cry?

This wasn't a clue. It was another dead end.

Maybe I had got it all wrong.

But Erin was still staring at the frame. 'No, Lil. I *think* you're on to something.' She did? 'I recognize that picture. Those statues. I *really* do – I just don't know where from.' Wow, so Erin really *did* believe me. 'But we've not got long to work it out. Notice anything special about what's next to the gold frame?'

Nope. I zoomed back in on the photo Erin had taken. Next to the frame was a wall calendar of the year. This year. And only one date was circled. In big red pen.

This Saturday.

I looked at Erin. She looked at me.

Whatever Agatha was trying to tell us, we had less than forty-eight hours to figure it out.

Or I wouldn't just be spending my thirteenth birthday stuck in my sister's body, I could be spending for ever.

CHAPTER FOURTEEN

Weird. I'd thought going bowling in my sister's body with her next to me in my body, while trying to avoid her boyfriend, while simultaneously trying to talk to my best friend, who thought I was someone else and was trying to hang out with my sister, who wanted to speak to her boyfriend, who was trying to spend time with me, would be a fun way to spend a birthday.

Turns out it was relatively stressful.

Still, it was Friday night, I was officially thirteen, the lights were down, the UV lanes were up, and despite being terrible at bowling – whichever body I was in – I was having the most fun I'd had since that stupid Shakespeare conference with Erin had ruined my life.

And I *needed* some fun after this week.

I was exhausted from constantly treading on eggshells at home and school, and pretending I knew what words like 'egregious' meant (apparently it meant 'shockingly bad' which summed up everything really). And Mrs Saddler hadn't been any more impressed by my performance today. Plus Erin's apology to her had achieved zilch, as when she found out my sister was also leaving rehearsal early, she was even more furious than yesterday. I'd been at the receiving end of a teacher-rage before (many times – too many times?) so knew the best strategy was silent acceptance, but my sister, who had no experience of adults being disappointed, panicked and offered to come in on Saturday morning AND Sunday to finish the scenery so the precious play didn't fall behind.

So now Erin and I were back to arguing – she'd gone and made a plan for the *one* day I'd asked her to keep free. Sunday. Micha's big football tournament that I'd promised I'd be at.

I was so *done* with Erin being me. And even more done with being her.

And the one person who would find something positive to help keep me going didn't have a clue about any of it. I *really* missed having Micha to talk to. We normally talked about *anything*.

Last night instead of working on my blog under my duvet like usual, I'd started typing out some thoughts, just so I could get them out. I'd called it '101 Weird Things You Will Never Know Unless You Magically Swap Lives With Someone Else' but crossed out 'Will' and replaced it with 'Might' in case Mum or Dad found it and thought I'd eaten too much broccoli again. Without meaning to I'd poured out all the things this week had shown me, like how much about my normal life I took for granted, and how much less fun life was without your best friend. I figured it could be a reminder, just for me, when I was back in my own body, of how good it was being me. Well, that was if I could get back in my own body. With only one day left to figure out Agatha's clue, I was beginning to seriously worry that might never happen.

I *had* to figure out Agatha's clue. What *were* those statues?!

But my brain was so tangled trying to figure it out, I *needed* to give myself a break. Just a few hours off the Agatha search to enjoy my birthday. And being here, in the dark, the noise of the bowling balls hitting the pins, was already making me feel a little less on edge, as if maybe I could get away with being a tiny bit more myself. Especially as our parents weren't here to give me worried looks and ask if 'I meant my hair to look like that' like they'd done every day this week.

Dad had broken his little finger at Circus Skills attempting an 'over-optimistic cartwheel' (Mum's words), so instead of bowling they were popping to a pharmacy for painkillers and some plasters for the cut to his head. Oh, and something else because apparently Dad had done himself 'another mischief'. When Mum had said this I'd stared forward in the car not wanting to know more, which she'd mistaken as deep interest and followed up with, 'Athlete's foot. Your father's got a rather extreme outbreak of Circus Skills fungal infection.'

I made a note to send any future counselling bills direct to them.

'Love that you're testing the hypothesis.' Ben slid on to the padded bench beside me. I stood straight up, like a dysfunctional see-saw. He was updating his own scoreboard pad that he'd brought 'in case the machine's algorithm glitched'. Despite trying my best, I was doing worse than any other player, including the child who was refusing to take his BMX gloves off and couldn't even pick up a ball properly. I'd had to lie and tell everyone I was using Lily's birthday to experiment with various throws. 'I'm still in *awe*. Your theory about angle in relation to the friction . . . ?' Ben lifted up his spare hand and pointed down at my head. 'Girlfriend of the year right here!'

I turned so he didn't hear the groan that wouldn't stay in. But my phone was buzzing.

> Erin: If you make things weird between me and
> Ben then 😬

Couldn't she see this was me trying my hardest to be nice?!

> Me: Says the one who just declined a selfie with my
> best mate 😒

But it was my turn to bowl, so with Ben cheering me on, I stepped forward, pulled my shoulders back and looked down the lane. Hopefully this time I'd do better. Channelling every bit of Erin-confidence, and using the exact same technique she just used, I strode forward, bent my knee and lunged the ball down the lane with as much force as I could muster.

And it knocked down five pins!

Which was great!

If it hadn't been on the lane next to ours ...

Where there was now a small child crying over having their turn ruined.

'I'm *so* sorry,' I said, running straight over.

The dad clutched the child to him as if I was a bowling-ball-wielding maniac. Which I didn't disagree with. 'As long as it doesn't happen again.'

I promised him it wouldn't.

It accidentally happened three more times.

When the manager moved (evicted) us to a new lane, Erin suggested she and Ben get drinks so I finally managed to get a chance to chat to Mich.

'Nice game, Micha, or should I say The IncredibowlMich ...' She always had the best names – and scores. She was over seventy points ahead of me. 'I'm still waiting to hit my stride.'

Micha laughed. 'As long as you don't hit any more ninety-year-old men when you do.'

The small child's grandad had unfortunately discovered what a bowling ball rolling over a foot in socks and sandals felt like.

'I think it's just one of those evenings.' I laughed, and then some more when I thought how much this really didn't cover the scale of how weird my birthday was.

'You're telling me.' Micha grinned.

I smiled back, nodding along to the music, but really I was wishing I could tell her how much life sucked without her to talk to. How I needed her to stick with whatever weirdness my sister was dishing up until I was back in the right body.

'So how's it all going ... ?' I tried to sound as vague as Erin should. 'With football and things ... ?'

Micha scrunched her mouth. 'Depends who's asking.'

'Well, I am.' This wasn't the kind of conversation Mich would have ever had with my sister so I needed to try harder. 'Look, I know me and Lil can argue, but if you ever wanted to tell me stuff, your secrets would be safe.' I looked over to the lane we'd just moved from. 'Unlike anyone bowling near us.'

Micha fiddled with her straw – she was nervous.

'Thanks, Erin ...' She paused. 'I guess everything's okay. I'm on track for a place with Aston Villa's youth team if I do well this Sunday in the—'

'Inter County Cup.' Even in the low light it was clear she was surprised I knew. Oops. 'Lily told me. She's got you down for a hat-trick, you know.'

Mich snorted. 'As if. And anyway, goals are nowhere near as hard as staying up in chemistry. If I don't manage that, I just know Mum and Dad won't let me play, even if I do get into the team.'

So they hadn't found out yet. That was one good thing.

'How's that looking?' I was fishing for a proper update. It had been too hard to ask over message, and my sister hadn't paid enough attention to be able to give me details.

She sighed. Hard. 'Not good. I panicked in the spot test yesterday and . . .' She looked at me, worried. 'You won't tell your parents, will you?'

I shook my head. 'I can promise you your secrets are as safe with me as with my sister.'

She sighed. 'Well, in that case . . . I flunked it.' Exactly what I *didn't* want to hear. 'Majorly. So now Mr Sharma is making me sit a whole new exam.' That was bad! 'A week tomorrow.' That was even worse. 'Fun, huh?'

Wow. As much as I believed Micha was capable of anything, things were not looking great.

'Can I do anything to help?' I wasn't that great at chemistry either but maybe I could talk my sister into it.

Micha shrugged. 'Nah, I'll figure something out.'

That was the thing about Mich, she never wanted to make her problems anyone else's. But Erin and Ben arrived back and cut our conversation short, and soon I was cheering Micha on as she got yet another spare. But I couldn't enjoy her full celebration, as in the darkness I felt something move behind our seats. Someone.

I turned around.

It was the manager. And he was standing watching us. Or, more specifically, *me*.

His face was lit up by a giant UV bowling ball, so I couldn't miss him mouthing, 'I'm watching you,' and use two fingers to point at his eyes, then mine.

Way to make me feel less nervous.

Ben leant over. 'Your sister's *killing* it.' She'd just got her fifth strike. 'She's normally terrible!' *Thanks, Ben.* 'Do you think it's time you stop the experiments and show her what you're made of?'

I laughed. Which seemed better than cry.

'Er . . . I don't like to end an experiment early.'

Ben nodded solemnly. 'Of course. But look who's watching . . .' He jerked his head towards the manager who was still lit up like a ghost in a suit. I had a horrible feeling that one more wrong move and we'd be asked to leave.

I stood up.

'C'mon, Erin!' Micha whooped. 'Time to unleash your AMAZING!'

My sister smiled. 'Ditto to that.'

How was I going to pull this off?!

I just needed to relax. But as I picked up my ball the manager drew alongside me.

Was he going to reassure me it was okay after all? That bad spells happened to everyone?

'No more of your displays please.' He was looking down the lanes, arms crossed, but speaking to me. 'I've seen you here before and know this is all an act.' Little did he know it was actually an unfortunate case of an unexpected body swap. 'So unless you stop messing around and take this seriously, it's going to be a life ban. For all four of you.'

Well, that was one way to motivate someone. Who wasn't me.

Because now I was *terrified*.

With the ball shaking in my hands, I edged into the middle of the lane. The hand-sweating wasn't exactly helping.

What would Erin do? Guess she would just believe she could.

All I had to do was not overthink it.

I was *definitely* overthinking it.

C'mon, me. Just achieve a normal throw. Knock some pins down.

I looked down the lane.

Took a few steps back.

Lifted my arm up.

Swung it forward to check my aim, pulled it back and ...

Bowled a perfect, straight ball right down the middle of the alley.

Ben was so proud he screamed in admiration.

Except ...

That was what I'd *meant* to do. But as I'd prepared to throw the ball, Ben had decided to share his latest ideas on my angle theory. How he thought resting his chin on the back of my neck and putting his arms alongside mine to show me with his whole body pressing into me was helpful, I *did not* know.

Because all it made me do was release the ball with the momentum I'd built up.

Straight backwards, on to his foot.

CHAPTER FIFTEEN

'Aren't you having your *favourite* for your big one-three birthday?' Dad was shouting, it was so busy in Slice, Ice, Baby! We were all being extra cheerful to try to gloss over the fact Ben had his foot (which was now so swollen it wouldn't fit in a shoe) propped up on a catering-size tub of mayonnaise. We all said he should get it checked out but he didn't want to 'ruin Lily's birthday'. Little did he know Agatha had already managed that.

Dad looked at my sister's plate and put his hands (one bandaged) up to his face in fake shock. The cut on his head was now covered by the only plaster the pharmacy had – a cartoon princess one saying 'I'm a Very Brave Girl'.

But Dad's shock was fair – my sister's plate, which should be holding piles of delicious birthday pizza, contained just two meagre slices of tomato and mozzarella.

Two?!

Her plate was a criminal act! A cheese-based crime against

my birthday! And I had a reputation to keep up in this place! Last time I was here my ice-cream eating had earned me a place on the Mega Bowl Wall of Fame (and people said it was my sister who excelled!). I glanced over at the 'Lily Mavers' written on the wall and hoped it couldn't see what I'd become.

Erin *knew* my pizza rule.

Tomato and mozzarella is *not* a pizza flavour – it's merely a pizza skeleton to hang off lots of *far superior* stuff: Pepperoni! Peppers! Ham! Banana (but only when I was at Micha's as Erin didn't allow them in the house).

And *two slices*?! This was an eat-all-you-can pizza place! Not a nibble-till-you're-comfortably-full restaurant! Erin's plate made me sad – like seeing a dog that'd had too much hair taken off at the groomer's.

But I had to push it to one side – I was *not* letting my sister's poor slice options, or being in the wrong body, ruin my birthday. The last week and a half had been all quiz lunchtimes, teacher chats, embarrassing rehearsals and chasing magical hairdressers, but for the next hour the only important thing was pizzaaaaaaaa.

'Can I tempt anyone?' A waiter pushed through the packed restaurant to wheel a tray of fresh hot pizzas over, a full sixteen-slice pepperoni one steaming away next to me. A pepperoni pizza that vegetarian Erin would never touch.

Thank goodness the music was loud as I couldn't help but whimper at its beauty. *Oh pepperoni pizza – how I long for thee! One day we'll be reunited, my oozing friend. Oh yes, we will.*

Micha leant over.

'Erin, did you just say "one day we'll be reunited" ... to a pizza?'

Well, I'd *thought* I'd only thought it but my passion for pepperoni must run deeper than I realized.

'Hahahahahaahaaha.' Slightly manic laugh. '*No.* That would obviously be madness. I was just er ... practising my lines.'

I took a ten-second-long sip on my drink to keep me quiet, and because Micha's amazing she just smiled and said, 'Absolutely.'

Ignoring looks from Mum and Dad I asked the waiter to load up my plate with veggie deluxe. Sure, it wasn't something Erin would normally do, but there was doing my best to be believable in my sister's body so our entire lives didn't implode – and there was saying no to free pizza.

'Awesome pressie by the way.' Micha nodded over to the stack of presents I'd cunningly 'tidied' in a pile between me and Ben. Some would call it a full-on barrier wall, but I had to protect myself somehow. 'You literally chose the *exact* wheels Lily had been after?'

'Really?' I tried to look surprised, but it was definitely easier buying someone a birthday present when it was *yourself* you were buying for. Erin didn't usually spend that much on me, but I had to take the positives of this body swap where I could, and new skateboard wheels had been it. Shame she said, 'What on earth are these?' when she opened them. And then, 'HOW MUCH DID THEY COST?' But I think I got away with it.

And we had another surprise lined up. Mum had had the genius idea to tell the restaurant it was her youngest daughter's birthday – not only was it cute, but even better, Erin would *hate* it. When people had birthdays here they went all out – a special dessert with sparklers, a song with all the staff, even a Polaroid picture to take home. I couldn't *wait* to see Erin's face. She kept saying how much of a breeze my life was, so I was going to enjoy seeing her deal with this particular gust.

'Yessss, babes.' Ben chinked his glass of Coke against mine. 'You *never* match me slice for slice!'

I jumped – as I did any time Ben was nearer than one metre.

'Uh-huh,' was all I said, hoping the chewing excused me from a full sentence. But Ben didn't seem to care I was worse company than a piece of cardboard. He just smiled longingly at me like Barry the Hamster (RIP) used to when I carried over a tiny triangle of toast and peanut butter for him. Wait.

Why.

Was.

Ben's.

Hand.

Creeping.

Across.

The.

Table?

Ben smiled at me.

And I knew the truth.

THE HORRIFYING TRUTH.

His hand.

Was moving towards mine.

TO HOLD IT IN A LOVING WAY.

Groosssssssssss.

I leapt up so hard, I bashed my knees on the table, sloshing over most of our drinks.

I *may* have also sent a pizza cutter flying through the air. It *may* have landed in an old lady's handbag.

Mum, Dad, Micha and Erin all stared right at me.

'Everything okay?' Ben asked softly when I landed back on the bench. Good – both his hands were firmly back in front of him, just where I liked them. I *almost* felt bad for him but if he knew, I swear he'd be grateful.

'Just hiccups,' I said to the whole table, widening my eyes as if I too were surprised. 'One reaaaally big unexpected hiccup.' I hit my chest. 'Must be the nine slices of pizzas.'

Ben nodded. 'Our dog Martin used to do the exact same thing when he had too many treats.'

'Honestly, that dog.' I whistled happily, relieved Ben was taking the attention off me. 'I couldn't love that cute lil' fluffpot more.'

Ben's eyebrows scrunched. 'But Martin was a metre-tall Bernese Mountain Dog.'

'And of course I meant *little* in a . . . *big* way.' I avoided Erin's laser-beam death stare. 'That fella really gives the best doggie-cuddles ever.'

'But he died three years ago.' Ben sounded genuinely sad.

'I meant in my imagination. I am, of course, still very sorry for your loss.' I took an overly large bite of my pizza to stop any more words from leaving my mouth. It was the only way. But the cheese didn't snap properly and boiling-hot tomato sauce flopped on my chin. *Ouch*. Even the pizza thought I was a terrible person.

My yelp silenced the table, *again*, so I looked at Dad for some help. Rookie error. I should have remembered freestyle Dad wasn't safe territory. Especially not after a bump on his head. 'So, er . . .' Uh-oh. 'Talking of terrible losses –' said no one ever – 'Micha, how are things at football? Lily told me all about it.' I almost spat out my pizza. I definitely *hadn't* – my sister must have been blabbing. Didn't she understand the rule was to tell parents *nothing*?! 'I hear it's been a bit tense with the whole chemistry thing, but worry not.' He lifted up his fingers and crossed them. 'YOYO.'

I guessed he meant YOLO. Not that that made sense either.

I swallowed my pizza with a sense of dread. Micha was going to think I'd broken her trust. Blabbed her secret! I studied her face – was she mad at me? She'd have every right to be.

144

'YOYO indeed, Mr Mavers.' To my massive relief Mich smiled at Dad and didn't give my sister evil looks. 'I really think I could get picked for the youth team, so I'm just going to have to pull an Erin and ace my next chemistry test.' Her breezy voice was playing this down. I knew it was for our benefit not hers. Or was it so they wouldn't say anything to her parents? 'It's kind of lucky really that Lily's tied up with all those chores. All that early morning mowing –' which I'd *definitely* invented, and judging my mum's and dad's looks to each other, they'd realized as much – 'means loads of time for me to work on Mr Sharma's extra assignment.' Assignment? I knew about the exam, but he'd set her extra work too?

Eurgh. I hated being an outsider on my best friend's life. Normally I knew every single detail of it – Mich once rang me when her pencil sharpening looked like Chase Cheney's nose.

But something had caught my attention. Or some*one*.

And they were waving.

Frankie. And her entire cheerleader squad.

My stomach dropped so hard that, for the first time in my life, I doubted I could finish my pizza.

What were they doing here?! Other than eating delicious pepperoni slices that should be miiine?!

I waved back with as much of a smile as I could force.

My sister was waving too, which surprised Micha so much she looked as if she'd just bitten into an olive and discovered it was an eyeball.

'Is that ... Frankie?' Erin turned back to the table, grinning. 'Cooool.'

Cool?! It was so uncool, it was boiling hot! Why wouldn't Erin trust me about what Frankie was really like?

'That's who I'm doing backstage with ...'

Mum and Dad exchanged looks, figuring out that also meant the one whose phone I broke, and who I moaned about at least three times a week.

Erin flicked her perfect plaits over her shoulder. 'And she's coming over ...'

Well, *this* was going to be a disaster. Frankie didn't need any family-based ammunition to make my life more hell.

'Be normal. *Please*,' I hissed in my parents' direction, but Dad was smoothing his princess plaster and Mum was trying to calm down a woman who had just discovered a greasy pizza cutter in her bag, so the chances were low.

'Oh heyyyy.' Frankie waved, her cheer-friends traipsing behind her. 'Looks like I owe someone a happy birthday?' Frankie twiddled the balloon Micha had tied to my sister's chair. What did she want? I knew for a *fact* she didn't want any birthday of mine to be happy. Or any non-birthday either.

Erin swivelled and smiled at Frankie, making sure she caught my eye. I knew exactly what she was trying to prove. And to be honest a tiny bit of me wondered if Erin was right as usual. Maybe Frankie *wasn't* that bad. Maybe I was overreacting? It just really did feel like whenever I'd tried to be nice to her this term she'd thrown it back in my face. Or posted my life fails on the internet.

As my sister and Frankie hugged, Micha watched open-mouthed, as if an actual zombie were feasting on her best friend's brains.

Right. That was *it*.

If anything made me extra determined to track down Agatha before the deadline tomorrow, it was this. I needed no more weird things to happen with my best friend before Erin damaged them beyond repair.

Everyone started making small talk except Micha, who was in the fast-blinking stage of shock, but I needed Frankie to clear the Mavers zone *immediately*. Why were my parents (the traitors) laughing so much at what she was saying?!

Ben leant over. 'Frankie ... I've heard that name before, haven't I?' Trust him to not remember, considering I'd mentioned it at least one million times. 'Oh!' He clicked his fingers. 'Isn't that the one your sister's always going on about?'

I shrugged. 'Talking a reasonable and justified amount about – yes, I think so.'

'I thought she said Frankie hated her?' And for the first and only time in my life, I wanted to hug him. 'Although no ... *That was it!* You said it was just Lily being dramatic.'

My momentary bubble of affection I had towards Ben and his overly fragile limbs popped. But Frankie was wrapping up to leave.

'I'll head then. Leave you to enjoy Lily's bday. XOXO and all that.' Wow, Frankie was such a parent charmer. 'I'd offer to take a photo of you all together –' she paused – 'especially as I'm lovvving that plaster, Mr Mavers, so on trend.' My dad beamed as if it were a genuine compliment. 'But . . . my phone doesn't work so well since, y'know . . .'

So *that* was why she'd come over. To use my birthday meal to remind my family about the incident. Nice.

'And Lily is very sorry about that,' Mum said.

Frankie tossed her hair. 'Don't worry. Water under the bridge, right?' She squeezed my sister's shoulder. 'So happy bday, backstage buddy! Let's hope Mrs Saddler doesn't give you more detentions as a present.' She winked. 'Better not miss any more rehearsals, right?'

I found myself growling into my straw. As Frankie walked away, my parents asked what she meant, and Erin said there had been a mix-up which wasn't anyone's fault (Micha was still shock-blinking). *How could no one see what she's up to?!*

But in her hurry, something dropped out of Frankie's pocket. I picked it up when I went for a pizza refill. Her library card. I could give it back to her at the next rehearsal – I wasn't risking any more interaction with her today.

I chewed in silence, checking my phone as an excuse not to talk to anyone. But there was a name in my DMs I wasn't expecting.

Nic: Happy birthday Lil.

148

Wow – Nic had never messaged me before. This was a birthday present in itself!

> Nic: Let's celebrate on Weds – by draining you of
> all your ideas haha

My stomach lurched like a pirate ship at a theme park. I loved that she'd remembered my birthday – and hated that my only chance to impress her was in the hands of my sister, live and direct from the lion's den of Frankie's house.

> Nic: Oh – did you say you liked Chase Cheney?

Sorry, what?! I almost choked on a dough ball. Why was Nic asking? Was it something to do with his gigs?! The first one was tonight, and she'd given her backstage passes for tomorrow, his last performance, to her sister, but if she could help me get in, I would willingly never eat pepperoni pizza again.

How to answer?

> Me: HE'S GOD'S GIFT TO BOTH EYES AND EARS.
> MAYBE EVEN NOSES.

No, Lil. Remember who you are talking to. Nic. The coolest girl in school. I emergency deleted.

Me: Yeah, his music's all right. Why?

Nic replied straight away. She was so cool that even replying without a gap was still somehow aloof.

Nic: Tell you at the meet.

'Everything okay?' Ben leant over. I could *not* let him see my phone, he'd have too many questions. Probably starting with, 'Why do you have a picture of Micha holding a miniature hamburger as your wallpaper?'

Although . . . maybe this was an opportunity . . .

'Just getting some difficult yet satisfying quiz questions through from Les Quizerables. Mmmm. Heaven.' I'd discovered the easiest way of being a convincing Erin was to say the opposite of what I really thought. Ben nodded, confirming my fear that this was a totally reasonable thing my sister would do on a Friday night. But I'd had an idea. 'Don't suppose you know where this is from?' I opened up the picture of the frame at The Hairy Godmother, the photo of the stone sculpture filling my screen. 'I think it's local . . .'

Well, I hoped it was. Ben took my phone out of my hands. *Please don't let him notice the cover is plastered with stickers of skateboarding penguins in hats!*

'Hmmmmm.' He zoomed in. If he could tell me then maybe I'd forgive him for his arm and foot bones being so easily breakable. 'It *does* ring a bell.' He laughed to himself.

'Toll, the old clapper . . .' I felt a fizz of excitement. 'Yes, that's it!' Ben paused.

I held my breath.

This was it!

The best birthday present *ever* – my first real chance out of this mess.

CHAPTER SIXTEEN

'It is . . .' Ben turned the screen, pleased with himself . . . 'a wonderful example of sculpture in architecture!' *Is that it?!* 'Greek gods maybe?' *He'd better have more!* 'Well, goddesses.' *He doesn't have more.*

He nodded, happy. I tried not to face plant into my veggie deluxe. 'Top notch quiz question!'

I felt like a birthday balloon. That had been popped. Then melted. Then put in a blender. 'In fact . . .' He got his phone out and opened up YouTube. 'I saw a really interesting video about the origins of stone carving the other day – I meant to send it to you.'

Uh and indeed oh. I had a horrible feeling where this was going.

He typed in my sister's name and pressed share. 'Incooooming!'

He stared at my screen, but nothing arrived – due to the fact I was merely a girlfriend imposter.

'Reception, huh . . .' Could I bluff my way out of this?

'Weird.' He shook his phone. 'And when did your screen get so smashed?' Erin would never have let her phone get as bashed as mine.

I shrugged again. 'Oh, you know . . . *life*. And don't worry about sending the video – you can just . . . describe it?' Said no one ever.

'It's okay, it says delivered.'

Desperate situation alert.

I flung my arm out and pointed to the salad bar. 'IS THAT WOMAN PUTTING DOUGH BALLS UP HER CARDIGAN?!'

Ben spun round – well, more of an awkward twist considering he couldn't move one leg. I jammed my thumb down on my phone's power button. When he turned back, I was holding up a blank screen.

'Weird, huh. My battery is *so* unpredictable.'

'But it was on sixty-four per cent.' Ben was definitely starting to look as if this evening was getting a bit much. And we hadn't even had pudding yet.

But I had to be careful – Erin would kill me if Ben split up with her. So to smooth things over I asked about his latest Castles! Chaos! Cows! strategy, meaning I could finish off my food. His detailed description lasted all five remaining slices. As the plates got cleared one of the waiters caught my eye and waved. This must be the moment! The surprise birthday singing.

My hope *had* been that, as an extra birthday treat, Erin would die of shock, or embarrassment, or maybe both, but now that Frankie was here, I wanted it to be as low-key and quick as possible.

The staff lit the sparklers as the lights went down. Well, all except one. A spotlight on Erin. I was *sure* they didn't use to do that!

My stomach churned. This wasn't exactly the 'getting away without Frankie noticing' discreet situation I was hoping for.

The whole place had gone silent. Except for the loud whoosh of the sparklers which had clearly been upgraded to some kind of military explosive.

'HAPPY BIRTHDAY TO YOUUUU . . .' the staff belted out. It was so loud it sounded like a thirty-person opera! Erin realized what was happening, and instantly went redder than her 'I ♥ I ♥ Slogans' T-shirt (that she'd worn despite my pleas). The circle of eight staff grouped behind her – arms waving in the air as they sang, the whole restaurant joining in behind them.

Please let this be the moment Frankie had decided to go for a wee. A really long wee. My family weren't helping the whole 'don't make this mortifying' thing either. Dad was on his feet clapping (saying 'ow' every time he did) and Mum was filming with the world's brightest flash. Micha was dinging her spoon on a glass while she sang and Ben was using his good foot to drum on the mayonnaise tub. It was surprisingly bassy.

But none of them would be smiling if they could see what I could.

Because the staff had freestyled with Erin's birthday surprise.

Freestyled with the pudding on the plate.

I tried to catch Mum's or Dad's eye as it advanced towards Erin.

As the banana split moved in.

My sister had to be warned! I hadn't seen her in the same room as a peeled banana since I was six – when she'd jumped out of Grandad's window and had fallen in a compost heap.

But I couldn't even hear myself think above the singing and clapping.

'HAPPY BIRTHDAY TO YOUUUU.'

To other customers this was just two bananas, some delicious ice cream between them. But to my sister this was her nemesis.

'HAPPY BIRTHDAY TO LI-LY …'

One of the staff added, 'WHO IS NUMBER TWELVE ON THE MEGA BOWL WALL OF FAME.' But I didn't have time to be proud. I only had time to panic.

I flapped my arms, trying to stop this whole thing, but everyone just thought I was dancing. Ben even copied me, flinging his arms around with a big grin on his face.

But I was too late.

They put the plate down in front of Erin.

And for a moment our table was still.

Erin lit up in the spotlight.

Around her the whole place on their feet watching with excitement.

They say being confronted with a fear can help you get over it.

But as Erin leapt back from the table, screaming, 'NOOOOOOOOOOOOO!' pushing the bowl away so hard it flew through the air (causing one of the bananas to join the pizza cutter in the old lady's bag), I wasn't sure I'd define her reaction as 'over it'.

The singing stopped abruptly. I could almost guarantee they'd never had this reaction to a dessert before.

The lights flicked on, hundreds of shocked faces suddenly visible.

My sister was now standing on her chair. The firework sparklers were still exploding up to the ceiling.

Everyone was in stunned silence.

Everyone except Erin who was yelling, 'BANANAAAAAA!' at the top of her voice. Well, mine.

And Dad who accidentally pulled his party popper. And then said, 'Ow.'

Erin looked at me, panicked. But how could I help? Couldn't she just not freak out about a fruit when she was in my body? Or at least get a semi-normal phobia like buttons or clowns?

Something touched my shoulder. I was so on edge that I screamed.

Argh! It was Ben's hand! Surely that was worse than a banana?!

'Are you okay?' *Oh no. Ohnoohnoohno!*

I suddenly understood his concern. He thought *I* was the one with the phobia – and here I was mere centimetres away from Erin's yellow nemesis. I looked across the table – at least my sister was climbing down from her chair. Oh no – now she was holding the chair in front of her as if the remaining banana could attack at any moment.

This was mortifying.

I *had* to do something.

I grabbed my glass. And with my knife hit the edge.

DING.

Well, here went nothing. Well, nothing but trying to stop the person hundreds of people thought was me stop loudly repeating, 'Bananabananabanana!'

DING, DING.

Everyone turned to look at me.

GULP.

I raised my glass.

'Ten out of ten, Lily.' I cleared my throat. 'Great impression of me there. Of course everyone knows it's me, ERIN, who's y'know –' I didn't want to say this, *whatever* body I was in – 'terrified of bananas.' Weirdest birthday speech ever. 'Oooh, look at it.' I recoiled back in fake fear. 'It's just so . . .' I had no idea what made them scary. '*Yellow!* And smells so much of . . .' I had nothing. '*Banana!*' Were the staff backing away? 'So, er, yes, Lily. A lovely birthday performance there to try to take the pressure off me. Inspired. So why don't you put down that chair, open your eyes, and we can celebrate your birthday! Here's to Lily! Who is actually, to be clear, very, very normal. Happy birthday, little sister!'

Mum and Dad were looking at me with a mixture of maybe pride and definitely confusion. As Dad moved the rest of the banana split into the middle of the table I said, 'Please no. Too soon,' for good measure. Everyone else in the restaurant half-clapped in a very similar way to when Mrs Saddler announced that we were going to make next week's final rehearsals even longer to 'let the magic shine'. But that's when I heard the laugh. Frankie's laugh. And I realized she was filming the whole thing. G-reat. And when I caught her eye she just blew me a kiss. Surely that was the icing on the worst-ever-birthday cake?

But no. There were some extra-terrible cherries on top yet to come.

After all the standing Ben's foot had gone the colour of Mum's car, so he finally agreed to go to A & E, and as his loving girlfriend I had to ditch the unlimited ice-cream factory (aka frozen heaven) and go with him.

Farewell sweet dessertio.

It was a quiet car ride even with Ben's sporadic whimpers of pain and Dad asking again exactly how it happened (and saying something under his breath that sounded a lot like, 'But this kind of thing normally happens to your sister.'). The journey was taking *forever*, the traffic jammed in all directions because of the Chase Cheney concert.

The concert I was desperate to be at.

Happy birthday, me.

As the car crawled along past the Artemis and Athena Arena, Ben started tapping on the window. Really tapping.

'I totally agree, Ben.' The whole place *was* lit up with massive pictures of Chase Cheney. 'Chase does look stunning.' I never had Ben down as a Cheneyator though.

But he groaned something that sounded like, 'Urun'. Was he trying to say Erin? And why was he still tapping?

I shuffled to the left back seat. What was he pointing at?

But when I saw it I *knew*.

And I knew that *despite* having to fake a banana phobia.

Despite Frankie telling my dad 'she'd never met a cooler Norman and she'd love to see his Circus Skills hula-hoop routine'.

Despite potentially crushing another body part of my sister's boyfriend.

Despite watching my best friend slowly think I'd lost the plot.

And *despite* walking away from free ice cream ...

Maybe this evening *hadn't* been a write-off.

Because at the top of the stadium, right where Ben was pointing, was a sight even more glorious than Chase himself.

Two stone statues. Two women touching hands.

The *exact* same ones in the frame at The Hairy Godmother.

And suddenly the circled date made sense.

159

The Hairy Godmother was going to be here. At Chase's concert. Tomorrow.

Sure, tickets were rarer than gold dust, and security tighter than Buckingham Palace, but Erin and I were going to HAVE to get inside that venue.

CHAPTER SEVENTEEN

I'd never seen anywhere so busy. There were people *everywhere*.

It was definitely not a normal feeling to be frantically scanning them all to find someone who looked like . . . myself.

> Me: Where are you?!!
>
> Erin: Chill your boots. Painting scenery overran. I'm almost there.

We'd agreed to meet outside the stadium at 3.30 p.m., as soon as the doors opened, right across the street from the huge entrance with the stone women.

Was there any way my plan would work?

The venue was totally surrounded by security guards, hundreds of people queuing, police officers and . . . yup, some police horses had just arrived. Were there sniffer dogs too?!

I was nervous enough without adding a potential mauling to the situation! And *where* was my sister? How could she be fifteen minutes late? Every second counted!

I breathed deeply and tried not to look at the dog that was pulling apart a Chase Cheney figure someone had dropped.

I couldn't believe we'd been so slow to put all the clues together. Agatha *had* mentioned she worked backstage at concerts – she'd even said something about Chase Cheney. We'd had the answer all along!

Which was why I was extra mad at myself, because if I'd figured it out before, I wouldn't have had to message Micha this morning to last-minute bail on meeting her in town. I'd done everything I could to try and keep the plan alive, but I had to admit defeat. And it sucked – we'd been planning it *for ever*. Still, as long as we swapped back this afternoon, I could make sure Mich and I had the best sleepover tonight and I'd be there cheering her on at football tomorrow. Just as we'd planned.

All I had to do was break into the busiest arena in the UK, with the tightest security, to get backstage with the world's biggest pop star, and track down an elusive magical hairdresser. Easy.

> Me: I promise PROMISE I'll make it up to you 🐁
> Me: Sorry. SORRY.

I saw Micha type. And stop. And type again.

> Micha: It's fine.

No emojis. No motivational penguins. No telling me it wasn't even a thing. I knew my best friend well enough to know 'it's fine' meant 'it's really not'.

And the worst thing was, I didn't just bail on today – I'd asked for her help too.

> Micha: You at least going to tell me why?

My stomach knotted. I hadn't been able to think of any other way Erin and I could be here this evening without Mum and Dad saying no. So despite hating dragging Micha further into this, I'd asked her to cover for us. Right now she was pretending to her family our sleepover had started super-early and that I was in her room, all so that my sister could be here undetected. I'd told Mum and Dad I was seeing Ben to cheer him up about his bruised (not broken, yay) foot. Being Erin was easy – I could do anything, no questions asked. If I were in my real body I'd have been asked to show them a plotted route and evidence my phone battery was charged.

Eurgh. I hated all this lying. To Micha. To everyone.

> Me: I promise I will when I can.

There was nothing I wanted to talk to Mich about more.

Micha: What time do you reckon you'll be here?

Me: 8-9?

Micha: Can you get here ASAP? I can sneak you
in the back way. I've said we're watching Up and
having an emotional time so no one comes in

I said sorry-thanks another ten times and reminded myself that I wouldn't be letting her down if I had *any* other choice, and that by this evening we would be leaping around her room, putting all this behind us. We *had* to be.

'Okay then. Tell me again. Are we really doing this?'

My sister had arrived.

'You're late.' And why out of all the T-shirts I had, including an official Chase Cheney one, was Erin wearing one of hers that read: 'Sorry I'm Late, I Didn't Want to Come'? I had to hope that in a crowd of forty thousand people, not one of them had remembered to charge their phone or bring a camera. 'And yes, we're *really* doing it. So we need to start the plan *now*.'

Erin raised an eyebrow. 'And you're convinced this will work?'

Her tone told me she wasn't. 'You're going to have to trust me,' I said. Truth was, I didn't know if we could pull it off either . . . but I knew we had to try. We didn't have an option.

'No offence –' here came the insult – 'but I think it could be a disaster.'

164

Dad really needed to talk to Erin about her motivational chat.

'Look, Erin. You're right, it might be. But ...' What could I tell her? That I'd spent all day on fan forums working out how we could do it? That I'd borrowed Mum's top so I could look responsible and wise? That I'd watched an hour-long video on the power of positive thinking? 'It's all we've got.'

And that was something even my sister couldn't disagree with.

It was weird feeling so nervous in the middle of thousands of people singing, shouting and living their best lives. I checked no one was paying any attention and got out my battered notebook with my carefully written-up plan.

MISSION BREAK INTO THE ARTEMIS
AND ATHENA ARENA + FIND THE HAIRY
GODMOTHER + SWAP YOU KNOW WHATS

1. Break into arena.
2. Find the Hairy Godmother.
3. Swap you know whats.

'I see.' Erin looked unimpressed. 'And you don't think the title sort of covered that?'

'Oh, there's more.' I turned the page.

3.30 – 4.30 p.m.: Find the press queue.
Get in it. Persuade them Lily Mavers
is on the list to cover the event for
GettingLilyWithIt.
(Idea: try and get on any backstage tours
to look extra legit!!)
Persuade them Lily has her big sister as a
chaperone.

4.30 – 6 p.m.: Get inside venue. Look
cool and calm and totally normal
(but on the inside celebrate my genius
plan working).

6 – 7.55 p.m.: Erin (real) to search
backstage pretending to be doing a piece
on 'Chase Unfiltered' – a behind-the-
scenes look at who and what goes into
making Chase's show. The perfect excuse
to scope out the dressing rooms and
FIND AGATHA!!!

My sister still looked unimpressed. I kept my voice low,
glancing from side to side as if we were undercover agents.
'Erin, treat this plan like it's homework, okay? Don't stop
until you think you'll get an A.'

'Star.' She smiled smugly, but at least the message had gone
in. I got back to the list.

Props: pad, pen, emergency hat
for disguise.

Which reminded me . . .

'Once we're inside I'll give you these.' I reached into Mum's
bag and checked the props were there. It was her super-formal
shoulder bag with a hundred compartments and she'd let me
borrow it (she honestly said yes to whatever Erin asked). The
perfect 'serious chaperone' accessory, as no Chase fan would
be seen dead with it.

Lily (real) will also be looking for clues
(secretly). Whoever finds HG first gets the
other one there ASAP to you know what!!!
(Put her magical skills to use.)
7.55 – 8 p.m.: (Or sooner. I don't know
how long body-swapping takes.) GET
SWAPPED BACK.
8 p.m.: Chase Cheney will still be on stage!!!
Get a glimpse before leaving.
8.30 p.m. – tomorrow: Lily (real) (which
will now be me) (in my own body) to enjoy
myself in my rightful place – at my bday
sleepover at Micha's

Erin nodded, taking the plan in (although ignoring the bad
drawing of a porcupine), but I hadn't finished.

1. Phones on at ALL times.
2. No doing anything embarrassing.

'Obviously that T-shirt already breaks rule two, but other than that, think you've got it?' I watched Erin giving it another read.

'Uh-huh. Shouldn't be too hard.' Hard? This was the concert I'd been trying to get into for *months*. Pulling this off would be harder than Erin trying to show her face at the bowling alley again! 'And you're *sure* the Hairy Godmother will be here?'

I nodded hard. I'd crept into my room as soon as I'd got back from A & E last night to explain the evidence to Erin. The statues on the venue. Today's circled date. What Agatha had told us about working for Chase. It all added up.

But as we joined the press queue, what was a scary plan on paper felt absolutely face-numbingly terrifying in real life. And every second we slowly moved closer to the sign that said GUESTS AND ACCREDITATION I felt more bits of me turn to jelly.

By the time we got to the front, I was a sweating, gibbering mess. Did we stick out like sore thumbs? Behind us were all thirty-somethings, on their phones, not even excited to be here.

'Names?' A bored-looking man the other side of a small window looked up from behind a stack of envelopes.

'Lily Mavers,' I said automatically, before remembering. 'Which is her.' I pointed at my sister. 'I'm her plus one.'

'She's my chaperone,' my sister said calmly. I lifted Mum's bag as if that was somehow the proof. 'I'm on the press list? Under "GettingLilyWithIt". I'm doing a piece on backstage.'

Wow. I could totally see why Mrs Saddler liked my sister – she was an *amazing* actor. My plan might actually work!

The man looked up and down the long list of names, then back up at us. 'Say again?'

My sister calmly repeated everything. 'You could try TheNicReport.' She sounded so confident. 'I syndicate my content.'

Syndicate my content?! I didn't even know what 'syndicate' meant. Although in fairness, right now I didn't even know what 'sandwich' meant I was so nervous.

The man pressed his pen into the list, then rifled through the alphabetically ordered sealed envelopes. I knew nothing was going to be there for us, but I also knew he had the power to hand out passes if we could just make him believe that there *should* be something. My mouth had gone totally dry. I couldn't cope with the tension – especially as a massive cheer suddenly roared out of the venue. It was 4.30 p.m. The first support band had come on stage! Sara and the Spacemen and Tortoiscca were both playing. It was really happening.

'Nope.' The man put the list down. 'Nothing. So move out the way so the people who are meant to be here can get through.' He waved the people behind us forward.

No. No, no, *no*! I gripped the ledge under his window, my hands shaking. It was a long shot but this *had* to work. We *had* to convince him! There was no plan B! My life depended on it! I turned to my sister — but she looked ruffled. Not a good sign.

Although she hadn't budged either.

'Can you check one more time? Please.' She was trying to keep cool but I could hear panic creeping out. If my sister who always got what she wanted couldn't make this happen, we really did have a problem. But the guy just rolled his eyes.

'Sorry, ladies.' He leant back and folded his arms. 'I wasn't born yesterday. So if you could move aside.' His patience had gone from low to zilch. 'Now.'

It was over. Our one chance to fix this had gone.

But as we turned round to leave, I saw it. A flash of black dungarees. A shaved head. A tattoo I'd recognize *anywhere*.

Agatha was here! She really *was*.

And she'd just walked through the door marked 'Production'.

And I'd just had an idea that could work. Even if I was going to pay for it for the rest of my life. Maybe beyond.

I couldn't stop to think about what I was about to do.

I turned back.

'Sorry . . .' I used my elbow to squeeze back in front of the two guys who'd been behind us. They didn't look impressed but then again, they weren't having to spend the evening with someone in a 'Sorry I'm Late, I Didn't Want to Come'

170

T-shirt, so I didn't have *that* much sympathy. I hit my hand down decisively on the ledge in front of the ticket window.

The press guy looked surprised to see me back. 'I should have said ... They might have swapped our names round. Lily could be down as *my* plus one?' My sister's eyes burnt into me. Please, *please* let me pull this off. 'I'm ...' I took a deep breath and prepared to seal my fate. 'Frankie. Well, Frances. Frances Walker?'

If she ever found out, Frankie would kill me. Then resuscitate me just to kill me all over again. Was I *really* stealing her backstage passes?

Yes ... yes, I was.

'And have you got ID?' the man asked, no hint of a smile.

Uh-oh. I blinked. And panicked. And blinked some more. Although ... Wait. I pulled out my wallet. 'Yup.'

As I pulled out Frankie's library card I felt like Arthur when he yanked out Excalibur.

'Hold it somewhere I can see, love,' the man said, confused as to why I was holding it triumphantly above my head.

I slid it under the window. Thank goodness Frankie had tried to be arty and had gone for a black and white shot, wearing a hat and sunglasses. You couldn't really make out anything except hair and someone blowing a kiss. I was a *genius*. A genius with questionable morals. I looked at my sister and mouthed, 'Tell no one.' She nodded. Regardless of how she felt about Frankie, if this worked it *had* to be between us, and us only.

The man slid the library card back, along with a white envelope.

'And you said she –' he nodded at my sister – 'was covering backstage? So should I add her name to the backstage tour?'

I nodded, confirming her name, not believing what was happening.

This had worked! Like a dream!

And maybe I shouldn't stress too much about the tickets – if Frankie hadn't picked them up by now, it surely meant she wasn't coming after all and would never even know anyone had 'borrowed' them.

Maybe this was the perfect plan after all!

As I walked away, opening up the envelope, it felt better than winning the lottery.

In my hand were two Access All Areas wristbands.

Clicking them on, I grabbed Erin and marched us towards the venue.

Straight to the door Agatha had just disappeared through.

CHAPTER EIGHTEEN

We stepped inside the arena and were immediately hit by a wall of sound. Music and chaos. Amazing chaos. In every direction, staff dressed all in black were rushing through corridors, shouting into headsets and looking stressed. Yet right next to them, as if it were the most chilled-out place on earth, super-glamorous people were clutching drinks and leaning back against the brick walls casually chatting.

What I'd give for Mich to be here.

Even seeing a CHASE CHENEY RUBBISH COLLECTION sign made my brain wobble.

But there was no time to look lovingly at bins. We were on a mission. Erin and I did a speedy lap of the level we'd walked in on, but there was no sign of Agatha so we headed upstairs. At the top a group of people were huddled together touching their toes and bending backwards like the concept of spines had bypassed them. Oh holy moly.

They were Chase's backup dancers!

'Can we wait here for a sec?' I pulled Erin into the doorway opposite them.

I needed a moment. A *serious* moment. I was centimetres from someone who had touched a trainer – maybe even a little finger – with Chase!

Which gave me an idea. Probably a bad one, but I *had* to try it. It was what Micha would want.

I reached into my bag and grabbed the chunky highlighter pen I'd packed as a prop. As casually as possible, I turned to pass it to Erin. My plan was to 'accidentally' flick it so it fell and rolled on the floor near the dancers. Then I could pick it up, maybe even say hi, and brush my arm into one of them meaning there'd be a 0.00000000001 per cent possibility that some Chase DNA would end up on my elbow. *What a time to be alive.*

Except at the exact moment I flicked the pen, I saw something even more magical than Agatha.

More magical than a unicorn! Being ridden by the Easter Bunny! In a race with the tooth fairy!

Chase Cheney had walked into the corridor!

CHASE actual CHENEY!

Who looked even more perfect in real life!

My legs buckled. Even my knee tendons knew this was a huge, *huge* moment.

And he was talking! Sounding all American and amazing. 'Oh, my lace has come undone.'

Oh, my lace has come undone. What sweet sound? Forget

Shakespeare, Chase had the perfect way with words! And now he was bending down to do his lace back up!

I would remember this sight for ever!

Although ... what was that ... ?

Something was flying through the air.

Right towards his nose.

And Chase was looking up. Scared.

And the dancers were shouting, 'Waaaaattttccccchhhh ooooouuuuut!'

And then as if in slow motion I realized. The flying missile was the thing I'd just yanked from Mum's bag.

That in my surprise had flown out of my hand waaaay too hard.

And it had just made impact.

With Chase Cheney.

Right on his nose. His perfect nose. His *previously* perfect nose.

'Er ...' Chase stood up. *THERE WAS AN ACTUAL SPOT OF BLOOD FORMING ON HIS NOSE!* 'Does this belong to anyone?' *Please, no, no, no.* He held it up. 'This ... er ...' He squinted at it. 'Athlete's foot cream?' *How did I grab Dad's cream from Mum's bag thinking it was a pen?!* He read the tube. 'Putting the fun back into fungal?'

His dancers broke down in fits of laughter but I was officially deceased.

Out of all the bad things that had ever happened in my life – this was it.

The absolute worst moment.

The only, *only* silver lining was that I was never *ever* going to admit that it was me who threw it. Chase would never know. Not if the world was ending and humanity depended on it. It didn't even matter that I was in Erin's body – the difference between Chase-assaulter and sister-of-Chase-assaulter was too small for my liking.

'Anyone?' Chase held Dad's cream out, scanning all the people who had paused to stare. I stopped breathing. I couldn't risk moving a single muscle in case Chase looked over.

'Yup.' Erin stepped forward. *What was she doing?!* 'It's my sister's. As in, this person here.' She pointed at me. *How could she?*

'I hate you.' It just popped out.

But when I looked back Chase was standing right. In. Front. Of. Me.

'You hate me?' He held the tube out. It definitely had a nose-shaped dent in it.

My mouth opened. And closed. Then gasped as it realized I hadn't breathed in over a minute.

'No!' I grabbed the stupid tube hoping it could disappear for ever. 'My *sister.*' Could I play this cool? 'I hate *her.* I love *you.*' *Did I just tell Chase I loved him?* Probably not the definition of playing it cool. 'I'm sorry. It was an accident.'

Erin sniggered. I kicked her foot.

Chase smiled his mega-watt smile (*focus on the smile,*

Lily, not the trickle of blood). I couldn't believe I was talking to my life idol! I couldn't believe I'd maimed him! 'Well, I hope the foot trouble clears up soon. The key is breathable fabrics. Always.'

And with that Chase and his entourage walked off.

I had to crouch in a foetal position on the floor for two to three minutes to recover.

'So you've branched out from injuring my boyfriend to major pop stars?' My sister had not stopped chuckling the whole time. 'Good to know no one is safe around you.'

But I was fuming. And now no one was around to hear, I wasn't going to hold back . . .

'Why did you have to tell him it was me, Erin? WHAT IS WRONG WITH YOU?'

'I wasn't the one who threw foot cream in his face.' She was loving this. 'Those edges are deceptively sharp.' Not helpful.

'IT WAS AN ACCIDENT!'

'Isn't it always?!' She folded her arms.

'Says you! Who nothing ever goes wrong for!' Uh-oh. Now it had started to spill out, I wasn't sure it would stop. 'Everything always goes right without you even trying!'

Erin shrugged. 'I don't even know what you like about him. His music sounds like something Mum would listen to.' She *knew* this wasn't true as Mum mainly listened to news programmes about gardens or motivational rain showers.

Why did she have to be like this?

'And if you ask me he needs a serious haircut.' How could

she say that about the man who won Best Fringe Flick two years running?!

'As if—' But something shut me up. Or someone. Agatha herself just hurried past us, marching through the big swing doors. Our argument stopped dead. Because as much as we hated each other right now – we hated *being* each other even more. We had to follow her!

'Lily Mavers?' A woman with a headset marched over. 'Is Lily here?' She was shouting at full volume to anyone who would listen. 'LILY MAVERS?'

My sister raised her hand and the woman immediately shoved a lanyard over her head. 'Good, we've been looking for you *everywhere*. Didn't they tell you to wait downstairs? Follow me.'

As the woman beckoned her to follow, Erin turned back to me. For the first time in my life, I swear she looked worried. Was it because of where she was going, or because she was leaving me alone to follow Agatha?

'I'll do HG,' I hissed. Such cunning code. 'You do you. And remember, phone on at all times.'

'Please don't mess this up,' was all my sister said back. Such a confidence boost. But there was no time to stress. If Agatha's job was helping people get ready, she might not be hanging around for too long. I raced through the swing doors, but the corridor split three ways. This place was *huge*. Where had she gone?! As I spun round, I saw a reflection in the glass of one of the ginormous pictures on the wall. The Hairy Godmother!

I wasn't going to let her get away, not this time. My heart racing, I sprinted after her. This walkway circled right round the stadium, so if I kept going I'd *have* to catch up with her.

Another roar went up from the crowd as the support band finished a song. But it bounced right off me. All I could think about was Agatha.

And she'd just turned into a room.

A production office that backed on to the seating, so there was no other way out.

I stopped in front of it. I had no idea what I would say, but I was ready to do whatever it took to get my life back.

The risk of taking Frankie's tickets had paid off.

I'd found the clues and I'd found Agatha.

I looked at the big HG PRODUCTIONS sign on the door, took a deep breath and pushed it open.

Here went everything.

CHAPTER NINETEEN

It was locked. But the Hairy Godmother *had* to be in here.

So why, after hammering on the door for five minutes calling her name, was there no reply?

And worse. Why wasn't there a sound from inside the room? Not even with my ear pressed against the door. My stomach had cramped up. Was Agatha avoiding us? But she'd left clues for us to find her here!

Keeping one eye on the HG PRODUCTIONS sign, I checked the doors either side to be sure. One room was full of people frantically stitching and pulling outfits on to Chase's dancers – and none of them had heard of the Hairy Godmother. And on the other side was just a big empty room, a bored man watching walkie-talkies as they charged. He referred to Chase as 'Chris', so I wasn't exactly surprised when he hadn't heard of Agatha either.

But I wasn't giving up. I sat against the wall opposite the door Agatha had disappeared through, hugged my knees and waited. And waited. Waited so long Chase came on stage – I could tell from the deafening screams and shouts. But I wasn't budging. If I left this spot for a second I could lose our only chance of finding Agatha. And I was *not* letting that happen.

I messaged Erin again to tell her to meet me ASAP, but like the others it didn't deliver.

What was she up to?!

Wait.

What if she was seeing Chase in action? That would be *too* unfair! I'd just have to hope my eyes could replay it when I got back in my body. Although Chase being on stage meant time really was running out.

I tried the door again. Still nothing.

Feeling guiltier than ever, I messaged Micha to say I would be later than I thought. I got a 'fine' in reply.

Things felt very un-fine.

I slumped back on the floor and carried on staring at the door as if it were a peanut and I was Barry the Hamster (RIP). But as it hit 8.30 p.m. and the loudest cheer yet went up and stayed up, with a sinking heart I knew that was it. The concert had finished. It was all over.

And I was still in the wrong body.

People started to fill up the corridors – laughing, joking, singing Chase songs, as I sat on the floor trying not to cry. When my sister eventually turned up I'd never been more relieved to see her. She looked sort of . . . ruffled.

'You took your time.' I scrambled to my feet.

'I got away as quickly as I could.' She was out of breath. 'What's going on?'

'First.' I couldn't hide my frustration at how wrong this was all going. 'Why didn't you reply to a single message? Rule two was phones on. At *all* times.' She looked guilty. Good. 'Please at least tell me you kept to rule one? Nothing embarrassing?'

She avoided eye contact. 'Well, we all have different definitions . . .'

Great. I'd add that to the 'I don't want to know but suppose I'd better ask later' list. We didn't have time for this now. Quickly I filled Erin in on everything, and how HG Productions was harder to break into than Dad's extra-posh chocolate biscuit stash.

'She's definitely in there.' I walked over to the door. 'I promise.'

Erin felt around the edges of the door.

'So she went in and then this locked . . . for good?' She tried to turn the handle – she never took my word for anything.

But this time, it turned.

The door opened.

I could *not* believe it.

'You did *try* turning it?' Erin asked. And for a millisecond I stopped thinking about Agatha, about Micha, about anything except whether if I could kill someone with a tube of athlete's foot cream and a particularly organized handbag.

'Of course I did!' I hissed as I pushed past her. *Agatha, we're coming for you!*

But inside was *not* what I was expecting.

It was the exact same, *exact same*, room as the hairdresser's where we'd first met the Hairy Godmother. The desk, the chairs, the photos on the walls, the mirrors. Even the plants and photos were the same.

But there was no sign of Agatha. And no door she could have left by.

A chill travelled up my body. I put my hand out, hoping to make contact with my sister, needing to know she was beside me.

She'd done the same.

Holding hands, we edged further in.

Behind us people were walking along the corridor, chatting and laughing as if everything were normal. But I'd never felt less normal in my life.

'Is this ... ?' My voice was shaking.

'Weird? *Very*,' Erin replied.

Once the shock had died down, we started to look for any sign of Agatha still being here. We did a methodical sweep across the room, but there was nothing. I even pressed the walls to check I wasn't missing anything.

What *was* Agatha trying to tell us? There *must* have been a reason she'd brought us to this room. Today.

So why was she making this so hard? All I wanted was my body back!

I slumped in one of her chairs.

'Do you believe me that I saw Agatha come in here?' It mattered. It really mattered.

My sister stopped rifling through magazines and looked at me. 'Yup, Lil. I do.'

And despite everything being so rubbish, Erin believing me made me feel a tiny bit better.

'Five minutes.' Walkie-talkie man put his head round the door. 'Then we're locking up.'

It was almost time to leave. Time to turn our backs on the best chance we'd had of getting our lives back to normal. Maybe our last.

ARGHHHHHH!

I didn't mean to but as I did another rummage under the sofa cushions, I threw one against the wall. I'd thought that maybe Agatha had swapped us to try to help me and my sister understand each other better, but we'd done it now. We'd found out what it was like to be each other. Agatha's idea had worked. So why weren't we back to normal?

What have we done wrong?

What am I missing?

I looked at my reflection in the switched-off giant TV screen. At myself. At my sister.

'Erin, are we . . .' My voice faltered as my throat closed up, ready to cry. 'Are we definitely going to get back to normal?'

But Erin was looking right over my shoulder.

'Lil . . . Was that always behind us?'

I turned to see what she was looking at. The big mirror. Which had *definitely* not looked like that seconds ago.

Scrawled across it in red lipstick was a message.

IT'S EASY TO WALK A MILE IN SOMEONE
ELSE'S SHOES.
BUT HAVE YOU EVER TRIED TO PUT
ON THEIR SOCKS? ‿

Right now I couldn't have wished harder that Dad had found us *anywhere* else to get our hair cut.

I had no idea what was going on.

And even less desire to put on Erin's socks.

CHAPTER TWENTY

I'd recognize that crying anywhere. I'd only heard it three times in my life, but I'd never forget it.

I listened into the cubicle. I'd ducked into the girls' toilets because I wanted to spend lunch working on ideas for TheNicReport editorial meeting that was now less than two days away and knew if my sister spotted me she'd nag me to work on my lines instead. The performance was this weekend and tonight Mrs Saddler was making us do a full run-through. Mrs Saddler was a monster.

I'd had my phone off most of yesterday to help me focus on properly learning the lines. Well, that and avoid the pics of everyone who had actually got to see the Chase concert (not sit semi-crying in a corridor ten metres away). No phone was also helping me deal with the deafening silence from my best friend. But I couldn't blame Mich.

Despite my pleas, after the disappointment of Agatha my sister had refused to go round to save what was left of the sleepover. Apparently Erin needed 'time alone with her rocks to process that we might not be switching back anytime soon'. Even worse, my sister had then stuck to her promise to Mrs Saddler and gone into school on Sunday to do more work on the props with Singed Simon, meaning that, despite me yelling at her, then begging her, then physically clinging on to her ankles, she hadn't gone to support Micha at her football tournament.

Which is probably why I hadn't had any replies to my messages to Micha since Saturday evening.

I knocked gently. 'You okay in there?' The sniffing paused. 'It's Erin . . .'

Still felt weird saying that. But I heard a ruffle of tissue and a little cough.

'Er . . .' More loo roll being pulled off. 'One sec.'

Micha never liked to let people see when she was having a tough time. For her to be crying on her own in school, things must be rock bottom. And I hated that her best friend acting so weirdly was probably part of it.

'No hurry.' I didn't know how to handle this. 'Is it anything I can help with?'

The door opened, a miserable-looking Micha behind it. Her big brown eyes were all blotchy. I couldn't help it – I went right in for the hug.

'Whatever it is –' I held her hard – 'I'm sure we can figure it out.'

When I finally let her go, she mainly looked surprised

that Erin, who she'd never seen express any emotion other than the time she'd shouted, 'Don't be so dim!' at one of the chasers on *The Chase*, had just hugged her. Still, shock was better than sad.

'Er, thanks.' Micha dabbed at her eyes. 'It's nothing.' Oh yes, the classic nothing that makes you spend break crying in the toilet. But even Micha couldn't hold it in any more. 'Just Mr Sharma went off on one at me.' Her words spilled out. 'I thought I'd done okay with the homework, but apparently I'd missed a whole section.' Her voice shook. 'So he's written a letter to tell my parents that if I don't get above seventy-five per cent in the test and assignment on Saturday that's it. I'm going down a set.' Her face tightened as she tried not to cry all over again. 'They're going to freak, I *know* it.'

I couldn't help it. I gave her another hug. *But where was my sister?* Micha needed her best friend and they'd just had double chemistry together, so where was she?

'I'm sure they won't.' I lied. 'And I'm sure you can get seventy-five per cent!' I really wasn't – Mr Sharma's tests were notoriously hard. Maybe I should change the subject. 'How did the tournament go anyway?'

Micha gave me the saddest smile. 'Well, this morning our coach told me I'd got selected for the youth team . . .'

Wow!

'Congrats, Micha. That's *huge*.' Someone needed to remind her how amazing this was.

'Yeah, if it wasn't just in time for my parents to stop me playing.' Uh-oh. Was she about to cry again?!

'They might not stop you.' There was a 0.000000001 per cent chance, but still a chance. 'We just need to figure out how to get you through this test. I *know* you can do it.'

And Micha actually smiled. A small one, but it was *so* much better than tears. The only problem was it was because she thought she was talking to the clever sister, not to me. I was going to have to figure something major out. And fast.

'Although . . .' *Please* don't let this backfire. 'Have you seen my sister?' Micha's smile instantly disappeared. All I got was a shrug. Not good. 'Wasn't she in chemistry with you?'

Another shrug.

My whole body tightened with panic. Was Micha starting to give up on me? I couldn't let that happen!

'Y'know Lily was really sad yesterday . . .' Could Mich hear my voice wobbling in a very un-Erin like way? 'Missing you play. Apparently she was watching the whole thing on her phone.' Was I imagining it or did it look as if another tear was about to drip from Micha's eye? She headed to the sinks. 'And over dinner she said something about helping you study any second she's not in rehearsals . . .' I didn't care what Erin would want in return – for me to go on dates with Ben, take over the washing *and* drying, even swatting up for Les Quizerables – I would do it.

Micha splashed water on her face. 'If she even *has* rehearsals.' Did she roll her eyes? *What did she mean?*

'Er, she definitely does . . .' But I never got a response, as Lou's head popped round the door.

'Oh, Erin. *Thank. Goodness.*' She was out of breath. 'I've been looking for you *everywhere*. Frankie's on the *war path*.' My stomach dropped so hard I was surprised I didn't topple over. 'She wants to speak to you or your sister to –' Lou put on an extra-stern face – 'get "the full truth".' Lou paused. 'XOXO.'

'Errrrr, any idea what about?' I willed with every particle in both of my bodies for it not to be about Saturday. Surely Frankie couldn't have found out about the tickets?

Micha and Lou looked at each other, confused. 'Er . . .' Lou replied. 'You *really* don't know?'

I shook my head. 'You mean you haven't seen this?' Lou held out her phone. This felt bad. Very bad. And even worse when she pressed play on a video.

Chase Cheney. On stage. The crowd cheering at the end of a song.

Uh. And indeed Oh.

'So it's time for "Fandemonium",' he purred into the mic. 'The bit of the concert where I get a fan on stage.'

Chase looked round – and as he turned to the side of the stage his face lit up.

'You again . . .' He pointed. The camera whipped round to see who he was grinning at.

And that was when I knew my life as Lily had changed. *For ever.*

Because there my sister was, in my body, chatting away obliviously at the edge of the stage, studying an electrical box as if it held the secret of the universe – right up until lanyard lady tapped her on the arm and she looked up. At Chase pointing right at her.

She didn't even blink. As if this was normal. How dare my body betray me so badly! And with a nudge from the lanyard lady my sister walked out. Right up to the microphone. In front of *everyone*.

I couldn't believe what I was seeing. My sister, in the worst slogan T-shirt ever, standing on stage next to the world's coolest man.

At least she was in the dim bit of the stage.

Oh no. Scrap that. A spotlight flicked right on her. My stupid face beamed out of every single massive screen around the arena. My chin spot alone was the size of a small dog.

Deep breath, me.

Just a casual forty thousand people watching my sister, in my body, chat to Chase on stage. How badly could it go?! (*Note to brain – don't answer.*)

The stadium was hushed, just an occasional whoop and whistle coming from the crowd.

'Sorry,' Chase laughed. 'Did I disturb you?'

Please have remembered rule one, sister! Pleeeeease! JUST BE NORMAL.

'A little.' Erin didn't sound even the tiniest bit fazed! 'I was finding out how dry ice works.' She grinned. 'Freezing carbon dioxide. *Fascinating.*'

What hope I had of this being okay drained out of me and down one of the plugholes.

'Enough!' I flicked Lou's screen off. I didn't want to see the rest of that clip as long as I lived.

I'd thought Frankie laughing at me at the convention had been bad. But my sister had forgotten to mention she'd upgraded my mortification to include *the entire world.*

THE ENTIRE ACTUAL WORLD.

Neither Lou nor Micha knew what to say.

And Micha had started sniffing again.

Oh. No!

She must think her best friend bailed on her to go to the concert without her! As if she wouldn't have been the *first* person I'd ask to come if life were normal.

Great. Now I was about to cry too.

I needed to get my Erin game face on, get out of here and sort this out.

'Thanks, Lou. Not sure how I missed that one.' Fake smile to the max. 'Think I'd better go and find my sister . . .'

In a panicked blur, I pushed open the door, Agatha's message whirring round my head. *It's easy to walk a mile in someone else's shoes . . . but have you ever tried to put on their socks?* What did she mean? I needed to figure it out fast, because I couldn't go on like this. Messing up my life was bad enough, but not Micha's too.

I marched out of the girls' toilets. And right into Mrs Saddler. Who was chatting to Mr Sharma. A double whammy of misery.

'Erin! How nice to bump into you. I'm very much looking forward to seeing some serious improvement in the run-through later.' Mrs Saddler smiled, but I couldn't muster one back. All I had was a feeble nod. I was rapidly running out of ability to pretend things were okay. 'You know, it's not too late to recast any roles.' How could I forget when she kept reminding me?

'Yes, Erin.' Mr Sharma pulled his glasses down his nose. 'I'm looking forward to seeing the same big improvement with Les Quizerables. You're normally our star quizlete.'

Which isn't even a word.

I made a squeak that sounded like Barry the Hamster (RIP) and ran. And despite hunting everywhere (SAS style, peering round corridors and flattening myself against walls to avoid Frankie at all costs), my sister was nowhere to be found. And she answered none of my messages or calls. My phone, however, was getting so many notifications it sounded as if someone was playing high-speed ping-pong. I switched it off.

This was a disaster.

My life was a disaster.

And this time I wasn't even the one doing it.

I spent the rest of the afternoon trying to figure out how to mend things with Micha. Ideas for the editorial meeting would have to wait. I looked at the messages I'd sent her this afternoon – two blue ticks and no reply.

> Me: I can't explain right now, but whatever you've
> seen on the internet isn't what it looks like. I promise.

I knew how lame it sounded without an explanation but what could I say?

> Me: I had no idea what happened on Saturday
> was going to happen (would I really have worn that
> T-shirt if I'd thought I'd be seeing the god that is
> Chase Cheney???). I'm so sorry I didn't tell you. I
> promise you are THE ONLY person I'd ever go see
> Chase Cheney with!!!

No reply. But I had nothing to lose any more so carried on sending her anything I thought might help. More apologies. More GIFs of football-playing porcupines. More congrats about the team.

But by the time the four p.m. rehearsal rolled round I hadn't even got so much as a cross penguin back.

It was official – my best friend had stopped speaking to me.

And now I had to face Frankie.

I really would rather be anywhere in the world than sitting in front of the stage waiting for that to happen. Even at Circus Skills with Dad.

And where *was* Erin?!

I stared at my script while Lou chatted to Enthusiastic Mark. Even the words I spent all day yesterday learning had disappeared. Well, there were all still there but in no particular order.

Hoard thee . . . nuts and . . . squirrel?

I glanced down. *Nope.*

The squirrel's hoard, and fetch thee new nuts.

Not that that made any more sense.

BANG. The double doors flapped open.

Frankie. And if looks could kill, I wouldn't just be dead, I'd be erased from history. Luckily she was followed by Mrs Saddler. Although now all the sucking-up Erin had chosen to do by coming into school this weekend was going to be undone the second Mrs Saddler realized she was missing.

Mrs Saddler lifted her arms, her billowy top wafting out below her. She looked like a fabric bat.

'Well, hello, my future stars.' She waved her hand around the circle of chairs in a dramatic 360 spin. I caught Harley grinning. 'As you know, today is our first *full* run-through. And with five days to go until the *rrrrrrrreal thing*, I for one *cannot wait!*'

I for two could wait so long that my shoes disintegrated.

I glanced up. Frankie was staring right at me. *Gulp.*

'I know what you did,' she mouthed. I glanced right back down. Had Frankie wanted the tickets after all? And found out it was me who took them?! Wow. I'd managed to make her hate me in two different bodies.

'So, Erin!' Mrs Saddler turned her enthusiasm to me. 'As *the* defining character in this production, I know today you will lead by example and deliver your best performance yet.' *Oh hello, feeble nod, welcome back.* 'So ...' She clapped her hands. 'Shall we get on with it?'

But with Frankie refusing to take her eyes off me and my sister AWOL, my head was officially scrambled. Did I feel sick with guilt? Or terror? Or just nerves? Whatever it was, when I got up on stage, the rehearsal was my worst one yet. I didn't even feel better when Erin finally appeared. Apparently she'd been spending every spare minute in the art room giving some of the props a fresh lick of paint. Nice to know she was more bothered about making Mrs Saddler happy than replying to any of my frantic messages.

Out of all the days since the swap, this was the worst. And that was before Mrs Saddler summoned me over at the end of rehearsal. Erin came too, clearly worried about her precious play. Mrs Saddler waited until everyone else had cleared the hall.

'If I had one word to describe your rehearsal, it would be ...' Mrs Saddler paused as she looked at Erin. 'Am I fine to speak honestly in front of Laura?'

'Lily,' I corrected her. 'That's her name.'

'Horrible.'

'I quite like it.'

'No, Erin, *not her name.* Your performance – it was *horrible*.' Mrs Saddler took an overly dramatic inhale and stared into the distance. 'I didn't want to say this in front of the others, but if things don't change significantly, you've left me with no other option.' She nodded to where Lou had been sitting. 'I'll have to ask your understudy Lou to step up and play Titania.'

She couldn't! Playing Titania was what Erin was relying on to film for her audition to Chinyere Okafor's Drama Academy! Her only chance of getting in depended on it! 'W-wh . . .' I was actually stuttering. 'What do you mean?'

The colour had drained from Erin's face.

'Well, Clara would have to step up and cover Lou—' Mrs Saddler said, thinking out loud. But my sister interrupted, in a quiet voice I'd never heard from her before.

'But Erin could do at least one of the performances? Because that's what's being taped to send to Chinyere Okafor. For the audition.'

Mrs Saddler laughed. 'Oh no.' She tutted as if my sister were being ridiculous. 'That plan's all changed. I was going to tell you all today if things had gone better. Ms Okafor is coming to *watch* the opening night on Saturday. She'll be right here in the audience. So if Lou is playing Titania then . . .' She shrugged. 'I'm afraid that's decision made.'

My sister looked as if she'd taken a punch to the stomach. If we didn't swap back by Saturday, her dream was over.

To say the walk home wasn't a laugh-a-minute was an understatement.

Erin was gutted about the play and while I felt bad for her I was furious she hadn't told me what'd happened on Saturday – or been there for Micha. We snatched sentences back and forth, but it was hard to have a proper conversation when every ten paces we got interrupted by someone asking questions such as, 'Does Chase really smell of marshmallow?' It went something like this:

Erin: I was only backstage because *you* put me up for that stupid tour. Point one on the plan!

Me: And was part of the plan ever 'share your love of dry ice with the world'?!

Erin: I didn't tell you because I thought it wasn't that big a deal.

Me: My best friend's not talking to me, the world thinks I'm a laughing stock and Frankie wants to murder us both. DOES THAT SOUND LIKE A SMALL DEAL?

Erin: I can sort things out with Frankie. She probably doesn't even know it was us. She probably just reckons you had something to do with me ending up on stage. It'll be cool.

Me: She's never been cool about anything to do with me, Erin.

Me: *Annoyed grunt*

Me: I still can't believe I was the last to know.

Erin: I tried.

Me: But the rule was to be normal!

Erin: BUT THAT WAS MY NORMAL!

I had never needed to get home and flop on the sofa more.

But when we walked in Mum and Dad were sitting at the kitchen table.

'Have a seat.' Mum looked furious. 'Your sister too.'

The chairs were pulled out ready.

'You're both in trouble. *Big* trouble.'

CHAPTER TWENTY-ONE

I normally didn't have a clue what my parents were thinking. Like when they went to the car boot sale and came back with a 'warm tub' for the garden (like a hot tub, but broken so never heated properly). But right now I knew *exactly* what they were thinking. We weren't just in big trouble, we were in The Biggest.

Mum rested her chin on her hand, closed her eyes and inhaled deeply. Even Mrs Saddler would be impressed.

'Your grandmother rang.'

'Grandmoan,' Dad clarified. Mum gave him the Look. Now was clearly not the time for jokes.

'My mother, *yes*. She asked if we'd seen this ...'

My sister and I glanced at each other. Mum's mum normally only got involved in our lives if there was free food, free holidays or something to seriously moan about.

Mum grabbed something from the worktop. The local paper. She pushed it towards us.

**Aggressive Squirrel Goes On Sausage Roll
Stealing Rampage**

Why was Grandmoan bothered about that?!

But my sister was tapping the headline at the bottom of the page.

Local Girl Tells Superstar to Smarten Up!
Turn to page 2 for the full hilarious
encounter >>>

Never had the word 'hilarious' felt as if it was going to be less funny. I put my hand over my eyes and watched through my fingers as Erin opened the paper.

To say the picture of me on stage with Chase took up a quarter of the page would be a lie. It took up half.

Local Lily Calls Out Scruffy
Superstar Chase

Was it me, or was the room spinning?

'I honestly spat out my mint tea when I saw it,' Dad said quietly. 'So how about one of you tells us what's going on?'

I hated them being mad, but I couldn't even explain and make it better – I was almost as clueless as them.

Mum glared at me. 'And don't think we don't know you were involved, Erin. Ben's dad confirmed you weren't there

201

on Saturday.' She breathed in and out. Loudly. 'I don't think either of you need me to say we're very disappointed.' The ultimate parental burn! 'In both of you.'

I mumbled sorry and with shaking hands pulled the paper towards me. How many people read this?! I had a horrible feeling the answer was ... everyone.

With a shaky voice, I began to read it out.

'The biggest nights of pop Lemford has ever seen touched down at the Artemis and Athena Arena last weekend. But one local girl stole the stage with a dose of unexpected honesty for A-lister Chase Cheney.'

I stopped to look at my sister, but she was staring at her hands.

'After being invited on stage, Lily Mavers, 13, who was rocking a hilarious "Sorry I'm Late, I Don't Want to Be Here" T-shirt ...'

I'm sorry, how could the words 'rocking', 'hilarious' and that T-shirt go together?!

'... proceeded to school the superstar in science. A bemused Chase, who eagle-eyed fans noticed was sporting an injury to his nose, laughed it off.'

Thank goodness I'd had a few hours to deal with this discovery.

'But as he started playing his new hit "Honesty" he called Lily back out.'

I choked on my words. Back out? *Back out!* No one had mentioned a 'back out'.

'In an exchange some fans are describing as 'mega lols' while others have labelled it . . .'

I paused. I could see the shape of the words, but once I read them I couldn't pretend they weren't *that* bad.

'. . . the ultimate insult to the fandom . . .'

My stomach clenched so hard my voice went up an octave.

'. . . Lily played along with Chase's on-the-spot quick-fire honesty game, giving answers that took the audience, and Chase himself, by surprise.'

Not to mention it was also taking *me, actual Lily Mavers,* by surprise! I looked up at my family. Stony faces all round.

'Lily's honest opinion of Chase? In need of a haircut. Her favourite Chase song? She named a track by Coldplay.'

I was probably already a meme, wasn't I? I was never going on the internet again.

'Her review of the concert? Long. And not enough dry ice. But fans were left reeling by the possibility Chase might have previously met the mysterious Mavers, when he said, "Remember what I said to you guys. For foot problems, always keep it breathable." Insiders close to the star have suggested this could be a reference to some athlete's foot cream Lily and a close friend were seen hurling at the pop star backstage.'

Hurling?

And was that a zoomed-in close-up picture of my hand on the tube from some blurry CCTV footage?! They'd made it look as if we'd done it on purpose! I'd smuggled the cream back into the bathroom cupboard, but Dad pushed it forward on the table, as if it were forensic evidence. In fairness, it would give a positive DNA test for Chase's blood.

'Support band Ego Rhythm Radio, who have teamed up with Chase on new single "Final Chance" released this coming Saturday, confirmed Mavers had "made a big impression" on the global superstar and joked "after her critique he might even pull his style socks up". If you want to hear more from Ego Rhythm Radio, check out their debut album "▶Meet Me".'

Silence.

It was hard to know where to start. I'd only been in the paper twice before. Once when I was five and won a fancy-dress competition as a very realistic gherkin. And the time my school won a netball tournament and the photographer didn't realize I was only holding a bib while one of them went for a wee, and despite my protests made me stand in the photo.

'Lily?' Mum turned to my sister. 'Have you got anything to say?'

Erin was still staring down. I almost felt bad she didn't have a lifetime of disappointing Mum and Dad to help her through this. *Almost*, but not quite.

'It was . . .' Her mouth carried on moving but all that came out was a mumble.

'Speak up,' Dad said.

'It was . . .' She paused. 'An accident.'

I almost fell backwards off my chair! Did I actually just hear her say that?

Was my perfect sister finally realizing what living my life was really like?

Mum sighed. 'And was making poor Micha cover for you also an accident?' She paused to allow the guilt bubble up even more. 'And not telling your father and me?'

Erin still didn't look up.

I knew she'd be wanting to tell them the truth too, but we'd made a pact that under no circumstances could they find out.

'It was my fault.' The words popped out before I could stop them. 'I thought Lily could write an amazing piece about it.' Was I saying it for me, for if I ever got back in my body, or to get my sister off the hook? 'I didn't mean to involve anyone else, but I knew how much it meant to Lily, and what with being grounded with all the chores I thought you'd say no if I asked.'

Mum and Dad looked aghast. I guessed normal me doing stupid stuff was expected, but their eldest daughter doing it was a whole different thing.

Dad shook his head. 'Honestly, Erin, I don't know what's got into you lately.' Answer: her youngest sister. 'Your grades are going downhill, you've lost the captain spot on Les Quizerables.' Ouch, I didn't even know that one. 'Ben hasn't been round for weeks and now this.'

More silence.

Should I just tell them everything?

'To be honest ...' I started.

But Erin kicked me under the table as she interrupted.

'To be honest, it was my fault too. I'm sorry we didn't tell you but we didn't even know if it would work.' She looked at me. 'Erin was helping me out, she really was. More than I can explain . . . it just . . . well, it all got out of hand.'

Wow, she was sharing the blame.

Mum pressed her fingers across her forehead. 'I don't need to tell you two how dangerous what you did was.'

Dad sniffed. '*Anything* could have happened to you.'

I mean, anything *did* happen to us. My sister made global headlines, we'd potentially caused Frankie to want to commit double murder, and I'd discovered a portal to a magical room. But these finer details probably wouldn't help, so instead we both just apologized again. I knew going to the concert was risky – but it had been our only hope. I hadn't really thought about the what next.

'This is so out of character for you both.' Mum sighed again. 'Erin, I thought we could rely on you to be sensible. And, Lily, for all your . . . *accidents*, we've never known you to go this far.'

Dad rubbed Mum's arm, worried about her. 'It's as if we don't even know who you are any more.'

Well, the feeling was mutual. I was beginning to lose a grip on who I was too. And unless we figured out Agatha's cryptic clues and what she wanted from us, I was worried I might never get it back.

I'd hated what life had become, and all the lies.

Mum shook her head. 'The way things are going I'm half expecting a call from school saying, I don't know . . .' She racked her brain for something utterly ridiculous. 'Erin's out of the play or . . . Lily and Micha aren't friends any more.'

Wow.

Was there any way I could convince school Mum and Dad had changed their numbers just to be on the safe side?

Dad cleared his throat. 'I think it goes without saying you're both grounded. *Very* grounded. So this week, after school and rehearsals, we've got a punishment we hope might help you both take some time out and try to remember who the real Lily and Erin are.'

I think they were expecting a protest. But we both nodded.

Trying to figure this all out was *exactly* what we both needed.

CHAPTER TWENTY-TWO

My phone buzzed. *Finally*. It had been twenty minutes since we'd messaged the family group to let them know the rehearsal had been cut short. Erin and I had fled the hall at super speed to avoid Frankie, and had been doing stealth laps around the school playing field ever since. Normally we'd have probably just headed into town to kill time, but with Mum and Dad watching our every move, we figured honesty was the best policy, even if it meant going home to face extra chores.

> Dad: We'redoingtheTuesdaybigshop.Wait outside
> the caféforus.And nogettingintrouble.

That was his new way of saying goodbye.

> Dad: Ithinksomethingisstuckonmyspacebutton

'Guess we're off to ASDA café then.' I started to head to the corner of the field where there was an alleyway to the estate where the supermarket was. 'A dazzling end to a dazzling day.'

Erin nose-laughed. Today had been a disaster for us both. Mrs Saddler was so furious with how my first scene with Harley had been going, she'd stormed on stage and yelled at the whole cast to leave and work on our lines in private. She'd ended it by saying any final casting decisions would happen in tomorrow's dress rehearsal. All while staring Right. At. Me.

'Dazzling indeed. I swear if Mrs Saddler gives my part to Lou and ruins the *only* chance I have of getting into Chinyere Okafor's Drama Academy, I will never forgive her.' Erin paused. 'Or you.'

'Thanks for the vote of confidence.' I kicked at an old rounders ball on the path. Stupid ball. Stupid Agatha. Stupid everything. 'I am trying, you know. Although –' maybe I could flip this back on my sister – 'maybe I'd be better if you did a bit more to help things on your side.'

Erin sighed. 'Yeah, I know. I need to speak to Frankie. Find out what she actually knows.'

Rumour was she'd spent Sunday at the arena trying to track down any evidence of who took her tickets.

'And?'

'Explain it was all a big mix-up.' I wasn't sure how, but I had to rely on Erin to think of something.

'And?'

Erin rolled her eyes.

'Be a "creative genius" –' I didn't think the whiny impression of me was needed – 'with Nic tomorrow.'

'One hundred per cent.' Erin's dreams might be in the balance on Saturday, but mine depended on Erin majorly impressing everyone in tomorrow's editorial meeting. And so far my killer idea total was at . . . zero. Plus I hadn't heard a word from Nic since my birthday. 'But they're not actually what I meant . . .'

I'd meant the one thing that mattered even more.

It was day three of no messages from Micha and it was killing me. I didn't even get a reply when I asked how her parents had taken the news about chemistry.

'Have you noticed something's up with Micha?'

Erin shrugged. 'Sort of. I mean, I haven't really seen her.'

I tried not to roll my eyes at how this was *exactly* it. 'Well, yes, Erin. But do you not think that's . . . weird?'

She shrugged. 'I assumed she was busy revising for her test this weekend. And that big extra assignment she mentioned.' Sometimes there was no getting through to my sister.

I shook my head.

'What?' Erin raised her eyebrows. 'I apologized for what happened on Saturday. Twice! And for missing her tournament.' But when she had all Micha had said was that my sister had to 'do what she had to do'.

210

'And . . . since then, Erin?'

Erin's mouth twisted as if she were tackling one of her extra-hard quiz questions. 'Hmm . . . nothing.'

'We need to face it. She's not talking to you. Me. Us. *Whatever.*' I kicked the rounders ball so hard it flew into someone's back garden. 'And right when she needs our help more than ever.'

My sister stopped walking and turned to me, confused. 'You mean like . . . periodic table stuff?' She made it seem so black and white, as if that was what friendship was.

'Well, yeah.' I couldn't help but sigh. '*That*, but it's more, y'know . . . just being there for her. Because she's got all this stuff going on and her best mate has basically disappeared. And is being all . . .'

Erin raised her eyebrow. 'Don't say weird.'

'Weird.'

Erin hoisted her bag back up on her shoulder.

'If you want to know what I think.' I didn't. 'I think you're over-worrying.'

She started to walk off. I jogged after her.

'Well, I think you're under-noticing.'

My sister really didn't get it. How much Micha and I hung out. How we shared every detail of our lives. How bad things had got now.

I always assumed Erin knew everything, but maybe there were some things she needed to figure out too. I waited for the mood to thaw before I attempted conversation again.

'Look, if we've got to wait for the parents, shall we have another go at figuring out Agatha's message?'

Last night, while cleaning the car inside and out as our first punishment, Erin and I had agreed our next steps.

1. We had to try to find Agatha one more time.
   And this time *whatever happened* we *had* to speak to her.
2. We were going on a major suck-up mission to Mum and Dad until we achieved point one.
3. Maybe it was time I changed Erin's sheets after all.

'Good idea.' Erin nodded. 'Let's pick up hot drinks and go to the benches round the back. Maybe being somewhere different will help us, you know,' she waved her hands Agatha-style, '*see things differently.*'

But when we got there, instead of space to clear our heads, we ran straight into Ben. Erin had strategically forgotten to remind me he worked in the café. No wonder she'd suggested getting drinks.

'Well, hello!' He hugged me. Still gross. I tried to think of my happy place. The Ben & Jerry's counter in the cinema with Micha. 'I've missed you, babe.'

'Greetings ...' I still couldn't say 'babe'. '*You.* How's the foot?'

'Getting there ...' He raised one of his crutches. 'Still more sympathy breaks from my boss means more time to catch up on the important stuff.' I noticed what was on his table. *Rocking Out: The Hottest Palaeontology News!* magazine.

'Cool.' I lied.

'Well it's heading your way as soon as I finish it.' He grinned. 'Although shouldn't you guys be at rehearsal? Four days till opening night!' He actually jiggled my arm. 'You're going to be *awesome*.'

I couldn't help but snort. 'Hardly!'

Ben's smile dropped. 'C'*mon!* I know you wouldn't have cancelled our Castles! Chaos! Cows! sessions for anything less.' He was smiling again, but I could tell he was gutted his girlfriend hadn't spent proper time with him in weeks. For the first time it occurred to me maybe Erin missed being able to fully geek-out with someone too.

She tapped me on the arm. 'Hey, I'll go and grab the hot chocolates.'

I knew what she was doing – it was the same thing I did with Micha. Being around the people you missed most made this whole thing harder. But I was happy to have any excuse not to stay and talk to Ben about rocks (or anything really) so went to give her a hand. Cockapoo Karen was ahead of us in the queue but sadly her dog wasn't with her for joyous comparison. *Although* she did give me an idea. If it was my 'Top Fifteen Dog Walkers Who Look Like Their Pets' piece Nic had liked, maybe I could do a follow-up. That could be my first idea for editorial!

And amazing timing – when we headed outside, there Nic was, sitting on a bench, typing double-speed into her laptop.

I marched us over.

'Oh hey, Nic. Didn't expect to see you here.' She took off her headphones, unimpressed at being disturbed. 'You, er, come here often?'

'What, the bench outside ASDA?' How did she manage to make our school uniform look cool? 'I mean, it's not my number *one* destination.'

Why did I say such stupid stuff to her? I had to try harder.

'It's a great bench though.' Not exactly the gold I was after. 'St-unning. Very smooth ... Smooth wood.'

For once Erin had my back. 'Don't mind her. She's overdone it on the hot chocolate.'

But Nic didn't smile. 'I can tell by the foam moustache.' Okay, maybe Erin didn't have my back, or moustache, after all. I rubbed at it. Hard. 'Anyway, if you don't mind, can I get back to my piece?' Nic pushed her headphones over her ears again. 'Oh, and I'm sure you've guessed, but, Lily, we don't need you at editorial tomorrow.'

I choked on my drink. 'H ... How come?'

'Oh, I dunno.' Nic snapped her laptop shut. 'Maybe it's because I need to focus on people I actually want on my team. People I can trust.' She gave my sister a big, wide, entirely fake smile that looked alarmingly like her sister. 'Y'know –' she paused – 'not people who would swipe my sister's backstage passes.'

Nic let the words hang.

So Frankie did definitely know it was us.

And *of course* Nic would find out too. They were her passes. We'd betrayed Nic and upset her sister in the process.

How could I have been so stupid? I'd been so focused on getting into the concert and getting my life back, I'd not thought about who I might hurt in the process.

'Oh, Nic. I'm SO sorry.' I meant it. '*We're* so sorry. I mean, I *know* how it looks.'

Nic raised an eyebrow.

'Like you stole her passes so your sister could worm her way on stage?' Worm? She was comparing me to a worm? 'The press guy gave us a description of who picked up Frankie's tickets. A girl. Red hair in a messy bob. Got her friend on the backstage list to do a feature. The friend in a slogan T-shirt.' Nic paused. 'The clip of Lily onstage confirmed it.' She looked at my sister and shook her head. 'I thought I could trust you.'

Ground, please open up. All I'd ever wanted to do was stay off Frankie's radar and impress her big sister. And I'd failed spectacularly at both.

They must have thought I was a two-faced fake. And worse still, I couldn't blame them.

I looked at my sister, willing her to think of something, *anything*, to make this less awful. She knew how much I respected Nic. I couldn't have it all end like this.

But my sister was looking straight at Nic.

'You can . . .' Erin was standing tall, speaking slowly. 'Trust me, that is. *Really* you can.'

Nic rolled her eyes. 'I don't have time for this.'

'Please, Nic. Hear me out.' *Yes, Erin!* I didn't know where she was going, but I was willing her on. 'I'd actually gone down to the concert just to hang outside. On my own. See if I could get some content for my blog on . . .'

Erin shot me a look. She needed my help.

'Fandoms?' It was the best I had.

'Fandoms. *Yes.*' My sister looked pleased. 'But then Erin turned up. Out of the blue. She knew I'd had this idea for something with Chance Cheney.'

I coughed *loudly*. '*Chase* Cheney.'

Nic was staring at us both blankly.

'*Chase*, yes. I wanted to take a look at what really goes into making his show. Give a glimpse of his world we don't ever see.' Erin was parroting the idea I'd given her as a cover-up on the day. She had listened after all! 'I thought it could be an interesting angle.' *Did Cockapoo Karen just wave at me?! No, Lily, focus.* 'So as a surprise my big sister decided to come down and try to do something about it. When she saw Frankie's tickets hadn't been collected, but the concert had already started, she thought they were going to waste so said they were hers. I was *so* surprised when she turned up with them.' Erin laughed softly. 'She told me they were a late birthday present.'

Wow. Wow. *Wow.* I'd never wanted to hug my sister/myself

so much in my life. She'd shifted all the blame on to the real Erin to help me out with Nic.

Nic looked at me as if needing to check it was true.

'Lil didn't have a clue how I really got the tickets until it all kicked off at school.' I shrugged. I knew I looked guilty, as I genuinely felt terrible. 'I only told her the truth last night. I guess I just knew how much she wanted something that would really stand out for her blog. To get on your team. And when I saw those tickets, I thought it might be her best chance.'

I hardly dared look at Nic. Had we done enough to change her mind about giving me and my writing another chance?

'Not going to lie, that's not *quite* what I heard from my sister.' Nic paused. 'But ... I guess it all adds up.' It did?! 'And, Lily, I do like commitment. It was a nice angle you were going for.' She liked it?! Could this mean she wasn't totally mad at me any more? I stuffed my hands in my pockets and crossed my fingers. 'So while I don't exactly *like* that my sister was upset –' Nic tilted her head from side to side as if weighing it up – 'it wasn't exactly like Frankie had said thank you at any point. Or turned up on time to get them.' She paused. 'And I *did* get the impression she only wanted to go backstage to impress her new cheerleading mates.' Wow, I'd never thought of Frankie ever trying to impress *anyone*. 'Hmmm ...' Nic drummed her fingers on her laptop. 'Lily, your space at the editorial has already been filled.' They'd found someone else already?

My heart sank. 'But someone has dropped out of covering LOLCon.' LOLCon?! As in the super-exclusive invite-only event this Saturday with hundreds of influencers doing panels and events? There was even a huge secret guest yet to be announced. It was kind of like Erin's Shakespeare convention – but good. 'We could do with a spare pair of hands in the morning. So if you're up for doing some interviews for TheNicReport and do an amazing job, like *seriously* knock it out the park, then maybe, *maybe* I could have another think about you joining the team.'

What?! There was a glimpse of hope after all! I willed every bone in my body – both bodies, which was about 416 bones – for Erin to say yes.

And she did.

I could have kissed her, but kissing myself was a step too far.

'Great.' Nic stood up. 'I'll send you the list of influencer interviews we're pitching for.' I was going to have to brief Erin *so* hard. Even better, swap before then. 'You'll need to be fully prepped as it's all being streamed. Live. You're cool with that, right?'

Luckily Nic didn't wait for an answer. Which was good as Erin did not take the news well. In fact, she didn't manage anything more than a terrified squeak until we were back home and halfway through that evening's punishment. Cleaning the bathroom.

But I knew how my sister felt – my head was still whirring dealing with it all when I went to bed. As I climbed under

Erin's duvet I realized it was the first night since the swap I hadn't thought about the Hairy Godmother.

I was thinking about how to make Micha know I was still here, still her best friend, despite my body being inhabited by someone who was more interested in palaeontology than people.

I was thinking about how to keep Erin's place in the play.

How to impress Chinyere Okafor for her.

How to impress Nic on Saturday.

Instinctively I got my laptop out and began to type, spilling out my frustrations into the piece for my eyes only. The one about all the small things in my life I missed. (My random classmates! The skatepark! My crisp stash under my bed!) About how when things go wrong, it's normally okay, so long as you have the people you love around you.

Because right now, with all the lies we'd had to tell, I felt more alone than ever.

Feeling better for getting it all out, I saved it and closed my laptop. Then panicked Mum and Dad might find it when they did their random 'Can I borrow your laptop' check-ups on us. So I printed it, deleted it and folded the only evidence of it away in my notebook, never to be read again. But as I did, I knocked Erin's bedside table and with a *plip* something slid down the back of it.

It looked like a brochure, handwritten notes sticking out.

I hesitated. Erin and I had set ground rules. No rifling through each other's stuff was number one. (Number two was no permanent tattoos, and three was eyes closed in the shower.)

But I hadn't rifled – this had *thrown* itself at me.

I listened to check Erin wasn't still awake and picked it up.

CHINYERE OKAFOR'S DRAMA ACADEMY

It was the brochure from when Erin had visited last summer to see if she liked it. The corners were rounded where she'd read it so much. And it had fallen open on a page – the application criteria. Wow – I didn't know they only accepted roughly one in every five hundred applicants?! And you could only apply once. That was *intense*.

There was a super-long list of everything they were looking for in new students. Erin had stuck notes next to most of them.

- Have to get a main part!!!
- CANNOT let grades drop in run-up. Mum and Dad might tell me it's too much to take on extra stuff.

Some of her notes were from last year. Crikey – I knew she wanted to go, but I didn't realize how many months she'd been working on it.

- Think positive! Who knows if I'm any good, but I HAVE to believe I can be!!!

Did Erin really not know how good her acting was?

In the margin she'd written her own list.

Why It's Important
- I CAN'T take drama as an option at school – this is my ONLY chance of getting on to a drama course later.
- Chinyere is my IDOL. The best. There is NOWHERE else I want to go.
- It will make me SOOOO happy.

If I hadn't felt worried enough about the play, now I felt petrified.

Chinyere was Erin's Nic. And this play was her one and only chance.

Eurgh! I wish I'd never opened the brochure. I felt more nervous than ever.

I stuffed it back to where it'd fallen from, angry at myself for making things even worse. But as I did, another folded slip of paper fell out.

It was Erin's neat handwriting, everything perfectly laid out.

But this one said something I really wasn't expecting.

WORRIES

I couldn't help but read what came next.

- I can't just get in. I HAVE to get the scholarship. It's waaaay too expensive if not.
- Everyone expects me to be able to handle everything — what if I can't?

But the final one made me stop.

- Will spending every weekend away mean I never see Lily? She's already started to hang out with me less ...

And as I looked at Erin's words, I realized something.
I missed my big sister too.

CHAPTER TWENTY-THREE

I watched it again.

And again.

And one more time.

How could something get worse every time you looked at it?

I collapsed back against a packing box and contemplated how much simpler the world would be if the internet didn't exist. Or, more specifically, if my dad didn't have access to it.

'So explain to me how you thought this was okay?' I watched Dad shimmying away on my account, grinning in his 'Not Like Other Dads' T-shirt. Erin definitely got her love of a slogan top from him. 'And what on *earth* was that move?!'

'Well, we agreed to try to get them back onside ...' Even Erin looked embarrassed. 'And ... I think it was a swag walk?' I shuddered at the hip thrust now happening. Neither Erin nor I could look directly at it. 'Look, I was just sorting the recycling.' She paused to make sure I'd picked up that almost two weeks later she was still doing my chores. I had. And I liked it. 'And Dad was asking all these questions about GettingLilyWithIt, and why they hadn't seen Micha or Ben for a while, and I didn't know what to say. And the song came on. You'd left your phone out. And . . . one thing led to another.'

The more I watched, the more I saw my messages rack up. I had no intention of reading them. *Ever.*

'If it helps, Frankie liked it.' It did not help. It un-helped. 'I told you it would all be okay.'

'Hmm.' Before today's rehearsal my sister had grabbed Frankie and said sorry, and checked Nic had told her the ticket stealing was all 'Erin'. And that 'Erin' was really sorry. Apparently Frankie had been cool about it.

'C'mon, Lil. Frankie knows it wasn't "Lily's" fault. So she's only mad at "Erin". I told her "Erin" was sorry. Job done.' My sister really thought life was that simple. I dropped the subject and Erin went to get emergency snacks – arguing with her wasn't what I needed when this evening was challenging enough. It was night three of our punishment – today we were clearing old stuff out of the loft for the charity shop.

At the start, rifling through boxes had been fun – uncovering forgotten treasures and laughing at bad outfits. Why our parents had thought it was appropriate to send us out of the house in matching rainbow tracksuits that said 'Sassy Sisters' I'd never know. One hundred per cent a Dad purchase. But seeing all the souvenirs Mum and Dad had kept of me and my sister's terrible hobbies together had made me sad. (Our two-person nativity. Our yogurt pot walkie-talkies to gossip between rooms. Our matching tie-dye phase.) So much had changed.

Erin and I had worked super hard, so we could finish up and spend the last hour before bed clearing up a different mess – our own lives. LOLCon and the opening night of the play were in three days and there was still no sign of Agatha.

'Incoming . . .' Erin poked her head through the loft door and lifted up the mugs.

'Mini marshmallows?' I blew a chef's kiss as she clambered up and shut the hatch behind her. 'I thought we stopped getting them?'

'Shelf above the sink, teabag tin.' She patted her nose. 'Classified info.'

Wow, hanging with my sister could have its perks.

'So . . .' She reached behind her and plonked down two massive wodges of paper, Post-its sticking out. 'I did a thing.'

I picked up the stapled pile with my name on it. *Wow.* I wasn't sure where, in-between homework, chores, making notes on everyone at LOLCon, messaging Ben and dancing with Dad, she'd found the time, but Erin had printed off the *A Midsummer Night's Dream* script and made notes on every page I had lines.

I flicked through. It was so thorough!

Tips on how to approach it. (Although she says 'trifles', it's actually quite sad. Think of Barry the Hamster RIP)

225

Tips on how to remember certain lines. (I think this sounds like a Chase lyric – and yes, I've now listened to the album.)

Even little notes of encouragement. (This is a v funny scene, you're going to really make people laugh. Enjoy it! ☺)

My big sister grinned. 'Just in case we haven't swapped by then. Thought it might help.'

'Wow, Erin ...' I couldn't stop looking through. There were *hundreds* of pages. I didn't even know how to feel. Touched? Emotional? Terrified Erin had discovered how to fit twenty-seven hours into a day? 'It *really* does.'

But maybe not just in the way she thought. Until now it seemed Erin hadn't been sure I could pull it off, but this stash of paper felt like her believing I could.

'I had another idea too ...' Erin opened up a folder full of tiny bits of paper. 'If you do have a mind-blank, I've made prompts for all your lines. I'm going to hide them on the back of the props in your scenes.' She smiled. 'So no more stressing about forgetting anything.'

I couldn't believe she'd done this.

'You're an actual lifesaver!' I leant over and gave her a hug. 'Thanks, sis. This is *awesome*.'

It definitely felt weird to be effectively hugging myself.

'Well, Ben mentioned that every time he's seen you, well, *me*, this week, I've had my head stuck in a script. So thanks ... Y'know, I didn't think I'd miss him this much.' She sighed. 'And yeah, I know you don't rate him much, but he's like my Micha. Maybe even more, because we also have kissin—'

'*Enough.*' I had to cut her off. That mental image wouldn't help *anything*. I waved my script. 'Shall we get cracking? Cos if I'm going to keep us playing Titania, I need *all* the help I can get for tomorrow's dress rehearsal.'

The only time my sister and I had ever tried to study together before had ended in me slamming a door so hard, a porcelain badger fell off a bookshelf and almost hit Barry the Hamster (RIP).

But up here in the loft, after an hour, not only had no fake or real animals been hurt, but Erin and I had made real progress. Mum even popped her head up and, seeing we hadn't murdered each other, passed us some chocolate brownies Dad had just baked. Apparently they were 'an improvement on the ones where he forgot the chocolate'. Today really was a day for growth.

'So.' Erin opened up her laptop. 'Shall we ...' What she meant was use the last half hour to tackle the final item on our agenda. The thing that made her go pale whenever it came up. Her going live on TheNicReport channel, with its thousands of followers, to interview the biggest influencers in the world at LOLCon. 'Any news from Nic?'

She'd said she'd email today with a list of all the people who had said yes to her interview requests. I was hoping she might have news on the secret guest too.

'One sec ...' I refreshed my inbox. 'Oh ... yeah. Just!'

Erin leant over as I read the email out loud.

'Hey, Lily. Good news! Fifteen people have said yes so far (list below). So you should get to chat to some decent names.'

Fifteen?! Erin was going to need to know *a lot* about *a lot* of people. I scanned the names. They were all *massive*! KingKoalaFiguresItOut had over a million followers! Erin was going to freak.

> You'll need to be there 11 a.m. – 1 p.m., and
> any probs message me. Good luck!
> Nx
> PS If you can keep secrets, I also messaged
> the secret guest to ask him to fit you in.

Him? Apparently it was a *huge* name, so who would Nic know well enough to message? Erin and I looked at each other, the same thought hitting us at the same time, like a big, wet fish to both our faces.

> I figured you're a big Chase fan, and had that
> viral moment together, so it could be great to
> get a follow-up with him?

What.

Had.

I.

Just.

Read?!

'Erin?' I jabbed at the screen. Was Nic casually saying she might have a one-on-one Chase interview?

'Uh-huh.' My sister nodded grimly.

My head dropped into my hands. I felt Erin's arm go around me.

'I'm so sorry, Lil. I know this is your dream.' It really was – repping the TheNicReport was incredible enough without working with all those content creators . . . and maybe even Chase. 'So we just have to make sure we find Agatha before then.' I nodded but no sound came out. We'd both been ignoring the elephant in the room. Not the stuffed toy one in the charity bag that said 'Let's get Ele-funky!' but the one that was much more Hairy Godmother shaped. Despite her lipstick message to us, we still had no clue how to find her. 'And look . . . if we don't . . .' Erin gave me a little smile. 'I promise I won't do anything weird this time. I'll even let you pick my outfit.'

I put on the bravest face I could. Yes, it *was* my dream, but it was just as much Erin's nightmare. 'Thanks, Erin. You'll be great though. You always are.'

I munched my final bit of brownie, hoping my brain might forget it wanted to cry. I wished I could talk to Micha about this. About everything. But she wasn't talking to me. Which made me want to cry even more.

Erin noticed my semi-chew-sniff hybrid and grabbed her folder.

'HannahHuman seems really funny!' My sister was being extra cheery, trying to pick me up and show me it could all be okay. 'And the Pham Brothers do really coolio pranks.'

I nodded encouragingly, but since they were called HollyHuman and the Pham Sisters I didn't hold out too much hope.

'You know I was reading your blog.' Erin shuffled next to me. 'That piece? About the people who look like their dogs? Cockapoo Karen *still* makes me laugh.' Wow. I had no idea Erin had ever read my blog. 'And you've got so many readers now. Over ten thousand, right?'

I tried to look as if I was struggling to remember despite checking every day. 'Sort of ... around 14,231 a month.'

Erin whistled. 'That's all kinds of cool, sis.' I knew it was nothing compared to Erin being top of every class, but I still felt a twinge of pride that she said it.

I smiled at my sister, and she smiled back.

And for a second things felt normal. Better than normal. Like how they used to be between us. Like how they were in all the pictures all around us that we'd been boxing up.

'Although ...' Erin grinned. 'There are 7.8 billion people in the world, so you've still got 7799985769 people to go.'

My twinge of pride sat back down.

And we got back to coming up with questions for LOLCon. We even did a practice run-through where Erin pretended to interview me. I told her she was doing great even though she forgot her name, called LOLCon 'COLon' and signed off

230

with 'smell you later, alligator'. Which she hadn't said since she was eight. She even pinched her nose. It was so weird seeing her nervous. Up until last week I really thought she could take anything in her stride. But as she chatted away, writing more notes, I got distracted. Over Erin's shoulder, just by Ele-funky, was the newspaper from earlier this week. The one with Chase and my sister in. Did Mum drop it off with the brownies? I really didn't *think* I'd seen it earlier.

I leant back to get a better look. 'Erin, do you think we've missed something in Agatha's sock clue?'

'I don't see how we could have.' She scrunched her face. 'We've been through it, through *everything*, a million times.'

She was right. I'd even emailed random hairdressers around the world to ask if they'd heard of the Hairy Godmother. Or liked socks. But nothing.

So why did I want to pick up the paper again?

'I might just give this another read.'

'Sure, I'll pack up.'

But as Erin pottered around me, I was reading it.

Again.

And again.

And one more time.

Because I'd seen something that made me think Erin might be wrong.

Something that could change everything.

'Erin, look . . .' How had I not seen it sooner?! 'The support band . . .'

She peered over the scripts and paper she'd stacked up. 'Yeah ... And what?'

'And *what*?! Can't you see it?!' I pointed at their name again. Ego Rhythm Radio. 'Can you even remember seeing them on Saturday?'

She shook her head slowly. 'Ego Rhythm Radio? ... I think I only saw Sara and the Spaceman and Tortoiseca?'

'Exactly. *They weren't there*. And look ... their single. It's coming out on Saturday. This Saturday! And if you look at their name ...'

Finally, I saw the penny drop.

'Hairy Godmother.' Erin's mouth had dropped right open. 'Of course! An anagram! The letters are all there in their name!'

'EXACTLY!'

She grabbed the paper. 'Do you think this means the Hairy Godmother is going to make an appearance this Saturday?'

'Uh-huh.' I nodded and pointed at the other things that confirmed it for me.

The name of their single. 'Final Chance' and their album '▶Meet Me'.

'Just look at that symbol!' I pointed at the triangle. For the first time in ages I felt a rush of excitement that we could be back on track.

'Play.' Erin grinned. *Play*?! She's going to be at the play, isn't she?'

I nodded, knowing just how huge this was.

They'd even mentioned socks in their quote, just like Agatha's last message to us.

This couldn't be coincidence.

Agatha had spelled it out.

Our final chance was looming.

If we didn't switch back this time, we would be stuck like this for ever.

CHAPTER TWENTY-FOUR

Normally there was a lot of chatter before Mrs Saddler arrived, but today the hall was quiet. Eerily quiet.

Everyone was nervous about the final rehearsal. But I was stressed about something even bigger. Was Mrs Saddler going to replace me with Lou?

It didn't help that it was the first time seeing everyone in costume – and the whole cast looked amazing. Enthusiastic Mark's donkey head was so lifelike I patted him twice, and Harley looked like the ultimate majestic fairy king in his leafy cape. If I didn't feel awful, I might even be enjoying Titania's costume. I'd never worn anything like it – a long, flowy, light-green dress with billowy sleeves (Singed Simon advised me to keep at least three metres away from any naked flames) and a flowery crown for my hair.

I couldn't believe I'd got so far, but it might all be snatched away from me, from Erin, with less than two days to go.

'Cheer up.' Lou kicked my trainer. I glanced up from my script. 'It might never happen.'

'Or it might happen in ...' I checked the time. 'Less than two hours.'

I looked over at Lou's understudy in the corner practising her lines for Puck, ready to step up into her role.

Lou shook her head. 'Ignore that. There's *no way* Mrs Saddler would swap me for you. And definitely not when the show's in less than two days. You're way better than I ever could be! Just remember all the advice you've been messaging me this week.' She smiled. 'You've been a total ledge.'

Despite the weird circumstances, it was nice to hear she and the real Erin had been getting along – I never normally saw my sister with friends, and, from what I'd got to know of Lou, I thought she'd make a good one.

But another person was also boosting my confidence – Erin darting in and out of the wings, getting all my prompts ready on the props. She saw me looking and gave me a big thumbs up.

My sister *really* thought I could do this – keep my place, *our place*, in the play – and I couldn't let her down. But as I gave her a thumbs up back, Frankie walked over to her. And ... *hugged* her.

Maybe Erin was right – maybe Frankie really *had* forgiven her for the whole ticket thing? Either way, I needed to say an in-person sorry. And as much as I'd been dreading it, there was no time better than now. For everyone's sake, I needed to clear the air before opening night, so I said bye to Lou, and walked nervously over to Frankie and Erin in the wings. My sister mumbled something about 'needing to fix a wobbly donkey ear' and left me alone with Frankie.

I'd normally handle this by pretending I'd seen an intriguing squirrel through the window and run off to look at it. But that wasn't Erin's style.

I had to be brave.

'Sorry to interrupt.' I tried to channel my sister's normal confidence. 'I just wanted to talk to you about the whole Chase mix-up. Make sure you knew how sorry I was.' I paused. 'Because I am. *Really* sorry.'

'Oh yeah.' Frankie laughed to herself. 'Stealing someone's identity and their backstage passes is just a mix-up, isn't it?'

So she was still mad at me – and I didn't blame her.

'I'm so sorry. I really thought you weren't picking them up. Not that that matters. I shouldn't have done it.'

She folded her arms. 'Too right.'

Well, this was awkward. I'd never had to grovel while dressed as a fairy queen before.

'I'm not sure how, but I'll find a way to make it up to you.' As much as I was the world's smallest fan of Frankie, she hadn't deserved what I'd done. 'I promise.'

She looked at me.

And, after a long wait she ... *smiled*.

'Well ... in that case ...' She unfolded her arms. 'Apology accepted. I *guess*.' *Well, that went better than I thought!* 'Lily explained why you did it.' Maybe I hadn't given Frankie enough credit after all. 'So I'm sure karma will sort it all out. And there's enough going on anyway with getting everything ready for Saturday.' Frankie picked up Erin's props list. 'Less than forty-eight hours till your one chance, your big audition, in front of Chinyere Okafor. Your life idol, right?' I nodded. 'I'm sure you've got nothing to worry about. Who wouldn't *loooove* a Mrs Saddler eighty-nine-minute retelling of a Shakespearean classic?'

'Er, thanks.' I couldn't put my finger on it, but something about the way she said it didn't make me feel great. 'Although how come you know about the audition?'

'Oh, your sister was filling me in.' Frankie twirled one of the fresh apples we used for my first scene. 'Weird that we didn't speak much before, she's so . . . *fascinating.*'

Frankie calling me 'fascinating' definitely made my 'something's not right' alarm sound. But Mrs Saddler had arrived and was summoning us together.

'So it begins.' Mrs Saddler had her eyes closed, and was breathing so loudly through her nose it was like she was blowing up imaginary nostril balloons. 'TODAY IS THE DAY!' She spun in a slow circle, her arms out. 'Like when Da Vinci unveiled the Mona Lisa.' Well, that was one way of describing the dress rehearsal. 'Or when Michael Bublé released his debut album BaBalu.' She breathed out. 'Sssssssseminal.'

I looked at Enthusiastic Mark who was wearing brown

leggings covered in brown cotton wool and was gluing on fake sideburns. I wasn't *a hundred per cent* convinced I shared her vision.

'I am expecting *mesmerizing* performances. From *all* of you.' So why was Mrs Saddler only looking at me?! For five looooong seconds?! 'So let us BEGIN!'

Lou and I whispered, 'Break a leg,' to each other, but by the time I got my cue to walk out on stage, I was a nervous wreck. I strode out behind Harley, and that was when I saw it. A tiny piece of card stuck to the back of the foam tree.

> You've got this, Lil! Your first line is 'What, jealous Oberon!'

I looked over at the wings and smiled at my sister.

And knowing she thought I could do it meant I . . . did.

I said the right lines, I pulled the right faces, I even managed to bite my apple mysteriously enough for Harley to look impressed. Sure, I was nowhere near as good as the others, but thanks to Erin's help and hints all over the props, I'd definitely improved.

As we all gathered on the stage to bow there was only one thing on my mind.

Had I done enough to keep my part?

Well, that, and: must wear more deodorant as Titania's dress was *not* breathable.

Erin looked as nervous as I felt.

'Soooooooo.' Mrs Saddler stepped up to the stage. 'If I could sum that up I'd say it was ...' A *triumph*? A *relief*? A *miracle*? 'Adequate.'

There was a collective drop of shoulders. We'd all put *so* much into it.

'Good news? Backstage ran smoothly. Your detailed plan is working brilliantly – well done, Frances.' I'd never seen Frankie look so smug. Guess forgiving my sister didn't go as far as giving her the credit she deserved. 'Louise, solid performance. Mark, lots of *enthusiasm*. Harley, powerful, as always. But all of you can do better tomorrow. No ... sorry. *Must* do.' Was it good news or bad that she hadn't mentioned me? 'We're *incredibly* lucky to have the Swan Theatre to perform in.' It was a huge, grand theatre that backed on to the super-modern event space where LOLCon was happening. 'As most of you know, acting *icon* Chinyere Okafor herself will be in the audience so there will be *no room* for anything less than perfection.' I saw the looks go around. *Everyone* wanted to impress her. 'Which leads me on to my little surprise ... I've organized professional hair and make-up teams for the principle cast.' Mrs Saddler nodded dramatically, enjoying the excited gasp. '*Yes!* You're right to be excited.' But Erin and I looked the happiest of all. Forget magical make-up! Could she mean the Hairy Godmother? 'It's really going to add an extra layer of magic to the whole night. *Although*, talking of quality, we must discuss the outstanding issue. Titania ...'

239

My stomach knotted. Here it came. The moment of truth. Had I done enough to keep Erin's dream alive? I knew my sister felt as nervous as me, as she was rocking back and forth in her chair, her head in her hands.

'Today was an improvement, *of sorts* . . . but as your rrrole is so crrrrritical . . .' Mrs Saddler unleashed the most dramatic 'r' roll I'd ever heard. It went on for so long a bird landed on the window and flew off again. 'To the prrrrrrrroduction . . .' She went for it again. The bird returned. 'I'm going to leave it to the most important people to decide who they want as their Titania. Your fellow castmates.'

Er, what?!

'So on the count of three, all in favour of understudy Louise playing Titania, put your left hand up. For Erin, raise your right. And remember – this isn't personal, this is about one thing only. *Art*.' It really wasn't, it was about my sister getting her dream place at the drama academy. About her little sister doing her best to make it happen.

But the decision was out of my control. I looked round the room. The only person brave enough to make eye contact was Lou who mouthed, 'Sorry.'

I mouthed, 'Don't worry,' back. It wasn't her fault.

'Three . . . two . . . one . . .'

I stared at the floor, too scared to look. I heard the noise of arms going up.

Mrs Saddler started counting the hands. But then stopped. This was torture.

I *had* to look.

But . . . I couldn't believe what I saw.

Every right hand – Lou's, Harley's, both of Enthusiastic Mark's, Singed Simon's – they were all in the air. *Everyone* had voted for me.

Even Frankie?!

I did a double take.

'Thank you!' I blurted out, at the exact same Erin shouted, 'Yesssss, sis!'

I'd done it! By some miracle I'd kept Erin's place in the play!

Now all we needed was an even bigger one to swap us back before it started.

CHAPTER TWENTY-FIVE

Dad only made waffles for breakfast on big days.

And this Saturday morning he made waffles *and* pancakes. I arranged the berries in a smiley face, and sent a picture to Micha.

> Me: The waffle of truth says: Micha, you will be most excellent today. 👍🥚🌰🍖
> Me: And NO ONE messes with the waffle of truth

Just like the rest of this week I didn't get a reply. Erin had been trying to spend more time with Micha, but she'd been avoiding her, saying she had to study for her exam. I added the most motivational-looking penguin GIF I could find.

> Me: If you want to celebrate staying up in chemistry and taking YOUR RIGHTFUL PLACE in the youth squad I've still got a spare ticket for

later (if you fancy watching 89 mins of ~~Harley~~
my sister)

I knew Mich wouldn't come, but I needed her to know that I missed her. Especially as today was going to be the day Erin and I swapped back. It *had* to be.

We'd planned every second of it. We had to after Mrs Saddler sent a memo asking us to all arrive at the venue earlier than planned. She thought we needed more preparation time. Backstage crew were needed first, which meant dealing with the slightly large spanner in the works of my sister needing to be in two places at the same time. At LOLCon interviewing live on TheNicReport, and somehow setting up the props in the Swan Theatre with Frankie. The only bit of good luck was that the two venues backed on to each another.

I opened up my notebook and went through our plan for the millionth time.

MISSION IMPRESS NIC, IMPRESS CHINYERE OKAFOR AND GET THE HAIRY GODMOTHER TO YOU KNOW WHAT!

10.30 a.m.: Dad gives us both a lift.
'Lily' to head to LOLCon.
'Erin' to head to Swan Theatre to
find Hairy G.

BOTH BE ON ALERT FOR
POTENTIALLY YOU KNOW WHAT
(SWAPPING BACK) AT ANY POINT
FROM NOW!!!

My hope was that we could switch before LOLCon started.

11 a.m.: Interviews start at LOLCon +
backstage crew due at theatre.
Frankie to cover for 'Lily'.

My sister had told Frankie about the double booking, and
she'd agreed to cover for the two hours she'd be missing so
Mrs Saddler wouldn't find out. To say thank you, Erin and
I had spent last night loading all the props into the school
van, so Frankie would have one job less to do today.

1 p.m.: 'Lily' finish LOLCon + run
to theatre
1 – 4.30 p.m.: If we haven't already found
Hairy G IT'S NOW OR NEVER to YOU
KNOW WHAT (swap) *
4.30 p.m.: Curtains up. (Real Erin to
impress Chinyere Okafor! Get place in
drama academy!)
7 p.m.: Celebrate.

I tried not to look at the tiny bit we'd added below.

*Just in case worst happens, Erin and Lily
to run through lines for a final time and
make sure notes are on props.

I accidentally gulped a full mouth of unchewed waffle at the terrifying thought of maybe having to be the world's worst Titania in front of hundreds of people.

'So, Lil.' Mum sipped her tea. 'Big day. We'll be watching online later. Can't wait.'

'Absolutely.' Dad had a big grin. 'And if you see KingKoalaFiguresItOut, please tell him I'm a massive fangirl. Boy . . . Adult man.'

Mum gave Dad the sort of look she normally reserved for me.

'Are you feeling prepared? Your notes look . . .' She peered at Erin's folder which was meatier than my script. '*Extensive.*'

My sister nodded. 'Uh-huh.' She then made a noise like Barry the Hamster (RIP) had when he was picked up after a big meal. Speechless Erin was a rare thing but she'd been like this ever since I'd shown her the post of the queue outside LOLCon when we'd woken up.

Mum put her hand on her arm. 'We're all very proud of you, whatever happens. So just try to . . .' I knew what she was thinking. *Don't do anything ridiculous like normal.* 'Focus. And you'll be fine.'

My sister looked queasy and pushed her plate away. Pancake-refusing Erin was even rarer than silent Erin.

'You're going to be more than fine.' I nudged my knee into hers. In reality I worried it might be a total disaster – a disaster that would exist on the internet for ever. But my sister didn't need to know that. Through our bedroom wall I'd heard her playing Chase's entire back catalogue. She'd been really trying. 'You're going to be *great*. You're going to get to chat to *soooo* many amazing people.' I sipped my juice and tried to give her a mysterious look. 'So many amazing *hairy* people.'

She finally spoke, a little grin on her face. 'Very hairy.'

'Must be a young people thing,' Dad said quietly to Mum. 'Probably means *cool*.'

'Well, fingers crossed.' Erin stood up and took her plate to the sink. 'It's not easy getting picked for TheNicReport, you know. Nic only takes on one or two people a year. She once had an exclusive with Dua Lipa but didn't run it because she didn't like how Dua chewed her crisps.'

I knew Erin was trying to manage my expectations, *everyone's* expectations, but I couldn't help but smile that she remembered all the things I'd been telling her about why it was such a big deal for me.

'Well, we've got faith in you.' Dad gave her one of his lovely big smiles. 'And remember – a winner never stops crying.'

Mum coughed. 'Trying, Norm. It's *trying*. And, Erin? Knowing your father, just a warning we'll be in the front row for your performance.'

246

'*Please* remember Chinyere Okafor will be there . . .' I shot Dad a look. 'So can you keep any clapping to a *normal* level?'

'And no Mexican waves this time,' Erin said sternly. 'You know no one *ever* joins in.' At her last play, Dad had flung his arms up so violently his wedding ring had flown off and landed in Singed Simon's gran's hair.

Mum looked at me. Then my sister. Then me again. Were her eyes . . . misty?

She was either getting emotional or had waffle in her eyes.

'Supporting each other like this . . . who would have thought?'

A magical hairdresser who wanted us to stop arguing?

'Well, hold the pride until you've seen me in action. I just want to do justice to all Lil's hard work behind the scenes.' I looked at my sister. 'And I hope, hope, *hooooope* Chinyere Okafor is impressed.' But not as much as I hoped our plan to swap back worked before the curtain went up.

'When are you ever not impressive?' Mum smiled.

It was weird being Erin – no matter what I said, people told me to stop worrying and that I would be great. I think I preferred being me, when they just let me get on with messing up.

How did Erin deal with the pressure? I was at breaking point after two weeks.

When breakfast finished, and I'd done the dishes to help with Erin's chores, we headed up to my room. I jumped straight on the bed. Was it weird to miss a bed? Who cared. I lay face down and hugged it.

'Do you reckon our plan will go okay?' I really needed some reassuring right now.

'Do a reckon the pan will gherkin?' Erin repeated back. 'I'm not going to lie – you're a lot easier to understand when you're not talking into a pillow.'

I shuffled upright. 'I said, do you reckon it'll go okay. Today?'

Erin was checking herself out in the mirror. She'd stuck to her word and let me pick my favourite outfit for her to wear. Black jeans, trainers, slightly cropped jumper – and no tubes of foot cream in sight.

'It's *got* to, right? The clues you found all point to today. So if you find Agatha . . .'

'*When* I find her . . .'

'Ring me *immediately*?'

I nodded. 'Course.'

'And be warned. Ben might pop up backstage. He's into cute surprises.'

Cute + Ben = could not compute.

'Last year he made me a good luck rock.' *Is that a thing?* Couldn't only erosion make rocks?! (The geography fact Post-its in Erin's room were clearly getting to me.)

But Dad was yelling, so we headed out. Just in case this was my last car journey as Erin, I shotgunned the front seat and suggested we put on Chase Cheney to help my sister's vibe. What a selfless sibling I was.

When we saw LOLCon for the first time Erin and I both gasped (me in excitement, Erin in horror). It looked *st-unning*!

It was so, *so* big. Even outside there were loads of stands, and massive neon photo boards you could pose with – and the queue was streaming round the block. Dad and I wished Erin luck, but as she reluctantly waved bye, clutching her notes in her hand, she looked like me heading to a maths exam. Well, me heading to a maths exam in the middle of a crowd of thousands of super-happy people. I'd never seen her this scared! I, however – I was hanging out of the car window trying to glimpse a single guest.

'You okay there?' Dad turned the engine back on. I ducked my head back in. With Erin gone, it was time to focus on my mission.

'Definitely. Just, you know, pre-performance nerves can make you do funny things.' Which was the wrong thing to say as Dad turned the engine straight off for an impromptu mindfulness breathing session. But all I was mindful of was that it meant less time to find the Hairy Godmother. I gripped my fingers round the newspaper article about Chase Cheney tightly folded up in my pocket and tried to reassure myself. *Yes*, Agatha *was* going to be at the theatre. And *yes*, I could do this.

Eventually, we set back off. It was only a two-minute walk but Dad said I 'deserved to arrive in style'. As we pulled out back on to the road, my phone buzzed.

Nic: Good luck today. Hope you smash it xx

I replied with a thumbs up. So did I. But there was nothing I could do about it now.

Except feel sick with nerves, stress-eat Magic Stars, and then feel sick with nerves *and* Magic Stars. Which I did.

'Well, here we are ...' Dad's cheery voice snapped me out of imagining Erin on TheNicReport's live stream asking KingKoalaFiguresItOut whether they played Castles! Chaos! Cows!

Full body shudder.

'So just you remember, Erin doesn't do nerves!' He smiled. 'And if you're worried, just tell yourself my Circus Skills mantra ...' I wasn't sure it would be massively helpful considering he was currently supporting a semi-black eye. '*What doesn't kill you makes you stronger. Unless you land on your head.*'

I laughed. I had no idea when he was joking, but I loved him anyway.

'Thanks, Dad.'

'Anytime, oldest daughter.' But as he put the handbrake on there was something else I wanted to ask.

'Do you think Lily will do okay today?'

Without hesitation he nodded firmly. 'Of course. She's a superstar!' Wow – I thought he only said that to make me feel better. 'I just wish she knew how proud we are of her. She's always up to something interesting, isn't she? So impressive.' He pulled down the visor on the windscreen. Tucked into it was a picture of me and Erin messing around in the garden, giving each other a massive hug. I had no idea. He smiled the second he saw it. 'And the way she picks herself up? Always working on a new idea? There really is no one like our Lil.'

He wasn't expecting it but I reached over the gearstick and gave him a hug. A really long hug.

'See you later.' I opened the door. 'And . . .' I might as well go for it. This could be one of the last times I was in the wrong body with Dad. 'Love you. Lots. Lily does too.'

He beamed. 'Well, that was pretty hairy.' And before I could try to explain he'd got the wrong end of the stick, and it really didn't mean 'cool', he drove off.

With Dad gone, Mission Find Hairy Godmother was on.

I ran up the huge stone steps of the Swan Theatre. Mrs Saddler's old pal, who'd been in four episodes of *Holby City* (playing corpse one, two and three, and 'dying woman who soon becomes corpse') had loaned it to us for the week. I pushed through the stiff swivel doors.

And immediately stopped.

I'd never seen *anywhere* so posh. All the doorways were carved archways with ugly stone faces sitting at the top. And the walls were packed with signed photos of famous actors who'd performed here. My nerves shot up a gear, which considering they were already in 'most top gear possible' was a quite a feat.

But where should I look for Agatha first? Every second counted! I hunted for a sign.

Bingo!

251

A literal sign. I sprinted up the stairs and along the red carpeted corridor. But when I got to the first closed door I heard something behind it. *Strange*. No one else from school should be here yet. Feeling brave, I flung it open ... to find Singed Simon in a hi-vis jacket, walkie-talkie strapped to his belt, sellotaping up 'St Augustine's Fire Regulations'.

He looked at me, unimpressed. 'You're early?'

I tried to nod innocently, and not as if I was out of breath, hunting for a magical hairdresser.

'Yup.' How could I not arouse suspicion? 'Just wanted to get prepared. Familiarize myself with the venue. The ... er, evacuation procedures.'

'Well, it's your lucky day.' He pointed at a laminated poster *full* of writing. 'Emergency procedures are all here on my sixty-two bullet-point list.' Point one was 'read all sixty-one points below' which didn't seem the best first step in the middle of a blazing inferno (but I felt feedback would go down as well as an unattended candle).

'Wonderful. Very ... *thorough*.' I tried to look interested – he had voted for me to keep my part after all. 'Sooooo.' I looked back out into the corridor. 'Who else is here?'

Please say a super-cool hairdresser in dungarees.

Simon wrinkled his forehead – well, I thought he did, but it was hard to tell without eyebrows. 'Just Mrs Saddler. She's here to oversee the backstage crew when they arrive.' My stomach clenched. That was *not* good news. 'And Frankie.' Why was she here so early? 'She's been doing an amazing job getting the props sorted nice and early. Oh, and someone I didn't recognize.' Singed Simon wrinkled his nose. 'A lady. Who said something about . . . "the true meaning of art is in perception" and "the parking here is very tight".'

Oh, my Shakespearean sonnets! That sounded like Agatha all over!

My nerves switched to excited butterflies. We really might be able to switch bodies before the play *and* LOLCon!

'And, er, which way did this lady go?'

The millisecond Singed Simon pointed I sprinted off, his shouts of 'The loose carpet is a trip hazard' echoing behind me. I sped along the corridors, scanning every doorway. My heart was thumping, and it wasn't just the twenty-two seconds of running. Because on the final door I saw *exactly* what I'd hoped for. I couldn't help but punch the air.

HG PRODUCTIONS:

A CUT ABOVE THE REST

I'd done it! I'd found Agatha – all on my own.

Hello, normal life, I've missed you!

I knocked as hard as I could.

But . . .

There was no answer.

I knocked again. Even harder.

Not again! This couldn't be happening!

I gripped the handle and turned it. But this time it opened. Phew.

Relief flooded through me. And even more so when I saw what was in the room. All of Agatha's things – her chairs, mirrors, brushes, pictures, everything dotted around the place. To anyone else this would have looked like an organized hairdresser's, but to me this looked like pure heaven.

But ... one problem. One large problem. There was no actual sign of Agatha. The only evidence she'd been here was a steaming cup of the tea, which smelt as delicious as the one I'd had in her salon, and a massive bunch of flowers. I dared not sniff them in case they turned me into a guinea pig or something.

But there *was* a card in them. With two words on the envelope I knew very well: *Lily Mavers*.

Checking the door was closed, I took out the card.

> *Good luck today.*
> *May you bring the true essence of what it*
> *is to not just act as someone,*
> *but to understand them.*
> *And if you do?*
> *Expect to see me later.*
> *A xx*

I read it again. And again. Then out loud. Then very slowly.
But whatever way I read it, it made the typical amount of
Agatha sense – not a lot.

But 'expect to see me later' was *surely* a good sign? I HAD
to think positive. A swap was in sight. I grabbed the flowers
and headed out, ringing Erin to tell her the good-ish-bad-ish
news. She didn't pick up, so I messaged instead.

> Me: The eagle has landed!!!
>
> Me: As in HG is here . . . Somewhere. 😬
>
> Erin: Good work Lil!!! Go you figuring it all out 🦢 🦢

Wow – my sister was definitely nervous. She never gave me
compliments unless they were tactical for our parents to hear.
I sent her a picture of the door sign and the note.

> Erin: Hmmmm 'see me later'?! She does mean
> before the play right?!
>
> Me: I hope she means in the next ten mins!
>
> Me: How are things your end?
>
> Erin: 😬
>
> Erin: There are even more people here than at
> Much Ado About Something!

Only my sister could be surprised about this. I wandered
along the empty corridor, sort of hoping to see Agatha just
walking about.

Me: You're going to be great. I'll be watching
when I can!
Erin: 👌

It was 10.40 a.m. which meant twenty minutes till the livestream
interviews kicked off. And also probably time to admit my hope
of swapping back before then was almost at zilch, along with my
chances of getting on TheNicReport. But . . . I wasn't giving up
until Nic said it was over. And then I'd said 'are you sure?'. And
then she'd confirmed in writing it definitely was.

Me: Get back as quick as you can. Mrs Saddler is 💀
(but in a more dramatic way)

My sister had sorted that Frankie would set up all the props
and tell Mrs Saddler that Lily was doing all the carrying
from the van, which was why she wasn't around backstage.
Then when my sister got here, Frankie could take a break
while Erin double-checked all the props were in order (and
our backup plan – that her prompts on them had survived).
Once that was done Erin and I could track Agatha down
and finally get back in the right bodies.

Although if not . . .

The full horror of it hit me so hard I grabbed the nearest
thing for support.

A waist-height gargoyle.

It would be . . .

Me. In this theatre. On stage. Acting. In front of everyone. Including Chinyere Okafor.

Nope. Could. Not. Deal.

Maybe I should focus on something else. Like Micha.

I began to type.

> Me: I think you'll be setting off for the exam soon.
> Me: so sending you all the luck and periodic
> table thoughts
> Me: And remember, your brian is the best brian
> there is. 🐭

I'd once typed 'brain' wrong and now we always said it. I just wished there was something more me or my sister could have done. Erin had told me that Micha's parents had done exactly what she thought when they'd got Mr Sharma's letter – said football would be off until she got back into the top set.

It was all such a mess.

With no sign of Agatha I headed to the dressing room marked 'Principle Cast'. Maybe she'd put in an appearance with the hair and make-up team? But as I leant my flowers up in the empty room, rereading her note, I heard footsteps.

'Oh, hi, stranger.' It was Frankie. She was dressed all in black. 'Can't believe the big day's finally here! How are you doing?'

'Y'know.' *Freaking out about being stuck as my older sister for ever! Not wanting to sniff flowers in case I turn into a guinea*

257

pig! 'Getting there. Just hoping for something … magical to happen.'

She nodded as if she understood, but I very much doubted she'd ever swapped skeletons with Nic.

'Fair enough. Guess it doesn't get any bigger for you. So good luck!' She slapped her hand over her mouth. 'Oh, soz, is that bad luck?'

'Only if you believe in that kind of thing, so I'll take it.' I smiled, which seemed to annoy her. I really couldn't work her out.

'At least you don't have to worry about your props.' She patted the side of her nose with her finger. 'I've been sorting them all morning so Mrs Saddler won't suss that Lily's late.'

'Thanks, Frankie.' I meant it. 'From both of us. Do you need a hand?'

'No. You do you boo. It's a big day.'

Her walkie-talkie crackled.

'*Simon to Frankie!*' Singed Simon's voice boomed out. '*We need to move the fake olive tree in five.*'

And with a, 'COMING!' to him and an, 'XOXO!' to me Frankie ran off.

Which meant it was time to face my fate.

Time to do what thousands of other people had just started to do.

Watch my sister live and unleashed on TheNicReport.

CHAPTER TWENTY-SIX

If I was hoping that *seeing* it happen would be less stressful than waiting to for it to happen, I was mistaken.

Fifteen minutes into Erin's interviews the highlights already included:

- Erin calling my favourite creator, HollyHuman, MollyLooman.
- Erin saying to a very confused KingKoalaFiguresItOut. 'Don't worry, I'm on mute so no one can hear. If you need a nervous wee go have one! I just did!' Followed by: 'Why is there a microphone symbol? Are we not on mute? Everyone heard this, didn't they?' Then: 'My dad loves you by the way!' and the video cutting.
- Erin introducing her backstage tour by saying, 'Hi. People call me Lily. Because that is my name. That my mum and dad gave me.'

- And when one of the Pham Sisters asked if she was 'vibed to have got so close to King Chase' my sister said, 'Who?' and then, 'Oh yes, the one with great dry ice. Who I'm not allowed to say needs a haircut.'

I took a moment to respectfully mourn any hopes of Nic wanting me on her team. But I knew how hard Erin had tried so I couldn't be cross. Just disappointed.

Oh jeez. I sounded like Mum. Still, the one good thing was there was no sign of any special guest, which meant no sign of Erin doing anything even worse with Chase than what had happened at his concert. So with cast filling up the dressing room, I stopped watching and got back to my mission – tracking down Agatha.

But as I hurried out, Mrs Saddler grabbed me to go through a scene with Harley. And by the time we'd finished that, it was one p.m. And I still hadn't found Agatha. At least Erin would be here any second. I was sure together we'd be able to find the Hairy Godmother – and if not, we'd urgently need to do the backup plan of running through Titania's lines and preparing for the worst.

But an hour later everyone had arrived, *except* my sister.

Why wasn't she picking up her phone?!

'ALL CAST AND CREW TO THE AUDITORIUM.'

Mrs Saddler's voice boomed round the venue over the speakers and on all the crew's walkie-talkies. With a growing sense of dread I headed to the stage.

Although … wait?!

Who was that in the foyer?

Was the lady rummaging through her bag in a hat wearing … dungarees?! And a stripy top?!

Finally!

I ran at the Hairy Godmother like the wind!

'Agatha!' I shouted, leaping right in front of her (and a little bit on her). She jumped so hard she threw her cup of coffee in the air.

'I'm sorry, do I know you?' a very confused, very blonde and very covered in coffee woman asked. My apology took so long I was five minutes late for Mrs Saddler.

In a mad dash, I burst through the big doors marked CIRCLE SEATING. But when I saw the stage for the first time I stopped dead. The auditorium was *huge*. There must be … I tried to count … one hundred … two hundred … three hundred … whatever hundred too many seats! The stage was draped in red velvet curtains and looked like something from the movies.

How on earth could anyone be brave enough to step out there and perform?

In front of *all* these people?

Mrs Saddler strode on to the stage, a light shining on her as she looked down at us all. She looked like an angel. A really scary angel wearing enough material for five people. She billowed dramatically.

I slid into one of the red velvet chairs next to Lou, waved

hi to Harley and squeezed out the last drops of coffee from my sleeve. Surely Erin would sneak in any second?

'Now . . .' Mrs Saddler's clap echoed round the huge space. She inhaled with her eyes closed. 'And *that's* why we *love* the *theee-a-terrr*.' She was in her element. 'A few moments ago a very interesting lady said something I wish to share.' *Oh, here we go.* '"We can't truly walk in another's shoes until we've tried wearing their socks."'

Pardon?! Was Mrs Saddler quoting Agatha?! She must be here! I leapt up and scanned the room.

'Erin! Seats please.' Blushing, I sat back down. But my heart was racing. The Hairy Godmother was nearby! 'As I was saying. She couldn't be more right. Tonight isn't just about existing in the bodies of these amazing creations of Shakespeare, it's about truly becooommminnng them. So. Do. We. Think. We. Can. Do. That?' Mrs Saddler clapped between every word. 'I said, DO WE THINK WE CAN DO THAT?'

We all replied with a shaky, 'Yes.' Guess I wasn't the only nervous one.

'*Good.* Because we can't have a *single* thing go wrong in front of the queen of youth drama, CHINYERE OKAFOR HERSELF!' Well that was the opposite of calming. Mrs Saddler then paced about finishing her 'quick rallying speech' (which took another twenty-five minutes). By the time she stopped we only had an hour before curtain-up. I raced to hair and make-up.

Where was Erin?!

I was really starting to panic. Especially as the hairdresser turned out not to be Agatha, but Anita from Anita Haircut and when I optimistically asked her about her feelings on socks, all she said was they were good for mopping up blood. And told me to stop moving or it wouldn't be her fault if she stuck a hairpin in my eye.

Where was Agatha?!

And where was my sister?!

In desperation I headed back up to the auditorium. I pushed the heavy door open and peeked in. So. Many. People.

This was really happening. Mum and Dad were already in the front row, two empty seats next to them: Micha's and Ben's. Oh no. Had they both given up on us?

When Dad spotted me he blew me a shower of kisses and Mum mouthed, 'GO, YOU!' My stomach clenched with guilt at how disappointed they were about to be unless I managed to find the world's most elusive hairdresser.

'ERIN.' Mrs Saddler's voice thundered down the corridor. I spun round, the door slamming. 'What did I say? No letting the audience see you in full dress! AND WHERE IS THAT SISTER OF YOURS?'

Uh-oh, the one question I really didn't want.

'I, umm, think she was doing a final sweep of the van to make sure the props were A-okay. She's doing so much it's tricky to pin her down.'

'That's what Frances said.' Mrs Saddler glared at me

so hard it was as if she was trying to dredge the truth up from my soul. It *almost* worked. 'But you tell your sister, even if Lupita Nyong'o and Kate Winslet themselves had decided to take her for a pre-show chat, that would *still* not be a good enough reason for being late.' She swallowed. 'UNDERSTOOD?'

I thought I got what she was subtly hinting at, so as Mrs Saddler marched me back to the dressing room, barking on about meeting someone important, I messaged my sister again. It didn't make any sense. Why wasn't she sticking to our plan?!

> Me: TO BE CLEaR I AM NOT eXAGGERating
> IF YOU DON'T GET HER EIN THE NEXT 10
> MINS THEREIS EVERY CHANCE MRS S MIGHT
> KILL ME!!!!

But my messages were still being delivered, and not read. What could be more important than being here? My dreams were over, but this was the last chance at hers!

Feeling more hopeless than ever, I headed to my spot in the dressing room just as a confident, calm voice broke through the excited chatter.

'Hi, everyone.' The room fell instantly silent. 'I wanted to say break a leg.'

Oh my actual Shakespearean ruff! It was Chinyere Okafor. In the flesh!

I sat bolt upright. Seeing her felt almost as unreal as sighting Chase! I'd heard *so* much about her and she was even cooler in real life. No wonder Erin was obsessed!

Mrs Saddler was standing next to her grinning like the dramatic cat that had got the dramatic cream.

Chinyere looked round the room with a dazzling smile, which only got bigger when she saw ... me.

Why. Was. She. Walking. In. My. Direction?!

I urgently tried to bend my 'about to cry' face into an 'about to deliver an award-winning performance' face.

Do not say anything weird, Lily!

Make Erin proud.

In fact ... maybe just don't say anything, to be on the safe side!

'So you must be Erin.' I nodded sheepishly (although, tbf, I had no idea how sheep nodded). 'I've heard a lot about you.' Chinyere put her hand out. Even that was perfect – bangles jangled round her wrist and each nail was manicured with a rainbow polish. I felt a fraud even touching such a hand.

'I'veheardalot aboutyoutoo. Allgoodthings.' I was so nervous my words smooshed. 'The bactually.' *Nope, Lily. That wasn't a word.* 'I meant *best actually.*'

Chinyere smiled. Mrs Saddler did not. 'Well, as long as it was *bactually* then that's all good.' I grinned. Erin was right – Chinyere was amazing. 'Now I won't keep you, I know you'll be getting in the zone, but I wanted you to know that . . .' She lowered her voice. 'After everything I've heard you're *definitely* someone I'll be keeping a close eye on tonight.'

Well, that was petrifying.

'Oh great,' I lied, for the sake of my sister. The truth was I'd prefer if she told me she was using binoculars from at least two miles away. With ear plugs too.

'Your parents are coming?' Chinyere raised an eyebrow. 'If I wanted to grab them for a word?'

CODE RED! My sister had warned me that this might happen but only if she had Erin in mind for a scholarship!

'Th-they are.' This was the best-worst news ever. 'Front row. Although be warned, my dad doesn't know the definition of "too much cheering".'

Mrs Saddler pursed her lips. 'Erin is not exaggerating. Her father was once removed from a carol concert . . . over excessive use of an air horn.'

Weird – no one had told me about that, although it did explain why Erin was allowed two puddings that night, no questions asked, and why there was an air horn locked in a drawer that only Mum had the key to.

With a final 'break a leg' (and Mrs Saddler adding, 'Have a toilet break if you need one. We alllll remember what happened with Caroline. These costumes can be very hard to get out of,') they headed out.

But this time, instead of filling with chatter, the room stayed silent. The big moment was here.

After months of prep (well, days for me), this was happening.

My sister had totally disappeared and left me in the lurch but I could do this . . . I *had* to do this.

I could be a great Titania. Couldn't I?!

I picked up the script Erin had made me, even though it felt as if I was looking at the words for the first time. *C'mon, brain, don't empty now! I've fed you, and let you watch* World's Funniest Dogs *for a treat. Don't fail me now!*

'Call time for Lou, Mark, Jade, Petra. Can you come to the stage?' Frankie smiled at the roomful of nervous faces. 'And the rest of you, all I can really say is . . . Don't mess it up.'

I hugged Lou and stared out of the door, willing Erin to walk past it.

'*PLEASE TAKE YOUR SEATS,*' the tannoy blared out, '*THE PERFORMANCE IS ABOUT TO BEGIN.*'

I rang Erin for the hundredth time, but still no answer.

This was ridiculous.

I had to focus.

Had to.

Although I wonder how Micha's exam went? I hadn't heard anything.

No. Come on, Lily! Focus! But my phone lit up.

Erin?! Micha?!

> Nic: Thanks for going. Shame it didn't work out.
> And sorry Chase didn't come through. Hope the
> play goes better x

Ouch. Worst timing ever.

Confirmation my TheNicReport dream was over. I knew it would have been a miracle for it to have gone any other way, but reading it still stung.

I didn't have time to dwell though, I had to get back to my script.

Erin had tried for me, and now it was my turn. I stared at my lines. But five minutes passed and all I'd achieved was blinking.

C'mon, Lily.

Just.

Look.

At.

Your.

Lines.

And.

Concentrate.

That was the plan – until my phone buzzed again.

> Frankie: Hey Lil. I saw what happened at LOLCon 😬
> But I just pulled a favour!!! Nic says she MIGHT
> have something for you after all! She's in the props
> van for a few mins now if you want to chat about it!
> Quick! XOXO

What, what, *what?* This was *huge!*

After everything, Frankie was helping me out? She really must have forgiven me!

I screen-grabbed the messages and sent them to my sister. Could she find a way to squeeze in meeting Nic? It would mean the world. But the play was starting any second, and I had no idea where she was.

'Erin?'

I screeched as a hand touched my shoulder.

Ben?! How did he get in here?!

'What are you doing here?' I didn't mean to sound so shocked. And was it weird I noticed he hadn't called me babe?

'Just wanted to say break a leg.' I waited for something weird like a good luck rock. 'Oh and here.' He pulled out a bag. *Phew.* He did have something. He *did* still like my sister. 'Can you give this to Lily when you see her?' *Lily? He got something for . . . me?* 'It was for her birthday, but with the whole broken foot thing . . .'

'Bruised bone.' I didn't mean to correct him. It was just habit.

'That, yeah. Well, I forgot. So I thought you could give it to her tonight. I know she was nervous about the play.' He shrugged. 'She doesn't need to know it's from me.'

Well, I hadn't been expecting this! I'd never thought Ben liked me, let alone was so thoughtful.

'Can I?' I asked as I peeked in the bag. It was a little wooden sign: KNOCK OR YOU MIGHT END UP IN MY NEXT ARTICLE.

'Thought she could put it up when she's working on her

blog.' Ben's cheeks flushed. 'Or is she going to think I'm even more of a banana?' He clamped his hand to his mouth. 'Sorry, not that word. I meant . . . nerd?'

I was almost speechless.

But not quite.

'She's going to *love* it. I know she will. Thank you. From both of us.' He looked genuinely happy. 'And I promise you she doesn't think you're a bana . . . you know what.' Maybe she used to, but maybe she realized she'd been wrong.

'*PLEASE TAKE YOUR SEATS AND TURN ALL PHONES OFF.*'

'Better dash.' Ben pointed at the speaker. 'You're going to be awesome. And after – are we okay to talk about the thing?'

'Thing?' But he was already heading towards the door.

'Yup. You and me. Taking a break?'

Sorry, was Erin's boyfriend really telling her he wanted to break up before the biggest night of her life?

But my failure to answer seemed to be interpreted as a yes and Ben disappeared.

What little focus I'd mustered disappeared into a corner for a little cry.

'*THE PERFORMANCE IS STARTING.*'

Finally a sense of total calm washed over me.

The play was starting.

We'd failed to find Agatha.

I was trapped in Erin's body.

She'd gone missing.

Her boyfriend was going to dump her.

My best friend was ignoring me.

And there was *nothing* I could do about it.

Turns out, the wave of calm had actually been a massive tsunami of sheer terror. As the audience clapped for the end of the scene before mine, I doubted I could even remember how to walk.

Singed Simon scurried behind the curtain and carried our props into place. Wasn't that my sister's job? Or even Frankie's? WHERE WERE THEY?! Thank goodness Erin had stuck all the prompts on them – they were my only way through this nightmare.

'You've got this,' Harley said confidently, giving me a hug. I was freaking out so much even a Harley hug didn't register. I blinked at him to imply 'you too' but he gave me a concerned look back as if he thought I had wig fluff in my eye.

He peered through the wings. 'Woah, it's packed. This is going to be *epic*.'

It was going to be *petrifying*.

But the curtain was coming up.

And Harley was walking out. I needed to follow him.

But I couldn't move! And my breathing was so fast I was technically panting. I was sure Titania never panted!

I scanned around to see if there were any loose floorboards I could plummet through, but as I did I caught a glimpse of someone in the wings on the other side of the stage. My sister. *Finally!*

I'd never seen her look so sweaty. Her hair was all over the place and her clothes were a scruffy mess. Wow – for the first time she really *did* look like me. When she saw me she stopped, grinned and gave me the biggest thumbs up, before running straight off.

Seeing her was *just* what I needed.

Time to face my fear. To do it for my sister.

With a deep breath, I stepped out.

The good news? Not a *single* thing went wrong.

The bad news? *Every* single thing went wrong.

CHAPTER TWENTY-SEVEN

The first thing I spotted was Dad's smiling face. Well, I didn't technically spot it – I couldn't miss it as he yelled, 'That's my girl!' and then, 'And my other girl backstage!' He did always like things to be fair.

I couldn't help but smile, which was a problem as Titania was meant to be in a queen-like serious mood.

Focus, Lily.

There were *so* many eyes on me. Literally hundreds. Maybe thousands? And there was Chinyere!

I had to calm down.

Getting myself together, I concentrated on doing my best acting to look cross at Harley as he strode around the stage. The audience were loving him. *Maybe* this could go okay?

I lined up my opening words in my head.

What, jealous Oberon! Fairies, skip hence.

Yes, that was it!

Harley had finished his line. My moment had come.

Mrs Saddler always nagged me that confidence and power were at the heart of my character. So I took a deep breath to belt out my first line more confidently and powerfully than *ever* before.

'JOT, EARLESS OBERON. SCARIES, HIP FENCE!'

There were actual laughs. I was aiming for impressed gasps! Not laughs. And a lady in the second row was full-on sniggering! Cockapoo Karen?! She was in the same row as PJ and Nic's dad (who actually did look like my mum after all!).

No, Lily. Not the point! FOCUS!

But my first line had vanished from my head!

'Er, one sec.' Not the most fairy-queen choice of words. But this was like one of those nightmares where you were on stage, everyone staring at you, with no clue what to say – but in real life. And in my sister's body.

I *had* to keep calm. Just look at the fake toadstool Erin had pinned the first prompt on. With relief I spotted it.

And there was . . . nothing.

My blood ran cold.

'Try again,' Harley hissed, his mouth not moving.

Where has my prompt gone? Where have ANY of the prompts gone?!

I turned to the wings, desperate to spot Erin, but all I saw was Mrs Saddler waving her arms so much one of her sleeves got tangled in a large fern.

The audience were starting to make awkward murmurs.

I dared not look at Chinyere.

But someone did help. Someone in the last seat in the front row who I *swore* hadn't been there seconds ago. And that someone mouthed the three first words I needed to get me started again.

Agatha.

She was here! She was watching!

I wanted to yell, 'ERIN, THE HAIRY GODMOTHER IS HERE!' but decided that would be the final straw for Chinyere, and Mrs Saddler might physically attack me with a prop sword, so instead I said the line she'd given me.

'What, jealous Oberon! Fairies, skip hence.'

There were actual sighs of relief from the audience, and Mum lifted her head out of her hands. Spurred on by seeing Agatha, I managed to get my next few lines out and waited for Harley to finish his bit while I reached for my drawstring canvas bag, ready to pull my apple out. The apple Mrs Saddler told me I had to bite 'mysteriously'. How a bite could be mysterious I still had no idea, but it happened at the end of my first big speech and I was going to give it my best shot. And by some miracle, my speech was going okay!

'And for her sake I will not part with . . .'

Yes! Only one word left! *Him*. And even I could remember that. I reached into the bag and pulled out the apple triumphantly. But my last word never came out.

It couldn't!

I was too shocked.

Which was why instead of 'I will not part with *him*' I actually said – well, *shouted* . . .

'I will not part with . . .' Horrified pause as I realized what I had in my hand. 'A BANANA!'

Where was the apple we'd always rehearsed with?!

There was a rustle of confusion at this unexpected fruity outburst. I couldn't blame them. Could I style it out?

'For what a fine banana specimen it is.' I bit it. Mysteriously.

I have never been more grateful for signs that said NO CAMERAS. Luckily Harley saved the rest of the scene as I chewed (mysteriously). It was fair to say Chinyere looked . . . surprised. But what was going on?!

Erin's notes that we'd checked last night had gone – and the props had changed since rehearsal.

And a banana of all things! Although maybe that was just bad luck. Hardly anyone outside the family knew my sister was petrified of them. Well, hardly anyone except . . .

And suddenly lots of things fell into place.

As they did, I forgot to be so worried about the play. And as the first half went on, the words started to come back to me. Sure, I did get my finger stuck in one of my ringlets and I *might* have been hit by three stress hiccups when I was meant to be 'sleeping gracefully', but I got through it.

Still, I couldn't have been more relieved than when the curtain came down for the interval. I tried to peek through the curtain to watch where Agatha went, but she'd already disappeared, so instead I raced to get my sister and take her to the HG Productions room. But Erin was nowhere to be found. And there was no sign of Frankie either.

Today was *not* going to plan. It was a relief when I finally found a familiar face. 'Have you seen my sister?'

Singed Simon wrinkled his nose. 'Kind of. She's got a lot on her plate right now.'

'Well, yes, but where exactly is that plate?'

'At this exact moment?' He shrugged. 'No idea ...'

But maybe he could help with something else. My theory.

'Weird question, but I don't suppose you put that banana in the canvas bag?'

Singed Simon looked horrified. 'Do you *really* think I would have put such a slip hazard on stage?'

He had a point. So, apologizing, I left him to prep for the second half and ran about asking everyone if they'd seen Erin. Not even Lou had seen her – but at least I got to tell her what an awesome job she was doing. I tried the last place I could think of. The toilets.

'Lil?' I called out to the one closed cubicle door. 'Lilyyyyyyy?'

Still felt weird shouting my own name.

'One sec,' a voice called back. But it was Nic. I didn't know she was still here?

When she saw me, her face lit up. 'Can I just say a big thank you? As in *big*. For making this thing a whole lot more entertaining.'

Entertaining. Not exactly the impressing-Chinyere-Okafor-acting-gold I was going for.

'Do you think it's going . . . okay?' I didn't know she'd been watching, but any reassurance would be good.

'Definitely. Although maybe get someone to double-check your dress. I'm not sure Titania's meant to have her fairy train tucked into her pants.'

So *that* was why a mum had been shielding the eyes of the small child beside her.

'Advice taken. If it happens again maybe you could, I dunno . . . gesture?'

Nic grinned. 'No probs. If you see a phone torch waving, get offstage *stat*.'

I laughed. Despite everything going about as badly as it could, at least I was nearer to this entire nightmare being over.

'I hope it's okay to ask.' Nic finished washing her hands. 'But is your sister all right? I was hoping to bump into her.'

'Er . . .' *How to answer.* 'I think it's fair to say she's going through a bit of a rough patch.'

Nic leant back against one of the sinks.

'I'm gutted she didn't make it on to TheNicReport team. But she really didn't seem herself at LOLCon earlier.' Nic sighed. 'Probably my fault for asking her to cover it at such late notice—'

'No,' I butted in, boosted by the fact Nic seemed genuinely disappointed I'd messed up. 'She was *so* happy you did. She loved that you trusted her with it – and if this had come at *any* other time you would have seen a really different Lily in action.'

Nic nodded slowly.

'Yeah, you're probably right. She's definitely unique!' She dried her hands on her jeans. 'I love the angles she takes on her blog. The funny stuff is great, but the personal stuff really hits different.'

And despite knowing it hadn't worked out, a smile was creeping on to my face. Nic thinking my writing was worth reading was the best compliment I could ask for. Although, if Nic was hoping to bump into my sister, did that mean Erin hadn't managed to do what Frankie suggested and see Nic in the props van earlier?

'So did you not see Lily before the play then?'

Nic shook her head as if she didn't have a clue what I was talking about.

'Nope, not me. I was at LOLCon right up to the start.' She winced. 'In fact, just after. Mrs Saddler did naaaat look happy about me sneaking in.'

So Nic wasn't with Frankie before the play?

Things were getting more alarming than Dad's latest ribbon gymnastics routine.

I wasn't sure what was going on, but I had a bad feeling that if I didn't figure it out before the end of the interval, things might be about to get even worse.

CHAPTER TWENTY-EIGHT

I pushed through the people chatting in the packed corridors as if my life depended on it. Because it did. Agatha's clue had said this was our final chance, and it really felt like the last shot to stop everything going wrong.

I just had to hope Erin had the same idea and was heading to the same place.

Yes, I kept tripping over my dress (how fairy queens ever did anything in a hurry I did not know), and yes, I did stop and do a double take at my parents laughing with Mr Sharma as if it were fine to hang out with teachers, but I still got there in record time.

HG PRODUCTIONS

At least the sign hadn't gone.

Agatha was still here. Somewhere.

As one hand knocked the door, and the other rang my

sister, I stared out of the huge floor-to-ceiling windows that stretched the whole length of this side of the building. The car park below was quiet with everyone still inside LOLCon. Up here I had a perfect view of the secret entrance just for the influencers. A big black coach had pulled up by the door, its hazard lights flashing, with the driver stretching his legs outside.

Ring, ring.

Why wasn't my sister picking up?!

Ring, ring.

'You called?' And there she was. Wrong body, but same unflappable sister. She clicked REJECT. 'Figured we could speak in person.'

What should I start with? Where had she been? What really happened at LOLCon? Had she got news from Micha? Did she see Chase? How much would she murder me if Ben broke up with her? Would she forgive me for how badly I'd done in front of Chinyere Okafor?

But all of the questions bundled together into one thing. A point at the door.

'Good work. Guess you've tried this.' As Erin rattled the handle, I noticed she had a plaster on her finger.

'You okay?' I gestured at it.

'I would be if this door would open!' She rattled the handle again, but the door was firmly locked.

I paced over to the window. 'Agatha was in the audience. Did you see her?'

Erin shook her head. Her hair was a mess, her clothes were untucked and she had a mysterious stain on her top. I'd never been more proud. 'I did see you though.' Uh-oh. But instead of pointing out I was doing worse than any Titania in the history of Titanias, Erin put her arm round me. 'I think you're doing an awesome job. Thank you.'

I squeezed her right back. 'You did great at LOLCon too.'

But as she smiled, behind her I saw someone coming out of the LOLCon venue.

WAS THAT CHASE?!

I pushed my face against the glass.

Oh. My. Hairy. Godmothers.

It was! And he was chatting to the driver of the coach! Was that his tour bus?

'L . . .' My voice finally gave up. 'L . . . look.'

Even though I was in the wrong body, and had shouted about bananas in front of hundreds of people, this was somehow still the weirdest thing to happen all day! If I ran down the stairs and through the fire exit I would literally be hanging out with Chase Cheney.

A thought hit me. 'I could speak to him?'

Get that genuine scoop I'd dreamed of!

'Get something to change Nic's mind?' Erin grinned. 'You should go.'

Wow. My sister really did care about my blog after all!

But I had only ten minutes till I needed to be back on stage.

And we still hadn't found Agatha.

'But what about . . .' I looked at the door.

'I'll try to open it while you're gone. Remind Chase you're dry ice girl's sister. And be as quick as you can. I don't want to get swapped back into Singed Simon by accident.'

I gathered up my dress, ready to sprint like Titania had never sprinted before.

'I'll be four minutes. Less than.'

I was already off, as Erin shouted after me. 'And say bye to Chinyere while you're there!'

What did that mean?

But as I raced outside I understood. The only other person in this sectioned-off car park was Chinyere, coat on, bag on her shoulder, walking to her car. She'd seen enough and was going. I hadn't even impressed her enough to make her want to stay for the second half. She'd made up her mind without ever seeing the real Erin in action.

This sucked.

But as the fresh air filled my lungs, for the first time since being in the wrong body, I knew exactly what to do.

'Well, that was quick.' Erin was on her hands and knees peering through the tiny keyhole into the Hairy Godmother's room. I couldn't speak properly I was panting so hard.

'Nooo.' *Gasp.* 'Joy?'

'Nope. No answer. No key. No nothing.'

What were we missing?

'FIVE MINUTES UNTIL CURTAIN-UP FOR THE SECOND HALF.'

The announcements weren't exactly helping me not freak out.

But a voice I recognized interrupted us.

'Well, there you are ...' Along with Agatha's, it was the voice I most wanted to hear. I scrambled to my feet.

'Micha?!' I hadn't seen her look this happy in weeks. 'How did it go?'

She gave me the biggest grin. 'Didn't Lil say?'

Erin stopped trying to use a hairgrip to open the lock and looked up. 'I was just about to, but you do the honours.'

Micha pulled a piece of paper out of her pocket. 'Well, thanks to the most awesome revision session earlier.' She was bouncing from foot to foot. 'And a brainiac friend who helped me last-minute rewrite my whoooole chemistry assignment I ... well ... I smashed it!' She unfolded the paper. 'Over ninety per cent in both!'

Forget being in the wrong body, I couldn't help it. I hugged Micha so hard. So *so* hard.

'BEST NEWS EVERRRRRR!' I hugged her again. 'Chemistry genius *and* footballing goddess, huh!' Micha blushed, embarrassed at the praise. But ... what did she mean about the last-minute session? And who was this chemistry whizz friend? I couldn't help but feel a twinge of jealousy. 'Pretty cool of your friend. Whoever that was.'

Micha tapped my sister's foot with her shoe.

'I know we agreed not to tell but I think we can trust Erin?'

Wait. Did my sister just give me a tiny grin?!

Micha was too pumped to wait for her to answer. 'Please don't be mad and don't tell *anyone*, not even Ben, buuuuut –' she tugged at her twist pigtails in excitement – 'as a surprise Lily ran straight from LOLCon to meet me at school. Apparently Mrs Saddler was raging!' Mich tried to grimace but was smiling too hard to pull it off. 'Your sister risked life and limb to help me out! If I play for England one day, it'll alllll be because of her.'

So Erin had jeopardized the play, the thing she cared most about, to help my best friend. To help me.

Erin was a *legend*!

It was too much. I dropped to the floor and gave my sister the biggest hug.

'Promise I'm not mad.' I squeezed her *so* tight. 'I'm the opposite. Best. Sister. Ever.'

My words came out like a human accordion as Micha piled on top.

We carried on hugging and cheering in one big happy heap. It was so nice to be celebrating my best friend's good news with her. Although ... I suddenly thought of an even *better* way for Micha to celebrate.

'Okay, don't freak out but ...' I stood up. 'I think there's someone else who would love to celebrate your amazingness.' I pointed down to the car park. 'And ... he's right there.'

Micha opened her mouth. And shut it. And pressed her

face against the glass which steamed up immediately as she let out the longest, 'Whaaaaaaaaaaaaaaaaaaaaaat?'

My sister put her hand on Micha's arm. 'I know, *right*.' Erin glanced at me. 'St and *unning*!' Micha was too shocked to reply. 'We have to get back to the play but you should definitely go. For the both of us!'

And after waiting to get her speech back, then double-checking we wouldn't mind – then triple-checking she wasn't hallucinating – Micha ran off to speak to Chase. Well, it was more a stumble, and she definitely bounced off at least one wall, but it was the general right direction.

Leaving Erin and me.

And the Hairy Godmother's door, which still wasn't budging.

My sister rested her forehead against it.

'Guess whatever we were supposed to do, we failed.'

'Guess we did.' I linked my arm through hers. Seeing Micha happy again had almost made me forget how bad things were. But standing in the now empty corridor with my sister there was no escaping them. 'I'm really sorry, sis. I promised I tried.'

'You did great.' She dropped her head on to my shoulder. 'Especially with all the problems.'

So my sister had noticed the missing prompts and been weirded out by the banana swap too?

'Look –' I wonder if she had the same theory as me – 'I know you'll say I'm wrong, but I've got a theory. I think it might have something to do with ... Frankie?'

Erin's mouth scrunched. 'Lil, I *know* exactly who it was . . .'
Of course Erin would be one step ahead. She pulled out a
car key from her pocket and dangled it in front of me. 'And
why.' She winked. 'But don't worry, I've got the second half
back under control.'

'*PLEASE TAKE YOUR SEATS. THE SECOND HALF
IS ABOUT TO COMMENCE.*'

Erin's explanation would have to wait.

It was time for me to say the thing that neither of us
wanted to admit.

'It's time to head back, isn't it?'

The dream was over. We'd had our last chance . . . and
we'd blown it.

Still, at least we had the sight of Micha outside getting the
biggest hug from Chase. Was she laughing? Or crying? Or . . .
fainting? It looked like all three.

My sister laughed softly. 'Well, at least it worked out for
someone. How did it go by the way? With Chase?'

Oh yeah. *That.* I hadn't even told her. I gave the HG
PRODUCTION sign one last look before I turned to walk
down the corridor.

'I didn't see him.'

She looked confused.

'But you ran off?'

'Uh-huh. But when I got down there I went to speak to
Chinyere instead. I told her part of Mrs Saddler's acting
development was to handle unexpected surprises. And the

banana had been mine. And … well … she agreed to stay for the second half.'

Erin's eyes lit up. 'You did that for me?'

'You would have done the same for me, sis.'

And as I said it, something happened that neither of us expected.

There was a click of a lock opening behind us.

And when we turned round there was a lady standing in the corridor, a smile on her face, arms out wide.

Agatha.

'Erin. Lily. I've been expecting you.'

CHAPTER TWENTY-NINE

TINKLE DING!

Despite making no noise before, the door made the same tinkling chime as the salon we'd walked into almost three weeks ago.

Stepping into Agatha's room was like stepping into another world. I swear it had doubled in size from earlier, and the photos on the walls were now all shots of the first half of the play.

Still, I wasn't surprised.

When we'd first met I thought Agatha had felt magical.

Now I knew she was.

The big clock on her wall showed 5.13 p.m. Less than two minutes before the play started again. So why did her room feel like an oasis of calm?

Unlike us, Agatha looked her normal cool, relaxed self. 'Tea?' was all she said. Not, 'Sorry about transforming your entire bodies, lives and souls,' or even, 'How are you?' Just did we want a hot drink.

We both said yes though.

Agatha sat down on the sofa and gestured for me and Erin to sit down opposite. There were already three steaming, fresh mugs of her delicious tea waiting for us.

'Have we been dying to see you!' I picked one up as Agatha held out a plate of cookies. They were freshly baked. Did her room come with an oven?! 'A *lot* has happened since we last saw you.'

Agatha raised an eyebrow. 'Really?' She sounded surprised. Did she not know that swapping people's lives and leaving them a trail of magical clues could lead to major drama?

I sipped my drink, thanked her for helping me with my line earlier and began to tell her everything about the manic blur of the last few weeks – but by the time I'd swallowed the tea I seemed to have come to the end of my story.

Panicked, I looked up at the clock – it was ticking away yet still said 5.13 p.m.

Although ... Why was I trying to make sense of anything? I should have learnt by now that when the Hairy Godmother was involved, *nothing* made sense.

I took a stress bite of one of the cookies. Delicious.

Luckily, Erin wasn't as easily distracted by biscuits as me. 'Agatha, *please* don't disappear on us this time.'

Her nostrils flared. 'Not after what happened backstage with Chase.'

But Agatha smiled, her perfect red lipstick looking as if it had just been slicked on.

'I remember that day.' Of course she did. It was only a week ago! 'I had plans, but when I saw you arguing I knew it wasn't the right time.' *Wasn't the right time? Please tell me it is now!* 'But you found my message? And followed my paper trail to find me here?'

Followed the newspaper trail, yes.

Erin nodded. 'Well, Lil did. She's been the one who's figured out most things to be honest.'

I swear one of Agatha's eyes twinkled. 'Interesting ... So you *have* been having fun?'

Fun?! *Fun?!* I'd never been so stressed in my life!

'You mean besides being stuck as my sister who fits a billion things into a day and impresses everyone, *all the time*, oh, as I simultaneously watched my own life crumble, my best friend start to hate me, all while panicking I'd never get back into my own body?' I paused for breath. 'Yeah. It's been a breeze really.'

After weeks of bottling it up, it was nice to be able to say it all out loud.

But my sister was chuckling. 'Uh-huh, a *total* walk in the park. Nothing like failing as a friend and being a meme ... twice.' *Twice?* What had happened at LOLCon?! I was *never* looking at the internet again.

'So this fortnight was . . . a success?' Agatha sipped her tea.

My normally composed sister spluttered.

'Noooo! Not at all! I don't know if you know . . .' She trailed off. 'I mean I feel as if you know *everything*, but just in case, I'll fill you in. I messed up Lily's chances to work on TheNicReport, her favourite site.' Erin looked at me. 'Even though I swear it was an accident.'

'I see,' Agatha said.

'The worst thing is if she'd been in the right body today, she would have done an amazing job and definitely got offered a place.'

I wasn't sure I agreed, but I was flattered Erin thought it.

'Thanks, sis. Although please don't blame yourself – you hated it and still really tried.'

Agatha lifted her hand up, her bracelets jingling.

'Lily makes a point.' It was so nice being called the right name for the first time in ages. 'Facing up to the darkest moments is how we truly shine.'

I nodded but I wasn't sure why. I always had the same feeling whenever the Hairy Godmother was around. I felt both incredibly wise – and also as if I didn't have the foggiest what was going on.

'I see.' Erin clearly didn't have a clue either. 'I'm not sure I'd call saying, "Toodleloo kangaroo," to one of the world's biggest influencers "shining" though. Lils, I don't know how you do it!'

'Well, same.' I guess I'd never really understood before how hard Erin had it – it wasn't that she breezed through everything, it was that she never stopped putting effort in. 'Your life is so full on! All those teachers breathing down your neck.' I thought back to the whirlwind of the last two weeks. 'The quiz team. The play. The A grades. Hanging up your clothes. Even having a boyfriend.' I winced. When should I tell her about whole 'taking a break' thing? 'I don't know where you find the time!'

Erin squeezed my knee. She hadn't done that in years. Maybe meeting the Hairy Godmother hadn't been all bad after all? And when I looked up, Agatha was smiling. And our teas had somehow been drunk, and all that was left on the cookie plate was crumbs. How long had we been in here?

I looked at the clock: 5.13 p.m. Still.

'Well.' Agatha leant forward and clasped her hands. 'I must say I've been enjoying the play very much. Lily, you really shone as Erin.' Did she mean Titania? 'And, Erin, you excelled in a test even you couldn't prepare for.' Did she mean helping Micha, or being me? 'I think it's clear you both finally understand what it's like to truly be one another.'

Wait. Did Agatha mean the acting? Or the swap?

She was so confusing!

Erin and I glanced at each other.

Could the switch be about to happen?

But no! Agatha had stood up and was gesturing to the door.

What was she doing?!

'But, Agatha,' my sister protested. 'Our last chance? We

thought if we came to see you today . . .' But it was too late. Somehow we were already at the door. And without knowing what I was doing, my shaky hand was pushing it open, my sister following behind me.

We were heading back out into the corridor.

There were people everywhere again.

And Agatha hadn't swapped us back!

'PLEASE TAKE YOUR SEATS. FIVE MINUTES UNTIL CURTAIN-UP FOR THE SECOND HALF.'

What was going on?

I stepped out of Agatha's room, blinking as the venue lights flickered off and back on. They really needed to sort the electrics out – Singed Simon wouldn't be able to survive three more nights of performances here with such dodgy circuitry. But now wasn't the time to worry about electrics! I had the rest of eternity of being Erin to deal with. I put my hand out, and felt hers in mine.

This was a disaster. But at least we had each other.

And I really needed her, as Ben was striding towards us.

'Babe, I've been looking for you everywhere!' he shouted as he broke into a run. Woah, he was with the whole crew. Micha, my parents, even Mrs Saddler. Which meant I'd just been called 'babe' in front of Mrs Saddler. Lucky I was feeling pretty resilient. 'I just popped out to pick these up.' He waved some train tickets. 'Even better than a lucky rock, hey?' Wow, my mind boggled. 'They're our "Erin's been so great as Titania we're joining my parents on a mini-break" tickets!'

So *that* was the break he meant? PH-EWWW! I sighed so hard I made Mrs Saddler's fringe flap up. 'Come here ... I need to give you a major one of these ...'

And with the relief, and weeks of practising holding in horrified looks, I finally felt I could do it. Make physical contact with Ben.

I opened my arms wide and went in for a big hug. 'Yes, baaaaabe.'

But he didn't give me the big bear hug I expected back – it was more like hugging a postbox. And when I twisted my head, Ben looked ... frightened? Oh well. I carried on anyway. In for an Erin-penny, in for a pound. I only stopped when I remembered I wanted Micha to have her moment too. 'And can I say from one chemistry star student to another, congrats, Micha Ndiaye!'

But Mich was looking at me the same way she did when people put beans *and* tuna in their jacket potato.

'Er, thanks, Lil. Everything okay?'

Why was Micha looking so weird?

Was it the shock of hugging Chase Cheney?

Wait.

What?

'SORRY, WHAT DID YOU SAY?' I shouted so loudly the entire corridor turned round.

Micha looked even more alarmed than Ben.

'I said ... everything okay, Lil?' Micha looked concerned. 'Or would you rather I said "porcupine"?'

But I'd heard right! She'd called me by my name?! My stomach knotted. Could this mean . . .

I slowly turned to my sister – who at the same time turned to me.

The moment of truth.

And the truth was . . . there she was. My big sister. Looking exactly like she should. WAHOOOOO!!! Never had I been happier to see her face! Her perfect, grinning Erin-face.

And with the biggest cheer, we gave each other the world's biggest hug.

We'd done it.

Being back in my own body had never felt so good.

CHAPTER THIRTY

I wouldn't have a clue what I was doing backstage in the second half but who cared? We were back in our right bodies! Micha and I were friends again! And Erin was going to get to show the world, show Chinyere Okafor, how great she really was.

But as Erin and I dashed back to the stage, my sister pushed a car key into my hand. It had the same keyring as Mum's.

'Don't ask. But head to the props van. Say I asked you to get the spare key because we were worried. And hurry.'

My sister wasn't making any sense, but we had just been eating cookies with a time-stopping body-swapping hairdresser, so I figured I should just go with it and darted off on my own. As I ran I pulled my hair out of the braid Erin had it in and tugged it into my normal messy ponytail. That was better!

But when I unlocked the back doors of the van something I wasn't expecting was inside. Something in among all the empty boxes, spare donkey ears and unopened apples.

A very relieved-looking Frankie.

'Finally!' She lunged straight for me and gave me a massive hug. 'I thought no one was going to come till after the curtain went down!'

First a body transformation from a magical hairdresser. Now a Frankie hug. Today was weird indeed. 'Er . . .' I think I was more shocked than her. 'It was Erin who told me to come. She found the spare key in the interval.' I remembered my sister's instructions. 'She was worried about you. We both were . . .' I trailed off.

Frankie laughed awkwardly. 'Well, thank goodness for Erin!' Did she just wince? 'I was worried about me too.'

'You . . . okay?'

'*I guess*. Bored. Cold. But better now . . .' She smoothed down her ponytail, and took the spare key out of my hand, giving it a weird look. 'I really thought I'd picked up the right key, but I must have been in too much of a rush to get the first-aid kit.'

'Did someone hurt themselves?' What had I missed?

And this time Frankie *definitely* winced. 'Your sister actually. She cut her finger.'

It wasn't my imagination. Franke was *definitely* being shifty. I couldn't help but think there was a lot more to this than she was telling me.

I gave her a hand down as she jumped out. Did I recognize those little bits of white paper sticking out of her pocket? They looked *very* much like the prompts Erin had made that had all vanished. Frankie saw me notice them and stuffed her hand into her pocket.

But it was too late. I didn't care what Erin thought, now I had proof Frankie had messed with the props.

How dare she?! She knew how much this performance meant to my sister. She'd said it to me herself! And then been so friendly to me earlier?!

'How's the play been going?' Frankie was trying to move my attention on. But after months of being too scared to stand up to her, I finally felt ready to call her out.

'Not . . . *ideal.*' Maybe I'd start by seeing how she'd react to all the problems. 'There was some unexpected banana drama.' Instead of looking shocked, Frankie just looked at the ground. I *knew* it. It had been her!

It was time for me to tell her I'd figured out her little plan to sabotage the play.

Time to tell her I wouldn't stand for her walking all over me.

'Look, Frankie,' I started. But as she looked back, I didn't see the Frankie who had been making my life a misery. I saw a Frankie who had been stuck in a van for over an hour, a Frankie who knew she'd been rumbled, a Frankie who I hadn't exactly been great to, in my body or my sister's, a Frankie who had her own problems, even if I hadn't seen them before.

'Can I just say . . .' But if I really did want things to pick up for Erin in the second half, was it right for me to start a huge fight – or would it be better to finally put everything behind us? '. . . that I'm really sorry, again. For your phone. And Chase. And just well . . . can we put this term behind us?'

Instead of smirking, Frankie nodded. 'You know what? I

think that sounds like a great idea.' I swear she mumbled something that sounded like a 'sorry'. But I didn't need one. What I needed was for the second half to go well.

The two of us raced back inside and in the nick of time. With Erin's step-by-step plan making it super easy, and Frankie and me both working extra hard, we got the stage ready for the curtain to go up.

And the second half went better than I could have ever wanted, because from the second she stepped on stage, Erin's performance blew everyone away.

Proud sister alert. And the audience looked equally under my sister's spell. She was channelling even more magic than Agatha! Dad kept dabbing tears from his semi-black eye, Mum was taking really unsubtle photos with the iPad hidden on her lap, Ben had unleashed his 'I'm With Titania' T-shirt, and Micha, sitting next to them, was grinning from ear to ear. Agatha looked content back in her seat, and Chinyere Okafor was furiously writing in her notebook. I thought I even saw Mrs Saddler smile. A tiny *dramatic* smile. There really was a first time for everything.

When the curtain fell the crowd *erupted*. I couldn't help it – I ran on stage and gave Erin the biggest hug.

'You were A-MAY-ZING!' I squeezed her so hard I almost knocked her fairy crown off.

'You think?' she asked as if she really didn't know.

'Perfectio. In fact, what's better than perfect?' But I was out of time. The curtain was rising back up. I needed to scarper.

Erin stepped forward, causing the whole crowd to roar (and then join Dad in his unauthorized Mexican wave). Now it wasn't just my family, *everyone* knew my sister was a star – and hopefully she'd start to believe it too.

But instead of soaking up her moment, once the rest of the cast had come out, Erin started a chant of, 'Backstage crew! Backstage crew!' Mum, Dad, Micha and Ben joined in so loudly that soon the whole place was yelling it. I looked a complete mess, and was pretty sure my pen had leaked when I was chewing it, but Frankie and Singed Simon grabbed me and out we went.

As we took a bow, the crowd went wild. But best of all was the front row – Dad had whipped out his air horn (he must have smuggled it out!) and was honking with wild abandon, Mum's free hand was waving around in the air like she just didn't care, and Micha and Ben had climbed on their seats. Mum and Dad seemed just as proud of what I'd done backstage as they were of my sister in her huge role! Maybe they didn't always think Erin was better after all?

Arm in arm with my sister, I looked out. At my best friend who was shouting, 'Brava, Lily!', at Chinyere Okafor who was on her feet for a standing ovation, even Nic cheering as she took photos. Although . . . was Cockapoo Karen yelling something?

I tilted my head to pick it out from all the noise. 'Stand up straight, Frances! Smile!'

Sorry, was she yelling at . . . Frankie?

Nooooooooooooooooo.

Please tell me that wasn't her mum!

Or at least that I was the only one who remembered the cockapoo thing.

'Your mum is Cockapoo Karen?' Singed Simon hissed to Frankie.

'Don't!' Frankie snapped back. 'I *never* want to hear that name again!'

And suddenly it all made sense. The reason Frankie had hated me all term.

My most popular blog piece had compared her mum to a cockapoo. It was meant to be a compliment! I guessed Nic had found it funny – she'd reposted it after all – but Frankie couldn't have done. And she couldn't just ask me to take it down, because then I'd know her mum was Cockapoo Karen. Weirdly, I felt . . . relieved. I grabbed Frankie's hand, Singed Simon's too, and lifted them both in the air, unleashing yet another roar from the audience.

We were all still buzzing when we eventually made it offstage.

Erin and I made our way to find Mum and Dad. When we spotted them in the crowd talking to Mrs Saddler and Chinyere, we rushed over. I just had to hope Mrs Saddler wasn't going to kill my vibe and give me another detention for being late earlier.

But someone else appeared from nowhere and beat us to them.

'Mr Mavers, how *superb* to see you again.' Agatha embraced my dad. 'And you must be their wonderful mum I've heard all about.' She'd bundled Mum up into a hug before she could respond. 'I really hope you don't mind me saying what an amazing job your girls did tonight.' Agatha paused. 'And in the events leading up to it.' Mum and Dad looked confused – but also as if they were willing to overlook that and enjoy the compliment. 'From what I can see, neither of them could have done it without each other. A true partnership. I think we can all agree?'

Mum and Dad nodded, but I didn't have time to say thank you as somehow Agatha had gone.

Mum's eyes were wide. 'Whoooo was that?! She was *incredible*.'

We all turned to look at where Agatha had disappeared into the crowd, but the only evidence she'd even been here was a business card Dad now held in his hand.

The Hairy Godmother:
Get ready for a **real** *transformation!*

'That, Mother, was Agatha.' I couldn't stop smiling. 'The Hairy Godmother. That Dad took us to.'

Mum nodded, impressed. 'Think I might book myself in.'

And with a simultaneous, 'No,' Erin and I burst out laughing.

Mrs Saddler coughed.

'Sorry to interrupt, but as you can imagine I've got some very busy and important things to be getting on with.' She waited for someone to ask what, but no one did. 'I wanted to congratulate you, Erin . . . In fact, both of you. That second half was one of the most spectacular pieces of theatre I've ever seen.'

'So spectacular.' Chinyere Okafor held her hand out towards my sister. 'You're not just looking at a stunning Titania – but also the newest student at my academy.' She grinned at Erin. 'That is, if you'd still like the scholarship?'

Erin's jaw dropped.

'So does this mean . . .' Dad's voice was breaking. Mum put her hand on his arm to help him hold it together, but her eyes were firmly fixed on Erin.

Who, with a shaking voice, said, 'Yes.'

And, 'Thank you.'

And, 'Sorry about the banana.'

With the hugest whoop of the whole night, arms flying everywhere, all eight of us – me, my sister, Micha, Ben, Mum, Dad, Chinyere Okafor and even Mrs Saddler – bunched up in the biggest, happiest hug.

It was *so* good to be back to being me.

Even if I had accidentally leapt on Ben's previously unbroken foot and very much had my arm round Mrs Saddler.

I guessed normal Lily business had resumed.

CHAPTER THIRTY-ONE

Never had meeting Micha in town felt so good. Having our regular fifty-pence chips at the greasy spoon café felt like the best treat in the world.

There really was nothing better than hanging out with my best friend and talking about ... well, nothing much. But that was the point. Even the small, stupid stuff was fun with Mich.

Erin and Ben were meeting us at four p.m. Lou was coming too – with her new boyfriend, Harley. They'd got together two weeks after the play. She'd told my sister he often quoted lines from it to be romantic. *Bleurgh*. Micha and I had since agreed maybe he wasn't that perfect after all. Still, the bigger news was that Lou had got an audition for Chinyere Okafor's Drama Academy too, and Erin had been helping her rehearse whenever they got a spare second.

Micha sipped her milkshake. Today's brunch was on me – I'd told the grumpy guy serving us to do double toppings.

Which meant I couldn't really see Micha's face behind the tower of squirty cream when she asked, 'So tell me again what we're doing with your sister?'

'Micha, they're spending the afternoon playing Castles! Chaos! Cows! The *team* version. They're just coming to say hi.'

Since the swap, things had changed between me and Erin – we were closer than ever. But … it would take a lot more than an entire body swap and the most stressful time of my entire life for me to willingly invite her to a whole Saturday with Micha.

Erin and I had been hanging out in the evenings though, just like the old days. I'd forgotten how good it was to wind up Dad together and gossip in her room. Which is exactly where I was when she'd given me the real story of what happened the night of the play. When I said I thought all the trouble with the props was Frankie, and Erin said she knew who it was, what she didn't have time to explain was that she *wasn't* correcting me. She was trying to tell me she knew for a *fact* it was Frankie.

Frankie hadn't forgiven us for the tickets like she'd said she had. So when she realized her backstage partner was going to be stuck at LOLCon, she'd spent the morning removing all the prompts to throw Erin's performance off. She'd even thrown in the banana for good measure. The next part of her plan had been even worse – to get Lily locked in the props van once she got back from LOLCon, so she couldn't put anything right, and would get in even *more* trouble with Mrs Saddler for disappearing.

So *that* was why Frankie had messaged pretending Nic wanted to meet Lily in the van. But when I'd forwarded that message to my sister, Erin was running back from helping Micha and had seen Nic outside LOLCon, which is when she started to think maybe it was a set-up. She went to find Frankie to talk about it, but instead ended up overhearing Frankie telling PJ she was waiting for Lily to arrive so she could get her stuck in the van and out of the way. So, determined to stop Frankie doing any more damage, just before the play started Erin had swapped the van key for Mum and Dad's car key, keyring and all, and pretended to Singed Simon she'd cut her finger. He'd then asked Frankie to run to get the first-aid kit from the van and it locked behind her.

I'd been so shocked I'd had to collapse immediately on Erin's bed! I never knew my sister could be devious! And I liked it! Especially as Mrs Saddler now reckoned I was a hero for managing the first half on my own, and then finding Frankie too.

Not that Frankie and I had talked that much since the play finished – now we'd called a truce I think we both wanted to move on. I'd realized Frankie's life wasn't as easy as it looked, and although she'd tried to ruin the play, we hadn't exactly been great to her. Which was why I was really happy Erin had managed one last thing when she'd still been in my body. Turns out she *had* managed to have a quick chat with

Chase at LOLCon after all – and had wangled two pairs of backstage passes for his next tour. My sister and I had already given them to Frankie and Micha to make up for what had happened last time.

Micha had immediately asked me to be her plus one – although with a warning that she wanted to approve my T-shirt choice, and I wasn't allowed to mention dry ice. More than fine with me.

Micha slurped her milkshake. 'I cannot tell you how much I've been looking forward to today.' She pushed the glass to one side – she had cream all over her nose. 'Just sorry I couldn't get here sooner.'

'That's okay.' I stuffed a chip in my mouth. 'You had your first youth squad practice to be amazing at.' After her chemistry turnaround, Micha's parents had bought her a new football kit to celebrate her getting a place on the team. 'I'm sorry but ...' I looked around the café. It was only us and one woman (who looked worryingly like the one I'd thrown a pizza cutter at on my birthday). I checked my cutlery was safely on the table before I threw my hand up to point at Mich. 'Top goalscorer right here, everyone!'

I couldn't be prouder of my best mate. And I was making sure we were celebrating her achievements in style. After this we were trying on some prom outfits, then stocking up on snacks, then swinging by the skatepark before heading to mine for a sleepover. Micha was choosing the film and Mum and Dad had promised extra-large pepperoni pizzas as a treat for doing so well in the play – and for doing all my chores the last few weeks without grumbling. When they'd said that, Erin had just smiled. A really big one.

'Lil!' a voice called. I turned round. It was Nic. And Frankie. I hadn't seen Nic since the opening night.

'Hope we're not interrupting.' Nic swung herself on to the seat next to me. Frankie stayed standing. The Chase tickets had definitely cleared the air, but I don't think either of us were in any hurry to upgrade to best-mate status. 'I've been meaning to talk to you.'

I put my head in my hands. 'If this is about LOLCon, can I just say, it was a bad day. A *very* bad day.' I'd deleted all the footage I could.

'Don't worry I'll never mention *toodleoo kangaroo* again.' Nic laughed. I couldn't – *not yet*. Maybe in twenty years. 'But nah, it's not about that. We're looking for a feature writer for TheNicReport to cover lifestyle – y'know, school, friendship, all the good stuff.' I braced myself for the next question. *Could I recommend anyone?* 'And the team took a vote. How would you feel about it being . . . you?'

Ping.

The chip I was about to put in my mouth dropped back on to the plate.

'Me?'

I looked at Micha, who was boogieing in her seat.

And I looked at Frankie, who was . . . checking her social media on her phone.

Was this for real?!

'Uh-huh, *you*. Your sister sent me that piece you wrote. "Weird Things You Might Never Know Unless You Swapped Lives" or something like that.' Erin did *what*? She must have found my printout! But there it was on Nic's phone – all typed out, mistakes fixed, formatted properly with names removed. Wow. Erin had done that for *me*? 'I loved it. We all did. Sooo high concept.' I tried to keep a straight face. *If only she knew.* 'A really unusual take. In fact, we wondered if you might be up for breaking it into a column.' I could have a column?!

Micha was waving her arms, singing, 'Go, Lily, go, Lily.'

'Oh wait . . .' Nic winced. 'Erin said I wasn't meant to tell you that. Something about you leaving it in her room?'

If my sister were here I'd give her a massive hug – which she'd hate. I couldn't believe she'd done this for me.

'Nic. It's a yes! A *massive* yes.' I wasn't going to let this opportunity slip through my fingers! 'And an even more massive-er-er . . .' Why couldn't I remember words? She might retract the offer! 'Thank you.' I lowered my voice. 'And for the record, can I say, just as a side note unrelated to anything, I think looking like a cockapoo is nothing but a compliment.'

Nic grinned. 'You can, but I don't think Franks will be getting over that one anytime soon.'

But Frankie was . . . smiling? 'Yup, I'm gonna need a while longer for that one.'

Erin, Ben, Harley and Lou bundled over, and due to the fact I had zero chill, I immediately blurted out my news about TheNicReport. Erin didn't make eye contact, but grinned the whole time, before swiftly moving the conversation on by showing us all the stuff they'd bought for prom. Erin and Ben had decided to go for the first time ever. And, laughing, chatting and messing about, the whole gang of us headed out – Micha and me to shop, Nic and Frankie to check out some camera equipment and Erin, Lou, Harley and Ben to 'unleash total Castles! Chaos! Cows! mayhem with her friends'. My sister's words.

But as we walked down the high street Frankie stopped.

'What's that?' She pointed across the street, to a new shop on the corner of the alley. 'Was that there when we walked past earlier?'

I couldn't remember it, but I hadn't been paying much attention. I read the sign out.

'The Crystal Mall . . . ? Haven't seen it before.'

Frankie was already crossing the road. 'C'mon, Nic. Let's pop in.'

But Nic didn't move. Frankie stood outside the door, put her hands on her hips and huffed. 'Don't be like that, Nic. I'll just be a minute.' Frankie rolled her eyes. 'There might even be something in here you like.'

'And there might not, so can we stick to the plan?' Nic pointed down the street. 'Camera shop first.'

But Frankie wasn't giving up. 'Come on. Just one

311

minute or I'm telling Mum and Dad you want your tongue pierced.'

'Fine!' Nic turned back to us and smiled. 'Guess I'll see you guys around. And, Lil, message me later, yes?'

I gave her a big happy nod. 'Absolutely.'

But as Ben, Harley and Lou ambled down the street, chatting away, something made Erin and me stop.

Was it the sound of Nic and Frankie bickering?

Or did we recognize that *tinkle ding*?

Simultaneously my sister and I turned and looked at the shop Nic and Frankie had disappeared into.

And as Erin put her arm through mine we both laughed. Really laughed.

Because inside the window, the lady who ran it was giving us a wink and waving goodbye to us.

Agatha.

ACKNOWLEDGEMENTS

Thank you so much for reading *Sister Switch* – and for reading the bit after it's finished. Erin would approve! I hope you enjoyed it. And I hope you also enjoy reading big thank yous to the people who helped make it happen, because that's what's coming up.

First up to the amazing editorial team of Amina and Lucy – even in the weirdest of times, you made writing this really fun. Thank you SO much. And Lucy, an extra thanks for absolutely everything from day one (and for taking out the furry youknowwhats).

A massive thank you to the brilliant people behind the gorgeous cover – Thy, Jesse and David. It's a beaut! Lucky me. Catherine, thank you for the copyedit and emoji patience ('This one isn't showing' ... Oh, it's just another hedgehog). And a huge thanks to the lovely people at Simon & Schuster, who have all been super supportive, even from afar, so thank you Rachel, Ali, Laura, Dani, Olivia, Fahima and the whole team.

As always, a huge, big, hopefully-one-day-not-virtual-hug to the best (and most patient) (and probably/definitely most fun) agent there is: Gemma Cooper.

And thank you to all the people who always cheer me on, especially this last year. Chris, who made being stuck in a house fun, Becca, the best big sister in the world (ja, ich habe eine Schwester), my parents, who I love so much I would (and did) camp out in the rain to see them, Rose, the coolest (and greatest book-writing) niece there is, and to Pam (the OG Oberon), James, Tina (hello Ellie!), Jess, Parisian sandwich guru Yasmine, Ida (skate consultant), Dan, Scall, Team Cooper, Simon, Ian, Julie, Val, Babs, Kev and Teddy, the N-Unit, my pain pals, my MTV buds, Switch team, Holly, Robyn, Ro, Becky, Sarah and all my friends who swapped wild times for walks. You really are the best.

And lastly, thank you to you for reading. I hope your next trip to the hairdresser's is super hairy ... I mean cool.

Tinkle ding!